KILL THE MOTHER!

Borgo Press Books by MICHAEL MALLORY

Kill the Mother! A Dave Beauchamp Mystery Novel
The Mural: A Novel of Horror

KILL THE MOTHER!

A DAVE BEAUCHAMP MYSTERY NOVEL

MICHAEL MALLORY

THE BORGO PRESS

MMXIII

KILL THE MOTHER!

FIRST EDITION

Published by Wildside Press LLC

www.wildsidebooks.com

For Brendan,
who is content being an only child.

KILL THE MOTHER!

ONE

It was a little after ten by the time I dragged myself to the office. After unlocking the door, I groped for the light switch, flipped it, and watched as the fluorescent tubes built into the ceiling flickered to life. That was a good sign; it meant the electricity hadn't been shut off yet.

Tossing the small stack of mail I'd pulled out of the box downstairs onto my desk, I went to the tiny sink in the office's kitchen cubicle and turned on the faucet. A jet of water spurted out, hit the bottom of the sink and splashed back up onto my shirt. In another time and another place, I might have been annoyed, but today I was pleased. It meant the water was still on, too.

So far, so good, kid, a familiar voice said. There was nobody else in my office; the voice was strictly inside my head. It belonged to Humphrey Bogart. Bogie was among the Golden Age Hollywood stars who talk to me regularly. Some people, I'm sure, would find this a sign of mental instability, if not outright insanity, but I find it comforting. I know I'm never alone. Besides, even if some people were right and I really was as crazy as a bedbug, it's okay. This is Los Angeles, and if you can't walk around insane in Los Angeles, where can you?

I took advantage of the water's presence to make a pot of coffee, after which I shuffled to my desk and took a closer look at the mail. There was yet another credit card solicitation; a begging letter from a charity to which I once gave twenty-five bucks, an amount they have far exceeded in postage by sending me junk mail; a bank statement, highlighting last month's activity of too much money going out and too little coming in; and an official looking letter from Hot Ticket Home Entertainment Rentals.

Oh, sheez. Was this thing ever going to go away? It started when I innocently rented a DVD of *The Big Clock*, the great 1948 film noir thriller with Ray Milland and Charles Laughton, from my local Hot Ticket and it was proving to be the worst decision I've made recently. I've never had any kind of problem with Edendale Video and Poster, an independent store that was presently my entertainment supplier of choice, but Hot Ticket, a national chain that seemed to be perpetually in bankruptcy, was a nightmare. Reluctantly, I opened the envelope and read the letter.

Dear Mr. Beauchamp:

Our records show that our last several inquiries to you, regarding your failure to return the DVD of The Big Clock *in a timely fashion, have gone unanswered.*

That was absolutely untrue. I did answer their last letter and told them that I had returned the disk more than a month ago. Okay, so it was a year-and-a-half overdue because I had lost it, but once it turned up at the back of the refrigerator (oh, like no one else has ever opened the fridge with something in their hand, and then absentmindedly set it down when a milk carton starts to fall and forgotten about it), I got it right back to Hot Ticket. I had neither the intention nor the wherewithal to pay the two-hundred-dollar fine they were attempting to levy.

Because you have made no good faith effort to resolve this situation we have no choice but to turn the matter over to a collection agency, a representative from which will be contacting you at their earliest convenience.

Fine. Let them contact me. I used to be an attorney myself, so I had a pretty good idea of how far they could actually go in making a claim. Maybe if I was able to clear the matter up to everyone's satisfaction, the collection agency would even throw some work my way. I put the letter in my less-than-crowded in box. The rest of the day's mail, except for the bank statement, got dumped in the trash.

The morning progressed without a single phone call, and since I did not have a pending case—yes, I am a private investigator, at least according to a piece of paper that fell off of my wall some time back—I occupied myself watching old film clips on YouTube. After discovering that someone had actually obtained and posted a clip of Linda Crystal from *Cry Tough* in her legendary state of undress—nothing by today's standards, but shocking for a movie made in 1959 (in fact, I was so shocked I had to watch it four times over)—I was about declare defeat for the morning and break for lunch. That was when she walked in.

She was a fox, all right, and she sashayed right through the door of my office. She was wrapped in fur and stunning, and my mouth dropped open at the sight of her. I wasn't used to having foxes walk in on me like this.

"Um…hi," I said, stupidly. I say stupidly because I knew there was no way I was going to get a response from her, because she was a fox. A real fox. Four paws, reddish fur, big ears, pointy snout, and two squinty black eyes, which stared straight at me. And no, I don't know for a fact that it was a female, but it was small and lithe, it looked like a vixen, and I did not particularly feel like examining its rear quarters to find proof for my theory.

The fox was neither frightened nor frightening. She simply regarded me with dark-eyed curiosity, as though I was the out-of-place element in a slightly rundown office building on Ventura Boulevard in Sherman Oaks, California, the heart of the San Fernando Valley. *Then again*, said a voice inside my head, a deep, raspy voice that I recognized as belonging to John Huston, *this is Los Angeles where, in the right time and the right place, you're liable to see* anything.

Ignoring John, I turned to the fox and asked, "You hungry?" I try to be a good host, even to forest animals. Never taking my eyes off the fox, just in case it suddenly turned feral, I got up and slowly went over to the kitchen corner, where I opened the tiny fridge and pulled out a carton of milk that I use for my coffee. Taking a plastic bowl down from a shelf, I poured a little into it and cautiously set it down on the floor, not far from the fox, who looked at it, then back at me, and then—I swear— appeared to shrug its shoulders and walk over to it. It stuck its tongue out and tried a bit, and apparently liked what it tasted, because it started lapping up the rest.

What a remarkable creature, Clifton Webb's voice said in my head, and I had to agree. You remember Clifton Webb, don't you? *Laura? Sitting Pretty?*

The fox had finished the bowl and I was contemplating giving it seconds when I heard footsteps coming down the hall. A man appeared in the doorway; he was middle-aged but dressed like Jungle Jim, as though he was on his way to a costume party... or wanted people to know he handled animals. "Hey, buddy," he said, "this is kind of unusual, but by any chance have you seen—"

Then he spotted the fox. "There you are!" he cried, rushing to it, and picking it up like a small dog. Glancing at the empty bowl, he then looked up and glared up at me. "Did you give her something to eat?" he demanded.

"Just a little milk."

"Oh, Christ! Don't you know that milk gives foxes diarrhea?"

I had never really thought about it one way or the other. "Sorry," I muttered.

"She's on a restricted diet!"

Like every other vixen in town, a cynical voice said in my head. Thank you, Richard Burton.

"It was only two percent milk," I told the guy.

"Doesn't matter, milk is milk!"

"Okay, all right, I'm sorry," I said. "But if you don't mind my asking, what's the thing doing here in the first place?"

"We're doing a photo shoot downstairs," Jungle Jim replied. "She's in the shot. Dammit, if you made her sick, I'll file suit!"

I doubted he had any legal ground on which to base a suit. Then again, this was L.A. "If you think she's going to become diarrheic," I said, "I'd appreciate your taking her out of my office first."

"Up yours," the man said. "I should sue you anyway." On the way out he glanced at the sign on my door. "Beauchamp Investigations, huh?" he said, mispronouncing my name the way virtually everyone does: it's not *bow-CHAMP*, it's *BEACH-um*. I had actually thought about changing it altogether at one point, right after I cracked open a brand-new, just delivered edition of the Yellow Pages only to find that the expensive quarter page ad I had taken out read *Be a Chump Investigations*. "Some investigator you are, giving milk to a fox," Jungle Jim sneered, then disappeared into the hallway, vixen in hand.

I must have been sick that day in criminal justice class that the teacher covered the gastrointestinal limitations of wild canines.

I sat back down and opened the middle drawer of my desk, where I keep my journal. It started as a record of cases, but cases have been in such short supply recently that I've been filling it instead with any observations, musings, and notes to self I might have. Opening it to the first clean page I wrote: *Never give milk to a fox. It gives them the runs and really torques their owners.*

You never knew when this information might come in useful.

Finding less in the fridge worth eating than had the fox, I decided to go out and drop some precious, declining dollars on the lunch special at Burger Heaven: a double-decker burger, fries and a drink for $4.99. I locked up the office, but only made it as far as the front door of the building before stopping. There, in the lobby, was a table filled with food: deli meats and cheese, bread, fresh fruit, chips, urns of coffee and an iced cooler filled with soft drinks. I knew enough about present-day Hollywood to know that it was a craft services table, an ever-present sight on a film set, offering a cornucopia of food for the crew. Apparently it applied to photo shoots as well.

As I was pondering whether a person taking pictures of a fox somewhere down the hall would miss a few slices of ham and cheese, a woman appeared in the hallway. She was, I guessed, late thirties to early forties, dark haired, and on the short side but dressed in a tight sweater-and-slacks outfit that did her quite a few favors. "Who the fuck are you?" she demanded in a low, hard voice.

"Um, I'm Dave Beauchamp, I have an office upstairs," I said. "I just came down to see what was going on."

"And steal my food?"

Apparently I was wearing a hungry expression. "Actually, I...."

"What do you do?"

"I'm a private investigator."

She studied me with an intensified expression, but one that was more of interest than annoyance. "A private investigator," she repeated. "You mean like a detective?"

"Quite like, yes."

"Are you a real detective?"

Using both hands, I felt around my body to see if I was real, instead of fabricated from mist, and then nodded.

She didn't laugh. "Licensed?"

"Of course."

"You look too young."

I sighed. I'm the same age John Garfield was when he did *The Postman Always Rings Twice*, but I have frequently heard from people that (unlike Garfield at any age) I look like a college freshman. "I promise you I'm old enough to drive," I said.

She smiled. "Upstairs, you say?"

"Office 218."

She studied me some more, then said: "I may have something for you. Will you be in later?"

"Yes, I was just going out for lunch."

Now the woman smiled. "Well, go ahead and help yourself

here." She waived expansively across the food table.

"That's very generous of you," I said. "This thing you may have for me, does it involve a fox, by any chance?"

"No, just a group of bitches," she replied, leaning down to get a cold Diet Pepsi from the cooler, and intentionally or otherwise giving me an eyeful as the top of her sweater slung low. "I'll come up to your office later." She turned around and walked back down the hall.

I looked at the food on the table. Page one of the Detective's Manual: *Never turn down a free lunch*. Grabbing a paper plate, I loaded up enough cold cuts and cheese for a real Dagwood special and grabbed a handful of baby carrots and an apple, and a couple cans of soda, then went back upstairs to wait. To occupy my time after polishing off the monster sandwich, I dug through my bottom drawer until I found my framed investigator's license, the one that had taken a swan dive off the wall some time back. I had been meaning to hang it back up, but never quite got around to it. Now seemed like a good time. I rummaged through my top drawer until I came across the small metal hook that had been rattling around there for months, and pushed its nail into the hole in the wall. Then I hung the frame on it.

And waited.

It was sometime after four when the woman knocked on my open door. "Hi, I'm back," she announced.

"Hello," I said, rising from my chair. "Please take a seat, Ms.…"

"Frost. Nora Frost."

Her face was now more relaxed than it had been during our first encounter. Nora Frost was really quite attractive. She had the kind of looks that *almost* made it to movie star or model level. But her dark, flashing eyes were just a little too large, her nose was just a little bit too big and her mouth just a little bit too wide for film, though her slightly exaggerated features would probably have served her well on the stage. She did not show any tell-tale signs of having work done to her face, which wore an expression of smooth determination, as though she was daring wrinkles to show up, and the wrinkles knew better. "So, Ms. Frost—"

"You can call me Nora."

"All right, Nora, what is it you would like to see me about?"

"Like I said, I've got a problem with a group of bitches."

"Do you mean you have a problem with other women, or in the literal sense, as in female dogs?"

"I don't see much of a distinction," she said. "And the problem isn't so much with me as with my sons."

"You're sons are involved with these women?"

"They're not *involved*—" she smacked the word like a tennis serve "—with *any* women. They're only twelve."

"I see. Well, perhaps you should tell me what the problem is."

She leaned forward. "Have you ever heard of the Brothers Alpha?"

"No."

"You will. Taylor and Burton are going to be the biggest draws in the industry. Bigger than the Olsons, bigger than the Jonas Brothers."

Taylor and *Burton*. Why not? "And the Brothers Alpha are your sons?"

"My sons and my clients."

"I see. And since they are both twelve, I assume they're twins."

"We don't use the T word," she said icily. "It's demeaning to them as individuals. They are two different, unique, brilliantly gifted personalities who happened to have been born at the same time."

"I take it that 'Alpha' is simply their stage name."

"It signifies that they are on top in all respects."

At least they'd always come first on a list. "Are they, by any chance, the subjects of the photo shoot that's going on in the building?"

"Yes, it's a public service announcement poster."

"For?"

"Not for, against. The subject is blood sport and the poster is for use in Great Britain. The boys are very concerned about animal rights. They're socially aware, so they're doing a campaign against the barbarous sport of fox hunting."

"I thought fox hunting had already been banned in Great Britain."

She glared at me for a second, and then snapped: "What if it comes back, smart aleck?"

I had nothin.' "Are your sons well known over there?" I asked, trying to rescue the conversation.

"They soon will be."

"You know, the fox you're using stopped by here earlier to say hello."

"Harvey, the fox wrangler, told me. He said you gave the thing milk."

"A mistake I will never make again, I promise."

"I really don't care," Nora Frost shrugged. "The fox is Harvey's problem, not mine. He's the animal trainer, I hired him to provide and control the thing for the shoot, which clearly he wasn't capable of doing, since it wandered away and came up here. But I'm not here to talk about the goddamned fox." She leaned forward even further and started drilling holes into me with her eyes. "What you need to know is that my babies are going to big. They've got *it*. You know what *it* is? That mysterious appeal that you're either born with or you're not? Well, they were born with it, and that makes the others jealous."

Some got it and some don't, Mae West said in my head, adding: *As for me, I'd rather* get *it*.

"And these others are the bitches you were talking about?" I asked.

"The mothers of all those other little brats." She sprung up from her chair in agitation and began pacing back and forth in my office. "I'm not going to lie to you and claim this is not a tough business, Mr. Beauchamp. There are a lot of sows out there who think their little darlings are God's gift to the world, and they are so wrong. So *fucking* wrong, and so vicious." She leaned across my desk, her cold dark eyes locking on me, and her face hardened into a look of determination that would have made a mama tiger abandon the cubs and run for the treetops. I struggled not to show any signs of intimidation, even as I shrank back in my chair. "One of those miserable bitches threatened my babies," she said.

"Um, uh, how did she threaten them?"

Nora Frost sat back down. "She said she would kill them. Kill them, cut them up, and mail the pieces back to me."

The sound of a whistle echoed in my head, and I knew instinctively it came from Bogart. If this revelation shocked him, how was *I* going to handle it?

TWO

"Um…have you gone to the police?" I asked weakly.

"No," Nora Frost said, deflating somewhat. "If I go to the police, they'll end up questioning the boys, and I'm trying to spare them the fear. I don't want them to know they've been threatened. I assumed a private detective could handle things more quietly."

"I see," I said nodding, glad she had turned the high-beams off. "Do you know who it was who made the threat?"

"If I did, I would go to her myself. No, I don't know, but I have a suspicion. You see, the boys have been auditioning for a new reality show, and they're blowing all the other little monsters right out of the room. A few days ago I received a letter telling me if I didn't stop bringing them to the try-outs I could start preparing for their funerals."

"And that they'd be cut up?"

"Those were the details."

"Did you save the letter?"

"Yes. My first instinct was to burn it, but I didn't."

"Good. I'll need to see it."

Her eyes narrowed. "Why? Don't you believe me? You require proof I'm telling the truth?"

"No, it's not that—"

"Christ," she muttered, "I can see I came to the wrong detective office."

"Nora, please, calm down," I said. "I need to see the letter to see if there are any clues on it that might point to the sender.

Ink, handwriting, even fingerprints, if we're lucky."

"Oh, yes of course. I'm sorry, Mr. Beauchamp, I guess I'm becoming distraught. It's just that the boys are all I have. I lost my husband two years ago."

"I'm sorry." There was an awkward pause, which I broke by saying: "So, if I understand you correctly, you want to hire me to find out who it is that sent you this threatening letter."

"Yes."

"When I do find her...or him...since we don't know for certain it's a woman—"

"It's one of the bitch mothers, trust me."

"Fair enough, but when I do identify her, I will be obligated to notify the police. As an investigator, I don't have the power to arrest anyone."

"As long as she's out of the way and my babies are safe."

"My usual fee is fifty dollars an hour." I waited for the inevitable protest, but it did not come.

"Can I retain you for a lump sum instead?" Nora Frost asked.

"What kind of lump sum are we talking about?"

"Say, ten-thousand dollars for the job, up front?"

I hope the gulping sound that came from my throat was not as audible to her as it was to me. Ten-grand was, what, two-hundred hours? Five weeks work.

"If that is adequate I could write you a check right now," she said.

I could write a check, too, John Wayne's voice cautioned inside my brain. *Course it would bounce higher than a butte, but...I could write it.* The Duke made a good point: I'd learned from experience not to trust every proffered checkbook. "I'll tell you what, Nora," I said, trying to sound like William Powell, and failing, "I'll take a cashier's check for half, five-thousand, as a retainer, and the rest on completion of the case."

"Still don't trust me," she said. "No matter, I can do that. I can't go to the bank now, though. I have to get back to wrap the shoot. If I'm not there, they'll screw it all up."

"If you don't mind my asking, why are you shooting a foxhunt scene in an office building in Sherman Oaks? Shouldn't you be out somewhere like Huntington gardens?"

"You can't bring a wild animal into a public place without a filming permit, and I didn't want the hassle of that," she replied. "So we're using the studio downstairs."

"Studio? What studio?"

"It was called Triex."

I knew that an outfit called Triex Distribution had offices downstairs, but I never knew exactly what they distributed. I saw the guy in charge every now and then, an older man with a perpetual smile and tinted glasses, but he moved out a couple of months ago. "So it's like a photography studio?"

She gave me a strange, probing look. "It was a film studio," she said. "You didn't know about it?"

"No, and I'm a film buff. How ironic is that?"

"Aren't you too young to be a film buff?" she asked. "Shouldn't you be a video game buff?"

Now cut that out! Jack Benny shouted defensively in my mind. "I come by it honestly," I explained. "My father is a walking movie encyclopedia. He saw everything on first release and re-release in theatres, and then when home video came out, he started renting and collecting. He even wrote some articles for fan magazines. I caught the bug from him." The truth was, as a kid I was so pathetically bad at any kind of sports that staying inside and watching movies on TV, or reading about them, became my replacement activity for playing outside. I didn't mind, and Dad didn't mind, though between the two of us, we drove my mom a little nuts. "Still," I said, changing the subject, even if in my own mind, "I can't imagine what kind of films anyone would make in an office building in Sherman Oaks?"

Nora Frost started laughing. "My god, you really don't know?" she said. "You can't even guess?" I shrugged, and she prompted further: "This is the San Fernando Valley, after all."

Okay, I was missing something, clearly. Then it hit me. "Sheez, a *porn* studio?" I cried. "*Downstairs*?"

She laughed even louder. "A helluva fine detective you are! You don't even know they're cranking out fuck films right below your feet!"

What could I say? The hard truth I had to face just about every day was that I was not born to be a private investigator. I'm not tough, and I try to avoid mean streets whenever possible. I even try to avoid mildly disagreeable streets. I've been in only one fight in my life, in ninth grade, and then I beat my attacker's fist with my nose so brutally that he had to put a band aid on one knuckle. I, meanwhile, went to the emergency room. But having been laid off three years ago by the Law Offices of Zacharias & Flynn, and finding that no other law firm in town was particularly interested in me, there was precious little else I could think to do. PI licenses aren't all that hard to come by—in fact, I hear in L.A. they're easier to get than a building permit—so here I am. A guy's gotta live.

Or die trying, a voice intoned. Robert Mitchum, ladies and gentlemen. Very mordant, Mitch, very witty; now please go get stoned and leave me be.

I could not so easily wave away Nora's point. I should have been able to figure out they were shooting shag films down there. If the smile etched on the guy's face wasn't enough of a clue, there had been a fairly constant stream of young women hanging around the hallway. Had I really thought about it, maybe I might even have realized that "Triex" is a spelled-out form of "XXX," the traditional advertising rating for skin flicks. But I just didn't put X, X, and X together. She's right; a helluva fine detective I am.

"I really have to get back to the shoot, Mr. Beauchamp," Nora Frost said, rising and heading for the door.

"Please call me Dave," I said. For five grand in advance she could call me Hitler McAsshat. "Might I come along? To the shoot, I mean? You could introduce me to the twi…I mean, to the boys."

"Fine, but haul it." Nora was back to being all-business.

I closed the door behind me but did not lock it. There was

precious little to steal in there anyway. Even if someone cared enough to lift the laptop, the insurance would pay for a newer, better one.

Sheez, I did pay my premium, didn't I?

While we were waiting for the elevator (I would have preferred the stairs, but it was her choice), I said: "I don't want to intrude, but the more information I have, the better. You mentioned that the boys' father died."

There was a slight pause, before she said, "That's right."

"What happened, if you don't mind my asking?"

"He was killed in Afghanistan. He died fighting for his country."

"Oh, I see. Again, I'm sorry."

"I try to honor his memory rather than grieve his death."

"Do Burton and Taylor go to public school?"

"Are you kidding me?" The elevator dinged, and then the door opened and we stepped in. Nora jabbed the button for the first floor. "LAUSD stands for the Los Angeles Unionized Sewer Department," she said as the door slid shut. "I wouldn't let my babies anywhere near a public school in L.A. They're tutored at home. But since it's summer now and school's out, they're on break. I like to give them the same advantages of common kids."

The elevator door opened and we stepped into the hallway. The former Triex studio was at the end of the hall; the door was open, and through it I could hear a hubbub of voices. Nora marched straight in and I followed. Inside the suite were about a half-dozen people, all of whom stopped talking and practically snapped to attention at the sight of Nora. Only the fox, frankly, did not seem give a damn.

Instead of the drop ceiling that existed in my office, there was no ceiling in this mini-studio, only a lighting grid. The lights that hung there were focused on a long, semi-circular piece of muslin, on which was painted an English pastoral land-scape, filled with hills and hedges, with a stately manor house etched into the background. Two young boys stood in front of it, and between them was the fox, resting comfortably on the floor. They were not identical twins, but rather fraternal. The truth was they did not even look all that much like brothers. One was on the tall side for an adolescent and slender, with sharp features and a focused expression, while the other was slightly shorter, a little rounder, and had a faraway look. What linked them was dirty-blonde color of their hair and their light blue eyes, which gave them a certain coldness that wasn't conducive to becoming teen idols. Even though they were dressed in classic fox hunting outfits—round, helmet-like hats, red coats, jodhpurs and tall boots—they looked convincingly like a pre-teen version of Sherlock Holmes and Dr. Watson.

The fox, which was standing in between them actually seemed glad to see me, and strolled over to accept a scritch between the ears. Maybe she wasn't aware that the bowl of milk I gave her was going to result in grievous stomach troubles. However, Harvey the fox wrangler, the guy in the Jungle Jim outfit who had shown up in my office, suddenly materialized at my side. "Now what do you think you're doing?" he demanded.

"He came with me, Harvey, so leave him alone," Nora snapped. Then turning to the boys, she cooed: "Taylor honey, Burton darling, this is Mr. Beauchamp."

"Hello," they said in perfect unison. Okay, so they were twins after all.

"Hey, guys. Having fun?"

They looked at me as though I'd asked a question in a foreign language.

"Must be kind of cool, working with a real fox and all," I went on.

Taylor, the taller one, said: "It would make a nice pair of gloves."

"Honey!" Nora shouted. "Don't make jokes like that!" Turning to me, she added: "They have a unique sense of humor."

The boys glared back at me with all the humor of a plane crash. I glanced over at Harvey, who looked like he wanted to backhand the little cyborgs, but knew he could not. He was on

Mommy's payroll like everyone else here, including, soon, me.

"All right, talk to me, somebody," Nora shouted, clapping her hands. "Where are we? Are we finished with this?"

A man dressed in white linen slacks and shirt with a light meter around his neck—presumably the photographer—came up to her. "I think I have what you want," he said. "Come over to the laptop and take a look." Nora followed him over to a table on which sat a portable computer and intently examined a slide-show of photos.

"They're grinning," she said. "Why are they grinning? This is a serious poster, for Christ's sake!"

"We took a variety of poses and expressions," the photographer explained.

"No...no...no...no...Jesus Christ, Jerry, why would you take a picture like that? Burton looks likes a zombie!"

I glanced over at Burton and found myself agreeing with her assessment.

"You've been wasting my time and money!" Nora shouted. "You should go back to the fucking DMV!"

Jerry the photographer sighed, and then said: "Just look at the others, Nora."

Glaring at the laptop like she was trying to burn holes through it with her eyes, Nora snapped: "No! No! No! Hell no! Jesus, God! No! Wait, that's it. That one there."

"There are more—"

"Why are there more? You should have stopped after this one and not wasted everyone's time! This is the one. Look at that... even the fox looks like he's pleading not to be killed."

My guess is by that point the fox was pleading to get away from the lights and the noise.

"Put that one on a memory stick and I'll take it with me," Nora told the photographer. "All right, everyone, it's a wrap."

There seemed to be a collective sigh of relief in the room as the harsh photographic lights were clicked off and the ceiling's one remaining bank of fluorescents was switched on. Then the small crew set about to breaking down the shoot. A young woman appeared with a box of wet wipes and began to remove makeup from the boy's faces, while a couple of college-age guys took down the backdrop. In no time at all, the equipment had been removed and the tiny makeshift studio looked like an abandoned office again. Knowing what I now knew, I could only imagine what sort of activities had gone on in here for the past year. That, in turn, led to another question, which I saved for a time when Nora Frost wasn't so busy. Right now she was handing out checks to people, and something else along with them: autographed glossy photos of the Brothers Alpha. I could tell that the two guys who had taken down the backdrop were having an awful time trying not to laugh out loud as they received their "gift."

Within minutes, Jerry the photographer and most of the crew was gone. The only one left was a young Latina who appeared to be in charge of the wardrobe, or at least in charge of picking up after the twins, who left their costumes strewn all over the floor of the makeshift dressing room cubicle. "Hurry it up, would you?" Nora said as the woman put the costumes on hangers, with the hats and boots going into large plastic bags, which she started to lug out.

"Can I give you a hand?" I asked her, and she smiled.

I helped the woman, whose name was Rosario, drag the stuff out of the suite and to her van, the back of which was filled with various costume pieces and boxes of accessories. "You must do this for a living," I commented.

"For small shoots and commercials, mostly," she said. "This is my second shoot with the Alphas."

"I hear they're real up and comers."

She looked at me with questioning eyes. "What was your name again?"

"Dave Beauchamp. I work in the building here."

"So you don't have a connection with the family?"

"Until today I'd never heard of them. Why?"

Rosario looked around to see if anyone was within earshot and then crooked her index finger for me to lean closer. "I'm not a show business veteran or anything," she whispered, "but as far as I can tell, the only way those two are going to become famous is if they're murdered."

"Nora thinks they're going to be superstars," I whispered back.

"I know, but she's the one who wants to be famous and powerful. The whole family gives me the creeps."

"Why do you keep working with them, then?"

She closed the door of the van. "A job's a job, particularly these days," she said, no longer whispering. "Last week I did an infomercial for a guy who claims he's invented a kind of tea that will cure cancer. Personally, I think I he's a con man who should be arrested, but a job's a job, so I worked it."

"*Rosario*," Nora's voice shouted from behind us, "did you get your check?" We turned to see her standing just outside the building, with the twins behind her, both totally rapt by the electronic game gizmos they held in their hands.

"Not yet, Nora," Rosario called back.

"Well, hurry up, we have to leave."

With a sigh, Rosario half-trotted across the parking lot to her, received an envelope (but no autographed 8x10—presumably she had one from her earlier shoot). I followed, but not as rapidly. In fact, Rosario met me half-way coming back. "Like I said, a job's a job," she reflected, holding her hand out for me to shake. "Nice meeting you."

"Same here."

As Rosario was preparing to leave, Nora Frost was talking on her cell phone. I tried to walk past her, but she held out a hand to stop me from going anywhere. "What do you mean you can't do it?" she shouted into the cell. "I need you right now, dammit! What am I paying you for? Well, plans have changed, and I have to run somewhere, and I need to get the boys home. No, I can't! Goddammit, you listen to me, you...*oh*! We'll talk about this later!" She cut the line off so forcefully I thought she was going to crush the phone in her hand.

"Problem?" I asked.

"Elena, my assistant," Nora fumed. "I need her right now, and she says she's doing something and can't come! Can you fucking believe that?"

"Well, maybe she is doing something."

She glared at me. "Nothing she could be doing is more important than the boys' needs! She knows that! Maybe Rosario can do it." Still clutching the phone, Nora ran after the van, which was pulling away from the curb, her arms waving furiously as she shouted, "Stop!" Rosario pulled back against the curb and rolled down the passenger side window. I was able to hear Nora asking her if she could take the boys somewhere, and Rosario answer that she had to get the costumes back to the rental house before six or else pay for another day. *"Shit!"* Nora screamed, turning back and letting Rosario drive away. "Everyone's against me! I don't fucking *need* this!"

"Um, Nora, I have a car," I said. "If the boys have to get home, just give me your address and I'll drive them there."

All of a sudden the world turned Technicolor. The sun came out, the scent of jacaranda filled the air, birds flew by singing sweetly, the atmosphere warmed up, a rainbow filled the sky, and the flowers, if they could have uprooted themselves and danced, would have. And it was all due to Nora Frost. "Ohhhh," she moaned, placing a hand caringly on my arm and all but tearing up. "Do you know what you are, Dave? A contributor. The first moment I saw you, I could tell you were going to be part of the team." It was the most remarkable transformation I had seen since Fredric March took his first drink in *Dr. Jekyll and Mr. Hyde*. "Could you also stay with them until I get back?" she asked.

"I could do that, yes," I said. "Just give me a moment to lock up my office and I'll be right with you." I turned away from her *my hero* gesture—both hands clasped and held up beside her face, in the best Lillian Gish style—and dashed back inside and up to my office, where I grabbed my laptop and switched off all the lights before locking up and leaving.

When I returned to the parking lot, she handed me a business card for *Alpha Enterprises*. "The address is on the card," she said, smiling. The zip code was for Los Feliz, an old Hollywood area of Los Angeles whose aging mansions once housed the likes of Cecil B. DeMille and W.C. Fields. "Thank you *so* much, Dave."

"No problem. Are you going to be long?"

"No, no, I just have to run to the bank." She winked. "You know why."

"Oh. The boys can't go with you to the bank?"

Instantly, the sun went back under a cloud and a couple of the singing birds got caught by stray cats. "I don't want them to know what the money's for," she managed to say in a low voice, without moving her lips. "They'd ask, too. They're so inquisitive."

I looked over at the twelve-year-olds, who came across about as naturally inquisitive as moss.

"Boys," Nora called to the twins, "Mr. Beauchamp is going to drive you home. You show him what gentlemen you can be."

Taylor's mouth cracked into a grin that would rate the Guinness prize as World's Smallest, but at least it was an expression.

"I'll see you in no more than two hours, Dave," Nora said. "Make yourself at home while you're there." She turned and started striding toward a silver Lexus.

"Wait, Nora," I called, running to catch up with her. "You didn't give me a key."

"Oh, God! What a space brain." I doubted that sincerely, but said nothing as she rummaged through her purse and pulled out a key on a ring that had, unsurprisingly, a photo of the twins encased in plastic. "Here you are. It goes to the bottom lock on the door."

"All right. See you later."

After watching her pull out of the lot, I led the twelve-year-olds to my Toyota, which was only a year younger. I had gotten it for my twenty-first birthday, and was managing to keep it going. It was nothing fancy, but it moved. The two looked at it with disdain before crawling in the backseat. "You may have to dig the seatbelts out. I don't often have passengers."

"I can see why," Burton sniffed. "When was the last time you had this thing washed and vacuumed?"

I didn't answer, mostly because I couldn't remember. I pulled out and headed down Ventura Boulevard toward the first freeway access street, figuring the 101 East to the 134 East to the 5 South was the quickest way to get to the Los Feliz area, which was just northeast of Hollywood. "You guys want the radio on?" I asked.

"No," they said in unison.

"Okay."

We had driven no more than a mile, when I could hear hushed conversation between the two. It sounded like variations of, "You want to ask him?" followed by "No, you ask him."

"Ask me what, guys?" I volunteered.

Taylor was the one who asked, and my foot involuntarily stomped on the gas pedal, which resulted in my nearly rear-ending the car ahead of me. I stomped on the brake and screeched to a halt. Maybe I'd heard wrong. I must have heard wrong.

No, sport, Errol Flynn's voice said, *you heard right. By the way*, he went on, *if you're not doing her, I will*!

THREE

"Did you just ask me if I was fucking your mother?" I said, driving ahead cautiously.

"Seems like an easy question," Taylor commented.

"How can I be fu…having se…I just met your mother a few hours ago!"

"Yeah, but if you want to, it's okay with us," Burton said. "I think she can use it."

"Um, guys—"

"She's kinda uptight," Taylor interrupted. "Of course, if you did start to fuck our mother.…"

Burton picked up the thought. "That would make you.…"

"A motherfucker!" they cried in unison, and then snickered.

I got it; a carefully rehearsed routine. "Very funny," I said. "You two should be on the road." *Flattened by a logging truck*, W. C. Fields added. I decided to change the subject. "I'm sorry to hear about your father. I understand he was a hero."

"We don't like to talk about our father," Taylor said.

"All right."

We drove for several more miles before I tried breaking the silence again. "So, what do you guys like to eat?"

"Food," they replied in unison.

After several more miles, I said: "You guys like to watch television?"

"If it's not retarded," Burton offered.

"Or gay," Taylor elaborated.

At that point I gave up. No further words transpired between then and the time we pulled into the driveway of the Frost home on Commonwealth Avenue in Los Feliz hills. It was a quasi-Tudor brick house, probably from the 1920s or '30s, and while not perhaps fully qualifying as a mansion, was certainly more upscale than my apartment in Studio City (which, if promises were kept, Nora Frost was going to allow me to keep through the end of the year.) "We're home, boys," I said switching off the ignition.

"No shit, Sherlock," Burton said, keeping his eyes on his Game Boy, or whatever the hell it was he was thumb-abusing. Neither he nor Taylor made a move to exit the Toyota.

"Well," I said, opening the car door, which set off the annoying dinging until I pulled the keys from the ignition, "you guys can stay here if you want. I'm going inside. Maybe I can find where your mom hides her good silverware and steal it."

Almost unbelievably, that drew responses from them. When they looked up from their games, they were actually smiling. "We get a cut from the sale," Taylor said.

"For not telling," Burton added.

"Fair enough, let's go."

I was steeling myself for what the inside of the house must look like, but the reality of it exceeded my most exaggerated expectations. I can't recall ever seeing shrines to living people, but that accurately described the Frost living room. Practically every square inch of the walls was covered with framed photographs of the two boys. One poster sized image, which was grainy and blurry, and appeared to have been blown-up from a very low-res phone picture, showed the boys standing outside a restaurant next to Tom Hanks, who smiled dutifully. I could only assume that Hanks was innocently having dinner there when he was spotted by Nora. Next to the leather sofa was a life-sized cardboard standee of the boys, dressed like Indiana Jones, and over the fireplace was an oil painting of the two boys that was of near photographic quality. I walked over to the standee, the sort of thing they have in tourist traps that allow you to pose for a picture with your arm draped around one cardboard shoulder so that it looks like you and your best friend Elvis are hanging out together. "Was this from a film or something?"

"No," Taylor said. "We were supposed to go on a safari in Africa and Mom was going to shoot it and make some kind of television show, but we ended up not going."

"I think she's planning on dragging us out to someplace called an Arborium or something, so that it looks like a safari," Burton said. "Then she'll film the lions at the zoo and cut it together."

"Probably the Arboretum," I said. "They have a whole jungle setting out there that has been used for films for decades. They shot some early Tarzan movies out there."

"I thought Tarzan was a cartoon," Burton said.

"Before the cartoon, there were about ninety live action...oh, never mind. Just let me look around for a rocking chair."

"I don't think Mom has one," Burton said. "Why do you want one?"

"Yeah, I thought you were after the silverware," Taylor added.

"Oh," Burton muttered. "Was that rocking chair thing like a joke? Like you're so old?"

My brain suddenly conjured up the image of a birthday party clown sweating his greasepaint off in front of these two and then deciding to go home and commit suicide. But before I could say anything, Taylor announced: "I'm going to get something cold to drink. C'mon, Burt." The two of them marched out of the room, presumably toward the kitchen.

"Nothing for me, I'm good, but thanks for asking," I called after their shadows. Perhaps I should have gone with them, not to keep an eye on them, but because number five on the list in my notebook is that you can learn more about someone by viewing the contents of their refrigerator than you can anywhere else. On the other hand, I was relieved to be away from the little brats for a few moments. I decided to use the opportunity to examine the living room more closely. A brick fireplace with an ornate grate was set into one wall, though it appeared not to have been used any time recently. Upon closer inspection, I saw that it was cleaner than my apartment. Its primary function was as a shelf; the mantle held several framed photographs, including one large, formal one of a man in military dress uniform. Examining it closely, I saw a small brass plate affixed to the frame that read: *Lt. Randall Frost.* This was Dad, the hero.

Perpendicular to the fireplace was the sofa, and across from it was a large plasma television atop a horizontal cabinet with containing the kind of equipment one would expect to find in the home of a couple of tween boys, chiefly a DVD player and a game console. There was also a VHS machine. Sliding open the large drawer as silently as possible, I found about two dozen games in PS3 format, but a lot more jewel boxes filled with homemade disks, each labeled "Brothers Alpha" followed by a situation or location: "Brothers Alpha on Horseback"; "Brothers Alpha at Space Camp"; "Brothers Alpha on Catalina"; "Brothers Alpha at the Art Museum"; and about fifty more. I stopped looking, afraid I was going to come across "Brothers Alpha Knocking Over a Seven-Eleven," or something else the knowledge of which would make me an accessory after the fact.

I closed the drawer and went to sit down on the sofa. The iron-and-glass coffee table in front of it was empty save for a large scrapbook, which I did not even need to open to gauge its contents. But curiosity got the better of me. Sure enough, it was a photographic record of the Brothers Alpha from what looked like preschool through to the present. The last third or so of the book consisted of professional acting headshots in a variety of poses and costumes, but virtually no changes of expression, like flesh-and-blood paper dolls. There was no agent logo on the shots, just "Nora Frost, Alpha Productions," and a phone number. I pulled out the card Nora had given me and checked it against the photos: the phone numbers were the same.

It was getting a bit dark inside the house, since the sun was sinking behind a hill, so I took the liberty of turning on a few lamps. It was quiet, too; the only sound I heard was the ticking of the clock that hung on the wall over the television, and which, miraculously, did not have pictures of the Brothers Alpha on its face.

I walked to the spacious dining room, which did not appear to have hosted many recent meals despite the large table. The table was covered with what looked like week's worth of mail, Hollywood trade papers, *BackStage*, which was a casting newspaper, and a box full of mailer tubes. I presumed these would eventually contain the posters of the boys protesting fox hunts. "You guys okay?" I called into the void.

"Of course we're okay," a voice replied, and I think it was Burton's. "It's our house."

"We're having soda, and Mom doesn't allow us to bring soda in the living room," Taylor's voice added. It stood to reason: what would happen if all those photos were to have something spilt on them?

"Okay, just checking."

A little while later, through the dining room window I could see headlights. Nora Frost's Lexus was pulling into the driveway and not a moment too soon for me. It had not been two hours, or even close to it, but it seemed like it. I went to the door to wait for her and she burst through a moment later. "Where are the boys?" she asked, not bothering with such formalities as "Hello."

"In the kitchen," I said. "They wanted sodas."

"I guess they can have a little splurge, since they performed so admirably today," she said. "Come with me." I followed her into the living room where she opened up her purse and withdrew not a cashier's check, but a stack of cash, which she flopped on the coffee table. "It's the whole ten-thousand, not half. I didn't think you would mind."

I had never before heard the sound of ten-thousand dollars in hundred dollar bills thumping down on a hard surface, but I enjoyed it. It was rich, warm and resonant. "I decided this would be easier than a cashier's check," she said.

I tried to think of a cool Bogarty comeback that would hide my astonishment at the sight of so much cash in one place at one time, but failed. Even inside my head, all I heard was an impressed, Bogart whistle. So after gaping for a moment, I said, "I don't mind at all. This is fine."

"Count it."

"Cases such as this are based on trust." I picked the stacks of bills up and forced them into various pockets. I probably looked like I was wearing bad stunt padding. *Do you have ten grand in c-notes in your pocket, or are you just glad to see me?* Mae West cooed inside my head. "I'll send over an agreement for you to sign tomorrow."

"Can't we operate through a verbal agreement?" she asked.

"A signed contract is standard procedure," I told her. "Sometimes people refuse to pay the investigator if they don't like the results of the investigation, so this is protection against that."

"But I've already paid you."

"All right, I'll send over a receipt for the cash, then."

"I would really rather prefer no paperwork of any kind, unless it's required by law."

"No, no, the law doesn't really have an opinion about it—"

"Then it's settled."

Why was she so resistant to having a paper trail? Well, I would worry about that later. Lots later. I had ten-thousand of her dollars already in my pockets, and I didn't want to push so hard that she would think better of the deal and ask for it back.

"Do you need anything else, or do you have enough to get started?" she asked.

"I'll need the names of any of the women you suspect might have sent that letter. Oh, and I'd like to see the letter, too."

"I have it locked away upstairs in my bedroom," she said. "I didn't want to leave it anywhere the boys might see it. I'll go get it. Stay here."

She left the room and I heard soft footfalls on a staircase. In less than a minute, they returned, this time coming back down. Nora's eyes darted around the room as she walked in, as though making certain the boys had not come in while she was gone. Once satisfied, she came over and handed me a piece of paper. It was plain typing paper on which was written in Sharpie:

TO NORA FROST....

EITHER KEEP THOSE KIDS OF YOURS OUT OF AUDITIONS OR I WILL. THIS IS NO JOKE! I HAVE HAD IT WITH TAYLOR AND BURTON GETTING ALL THE ATTENTION! UNLESS YOU WANT THEM TAKEN AND CUT UP INTO PIECES, YOU WILL RE-TIRE THEM FROM THE BUSINESS. THIS IS YOUR ONLY WARNING.

"Did this come in an envelope?" I asked.

"Yes."

"Do you still have it?"

"No, I threw it away."

I sighed. Doesn't anybody watch cop shows on television anymore? "Could it still be in the trash somewhere?"

"Trash pick-up was this morning. Did I do something wrong?"

"There is a lot the envelope could have told us. Its postmark could have identified the location of the sender."

"It didn't come in the mail," she said. "It was slipped under the door." She began pacing again. "That's what's so terrifying about it. Whoever sent it already knows where we live. But you said the letter itself might have fingerprints on it."

"There probably are, but the problem with fingerprints is that unless the suspect has a record, or was once in the military, or has a government job, there would be nothing to match them up against. But I'll see what I can deduce from this letter. Can I take it with me?"

She nodded.

"How soon can I get that list of people who might be responsible for this?"

"It will take me a little bit to put it together. How can I get it to you?"

"Email works," I said, reaching for my wallet and pulling out a business card. Taking a pen from my shirt pocket, I jotted my new email on the back of the card. One of these days I would have to get cards reprinted to include all the pertinent information, but I still had a box of the old ones, and I hated to see them go to waste. "The sooner the better."

"Tomorrow morning. Is there anything else you need from me?"

The question was asked with a pregnancy of tone that I did not really want to contemplate at the moment. So I settled for a legitimate question. "What do you do, Nora?"

"Do?"

"For a living. I'm looking around at all these photos and oil paintings and photographic cutouts, and you clearly paid for that photo shoot today, and you've just handed me ten-thousand dollars in cash, not to mention this house, so you clearly have money. I'm just curious what you do to get it."

"Well, I and the boys receive a military pension from my late husband, but.…"

"But?"

"I am what you would call independently wealthy through an inheritance. My parents were quite well off. Will that suffice, or do you need to know who they were?"

"Well, I think—"

"Have you ever heard of Steve Cousins and Natalie Strange?"

Had I? "Are you kidding? I loved Steve Cousins!" I said.

She looked at me curiously. "I trust you're not speaking literally."

I knew what she meant. Steve Cousins was an actor of the 1950s and beyond, and the epitome of what used to be called a light leading man. He had style and charisma to spare, if not outstanding talent, but he reliably got the job done while the Paul Newmans and Richard Burtons were getting all the attention. His biggest claim to fame was a 1960s television series called *Luger* about a private eye named Steve Luger, since television was never interested in a private eye named Bob Schwartz. Cousins died, to the best of my recollection, about ten years ago. It was a long-standing rumor that he was gay and that his marriage to actress Natalie Strange, who had been a starlet at Universal in the 1950s, and then later enjoyed a career renaissance on Broadway in the 1970s, had been one of convenience, since she was suspected of being a lesbian. They were the ultimate lavender couple, insiders hinted. But despite all that, the two were also known as the happiest couple in Hollywood because, it was said, they had a wide-open marriage in which neither had to worry about infidelity, since it was already a given. In the 1980s they turned up on shows such as *The Love Boat* and *Fantasy Island*, and even in late life were depicted as the ideal couple.

"What I mean," I said, "is that I love Steve Cousins' work. You're Steve and Natalie's daughter?"

"Their adopted daughter. Mother died six years ago, and Dad a few years prior to that. I'm the sole beneficiary of their estate, which was considerable. In addition to acting, my father was a rather astute businessman. He had real estate holdings on the side."

"Wow," I said, suddenly feeling like I had gained insight into Nora Frost. She had been raised by movie stars, and even though they were second tier movie stars, she felt she had to live up to the attention and glamour awarded to her parents, but did not have the natural equipment to do so. But now that she had children of her own, she was projecting the desire for that same attention and glamour that had escaped her onto them. Rosario, the costume woman, had intimated as much. "So you got everything when your mom passed away?"

"She didn't pass away, Dave, she died," Nora said softly. "In her final years she had become rather forgetful, and like so many other forgetful people, she refused to acknowledge that she was forgetful. She wouldn't remember whether or not she took her pills so one day she ended up taking too much."

"I'm sorry, Nora."

She shrugged. "Life goes on." Clearly she had managed to build a wall around her feelings.

"I will do my best to find out who is behind this letter," I said.

"I'm counting on that."

"Don't forget to email that information to me."

"I won't."

I walked to the dining room and called, "Goodnight, guys."

"See ya," a voice replied from a distance, and I think it was Taylor's.

I walked to the front door, but before I could leave, Nora asked: "Dave, do you mind if I ask a personal question?"

"Go ahead."

"How old are you really?"

"I'm thirty-two, Nora."

"Okay. You seem younger."

"So I've been told."

"Do you want to know how old I am, Dave?"

"I don't wish to be rude."

"I don't mind at all. I will be forty in October. How do I look?"

You look mahvellous! Billy Crystal said as Fernando Lamas inside my head, but I forced it away. "Do you really want me to answer that?" I said instead.

"I wouldn't have asked otherwise."

"I think you look damn fine for any age," I said. *Sheez*! I thought, hearing it bounce back. *Where the hell did that come from*?

"Take your money and get your ass out of here," she commanded, but neither her expression nor her voice registered displeasure.

"All right. I'll be in touch."

She leaned close and breathed: "Touch me any time." Then she closed the door in my face.

Bogart or Mitchum would have had something to say back. I simply rubbed my nose.

FOUR

By seven the next morning, the Barney's Beanery chili cheese burger and fries I had treated myself to last night after leaving Nora's were still reminding me why I don't treat myself more often. After getting up and downing an Alka-Seltzer, I stumbled into the shower and shaved, and by nine I knew I had a decision to make: I could stay home and feel lousy, or steel myself to go into the office and feel lousy. I opted for the latter. Grabbing my laptop, I headed out. My first stop was the bank, where I deposited the majority of my newfound wealth. "I held up a gas station," I explained to the young female teller as I handed over the bills and, fortunately, she laughed. Ironically, my second stop after the bank was a gas station, where Exxon/Mobil held me up.

I got to the office a little after ten, beating the mailman. Powering up the laptop, I saw that there was indeed an email from Nora. Opening it, I found no personal message of any kind, not even "Hi," simply a list of names. Nora Faust was certainly not one to leave a trail, even a digital one. Plugging the laptop into my aging laser printer, I put out a copy. The toner was starting to run out so there was a pale line running through the print (why is it that machines invariably know when you've suddenly come into money and respond by breaking or running dry?). The names on the printed page were:

Marta Wheeler, Denise
Leslie Brielle, Alexis

Carole Gould, Nathan
Monica Epper, Tiffany
Cristina Diaz, Hugo

The full names I took to be the mothers, and the second names the children, and of course, there had to be one called "Tiffany." Finding them should be a cinch because I have at my disposal a tool about which Bogie, Mitchum, Dick Powell, Alan Ladd and Charles McGraw could only have dreamt. Sure, they had snappier patter and cooler clothes, and their celluloid adventures were definitely more thrilling than the run-of-the-mill stuff a real PI engages in, but they would've had to start pounding the pavement and following leads and clues to find even one of these women. In today's investigative world, we have databases.

Within a half-hour I had addresses and contact numbers for four of the women on the list. Only Leslie Brielle remained elusive. But obtaining four was a pretty good start. Picking up the phone, I dialed the number for Marta Wheeler. After three rings, it went to a recorded message:

> *This is the Klaster-Wheeler household…if you are calling for Bob, Marta or Denise, please leave a message when you hear the beep…if however you are looking for anyone not named Bob, Marta or Denise, are selling something, or do not understand what I'm saying because you don't speak English, do us all a favor and just hang up. BEEP.*

"Hi," I began, "I'm calling for Marta. My name is Dave Beauchamp and I'm calling regarding a new television show—"

"This is Marta," a crisp voice suddenly burst in. It was the voice from the machine.

"Oh, you're there."

"I screen all calls. You just never know. Mr. Beauchamp, you said? Hi, how are you? I imagine you're calling about Denise.

Are you a casting director?"

"Actually, no—"

"Producer, then?" she asked before I could finish.

"I'm calling in regards to the reality show that Denise—"

"*Junior Idol*," she blurted. "You must be calling from Max Gelfan Productions. Do you need her to come in again?" There was a sense of urgency, if not desperation, in her voice.

I jotted down the name of the production company and said, "No, Ms. Wheeler, I'm not part of Max Gelfan Productions, and I'm not in a position to offer Denise a job. I'm calling on behalf of Nora Fr—"

The phone slammed down before I could get the entire second syllable out.

I waited two minutes before calling back. After listening to the recorded message once more, I said after the beep: "Ms. Wheeler, it's Dave Beauchamp again. I'm a private investigator. Someone has made a threat to the Brothers Alpha, Nora's sons, and—"

The line picked up. "And that broodmare is accusing *me*?" Marta Wheeler screamed.

"She's not accusing anyone in particular," I said, trying to sound soothing. "She has merely asked me to check things out."

"Let me tell you a few things about your client, Mr. Beauchamp. There isn't anyone in this town who's ever met her who doesn't want to push her in front of a bus."

I cleared my throat and said: "Well, I'll admit she is a bit insistent—"

"She's the stage mother from Hell! Nora Frost goes into casting sessions and insists that her two little cadavers be seen before anyone else since she considers it a personal insult that they are required to audition in the first place. I was at one call with her where she didn't just bring one headshot of boys, she brought dozens, all autographed, and handed them out to the other kids who are there to audition, telling them that someday they'll be able to say they had met the Brothers Alpha! She tapes their every breath with a cell phone camera, too, claiming that she's making a documentary about them. I was told that she once actually locked another kid in the bathroom at the casting office so the boy couldn't do his audition. When they finally found the kid he was in hysterics, and his mother, who thought he'd been kidnapped, had to be taken to the emergency room. *That* is your client, Mr. Beauchamp."

"Um, if she's that bad, why do casting directors put up with it?"

"They don't more than once, but there are a lot of casting directors in town. Word hasn't gotten to all of them, apparently. But she keeps coming back for *Junior Idol*. It's supposed to be an *American Idol* for kids, but I'm frankly starting to wonder if this isn't a talent program at all, but one of those conflict reality shows where they're going to pit the kids and the mothers against each other. Believe me, Mr. Beauchamp, the Alphas haven't been brought back because of their talent, because they haven't any. Denise has been taking dance lessons since she was four, and voice and acting lessons as well. She's a pro. A lot of the other kids are, too. There's one girl named Tiffany Epper who's got a singing voice you wouldn't believe. Another kid, Hugo somebody, does impressions. He's ten or eleven, but he can do the best SpongeBob you ever heard. And Denise, of course, like I said, she's got it. But the Alphas, they're synthetic, they don't respond like flesh-and-blood human beings, let alone normal child performers."

"Thank you, Ms. Wheeler, you've been very helpful, so please forgive me for asking this, but simply for the record, have you sent a letter to Nora Frost making any kind of comment about Taylor and Burton, even if it was not meant to be taken seriously?"

"No...I...have...*not. Were* I to send some sort of letter, it would not be to threaten the boys, who I actually feel sorry for. But as I've told you, I sent no letter of any kind. Until now, I never even knew their names, only the Brothers Alpha. Now I really think I've said all I need to say about this."

"Thank you for your time, Ms. Wheeler, I certainly appreciate it," I said, to a dead phone line. She had hung up around the word *you.*

I sat back at my desk and contemplated the best course of action. I could tell Nora that I would not be pursuing the case, and return the ten-thousand dollars, since there was no signed contract, or....

Oh, who was I kidding? Even if my client was a gene mix of the Wicked Witch of the West, Nurse Ratched and Elizabeth Bathory, I was not in a position to throw away ten-grand. Having finally discovered the price of my soul, I figured it was nonreturnable, like a damaged package. Besides, someone had threatened the twins, either seriously or frivolously—and let's face it, these days the latter can be mistaken for an act of terror—no matter what Nora Frost was like personally.

I managed to speak with two more of the mothers, Cristina Diaz and Monica Epper, each of whom basically reiterated what Marta Wheeler had told me on all levels. Cristina revealed that she could not cut loose with what she really wanted to say because her son Hugo, the pre-teen mimic, was within earshot, but Monica had no such problems. Her vocabulary made that of Nora Frost's sound like a kindergarten teacher's. I contemplated going to the emergency room to have my ear swabbed out. But both denied sending the letter. What was perhaps more pertinent, both had a reaction similar to Marta Wheeler's, which was that no matter what they would like to do to their mother, they would not have threatened the children. What I found particularly interesting, however, was that like Marta, Cristina Diaz and Monica Epper did not know the boys' given names. They were all familiar only with their showbiz moniker, the Brothers Alpha. Yet the writer of the note had mentioned them by name.

That shifted particular weight to either Carole Gould or Leslie Brielle as being the sender of the letter, but since I was unable to find a number for Leslie, and the message I'd left on Carole's machine had not yet been answered, I had no way of verifying my suspicion. But I really had no illusions that simply calling them up and asking if they were guilty was going to yield results. That sort of direct confrontation only worked on *Perry Mason*. I might have better luck with Max Gelfan, or someone on his staff who had seen all the women and all the kids in one room together. I Googled *Max Gelfan Productions* and learned that while it was not as well established as the operations formed by Merv Griffin or Vin di Bona, it seemed to have a solid enough reputation as a game and reality show producer. Finding an address for the company was easy, too; it was just over the hill in Hollywood.

I headed out, deciding to forego lunch, since the chili cheese combo from Barney's was still singing an aria in my stomach. *I don't know which is weaker,* a voice said inside my head, *your brain or your belly.*

Be quiet, Mitchum. I have a job to do.

Traffic on the 101 was kind, meaning I made it down to Hollywood in about forty-five minutes. Max Gelfan Productions was headquartered in one of those almost-studios that called themselves "production centers"—multi-level build-ings containing small television stages somewhere inside, but consisting mostly of offices. This one was located on Gower, south of Hollywood Boulevard. I managed to find a parking place on the street (which effective used up my quota of luck for the next two months) and walked into the lobby area. A young, dark-haired, heavily-tatted woman sat behind the desk. "Can I help you?" she asked.

"Max Gelfan Productions," I said.

"Who do you wish to see?"

"The person in charge of casting."

The eyes narrowed, and I was able to read her thoughts enough to well realize I had as much chance of actually coming face-to-face with the talent coordinator for Max Gelfan Productions as I had dining with the president. Maybe less.

"Do you have an appointment?" she asked.

"No, but I'm here on behalf of Nora Frost."

The woman's demeanor changed as though digitally morphed. The defiance disappeared and was replaced by weary resignation. She muttered something under her breath—I thought it was *Oh, Christ*, but I wasn't certain. "Are you an attorney?" she asked.

"I used to be, but I got over it," I replied. "Now I'm a private investigator."

"Oh, *god*," she moaned.

"Look, ma'am, I'm not here to cause anyone any trouble, I promise. I'd just like to put a few questions to the person who has been auditioning kids for *Junior Idol*. If you tell me I can't, I'll accept that and leave, though I hope you won't."

She sized me up and down and apparently decided I wasn't one of the Four Horsemen of the Apocalypse, even if my employer was, and so punched a number into her desk phone. "Terrence, it's Cassandra, down front. Could you come down here please? I know, I know, but I think you might want to anyway. Someone's here about the Brothers Alpha. Okay, thanks." She hung up and said, "Have seat. Mr. Holving will be with you in a minute."

"Thank you very much," I said, and made my way to a circular sofa that probably looked good on the pages of a design magazine, but was uncomfortable as all get-out to actually use. About three minutes later, a forty-ish, very thin guy with close-cropped hair appeared and Cassandra pointed him in my direction. "Hi, I'm Terrence Holving, talent coordinator for Gelfan Productions, and you are...."

"Dave Beauchamp," I said, sticking out my hand, which he wetly shook.

"What's this about, Mr. Beauchamp?"

"Can we go somewhere and talk?" I asked.

"My office," he said, turning and heading toward the elevator. I followed, and within seconds we were on our way up to the fourth floor. "So," Holving said, "how are the Brothers Alpha?" The last two words were delivered with the kind of sarcastic bite in which Paul Lynde would have taken pride.

"Creepy and unnatural as ever," I said, truthfully.

Terrence Holving burst out with a choppy, gaspy laugh, like he'd been punched in the stomach with a joke book. "Well, at least I know you're acquainted with them," he said, as the elevator doors opened onto the fourth floor. "This way." We went down a very convoluted hallway, which I doubted I could have navigated on my own, and past a reception desk emblazoned with the "Max Gelfan Productions" logo. The knockout blonde seated behind the desk smiled as we walked by. Finally we came to a small, but well decorated office. There were posters and mementoes from any number of past projects covering the walls. Holving closed the door behind us. "Please sit, Mr. Beauchamp," he said, motioning me to a chair, and then seating himself behind his overburdened desk. "What do you want to know about the Brothers Alpha?"

"First, Mr. Holving, please understand that while I am a private investigator who has been hired on a matter by Nora Frost, I am in no way here to threaten you or anyone else in Max Gelfan Productions. I don't as a rule start conversations with that kind of disclaimer, but in the short time I've known Nora Frost, I understand how it might be best to get that out in the open right up front."

"She's some piece of work," Holving said. "But hiring a detective? What in god's name does she think we did?"

I explained as best I could the written threat to the boys, and how I had already contacted several of the other mothers involved in auditioning for *Junior Idol*.

"Oh, good god," he muttered. "How like Nora to think everybody's out to get her little darlings. It's people like her that sometimes make me wish I'd stayed in Topeka and become a high school music teacher. All the moms want their kids to shine, but Nora thinks hers shit rainbows, pardon my French."

"But what about the other moms?" I pressed. "Could her fears be warranted? Have you seen anything that might be construed as vindictive behavior?"

"No. One of the mothers actually pulled her daughter out of the running because of Nora."

"Would that have been Leslie Brielle, by any chance?" I asked.

He smiled suspiciously. "You seem to have all the answers already."

"Not at all. It's just that Nora gave me a list of five other moms, which I took to be those she encountered in the course of these auditions, and the only one whose name did not pop up immediately on the database was Leslie Brielle. That would indicate that she doesn't really want to be found, which I would think is something of a liability for this kind of business. Or, it may indicate that she is overly protective of her daughter on a personal level, and is afraid someone is going try to get to her, which would be in line with pulling her out of a contest at the first sign of trouble. So was it Leslie Brielle, right?"

"Yes, it was Leslie, and she pronounces her name *Brie*, like the cheese. Lexy...Alexis...that's her daughter, desperately wants to be in the spotlight, but for some reason that makes Leslie nervous. She goes along with her daughter's wishes, but reluctantly. Lexy, in fact, seems to be the dominant one in the relationship."

"What does Lexy's father think of all this?"

"Leslie mentioned one time that she was divorced, but winced as she said it, as though the word itself hurt and frightened her. I think it must have been a bad breakup."

"So you don't think there's any way possible that Leslie could have sent a nasty letter?"

"No, no way. Lexy, now...."

"Are you serious?"

Terrence Holving gave me a wry look that indicated he was not. "Oh, in ten years, maybe. I don't know. Look, Mr. Beauchamp, all of us around here grit our teeth and do what we can to get through every visitation by Nora, but in answer to your question, no, I cannot think of anyone who would actually threaten the twins...oh, pardon me...the *brothers*, with violence. It's not their fault."

"True, but if someone wanted to hurt Nora, really hurt her, wouldn't that would be the easiest way? Do you happen to have a contact number for Leslie Brielle? Just so I can cover all the bases and earn the money I'm being paid."

Holving sighed and reached for the desk phone that was on the executive table, jabbing in a number and waiting. "Hi, Janelle? Could you get the phone number for Leslie Brielle and bring it to me right away? Thanks." He hung up. "Mr. Beauchamp, I'm not going to ask you what Nora is paying you to investigate this, but whatever Nora it is, I'll double it if you could somehow convince her to never enter this building again."

"Can't you do that by not calling her in?"

"That's just it, I *don't* call her in. I called the boys in for an audition when we first started work on *Junior Idol*, based on their photos, but it was clear from that session that they didn't have what we were looking for. Even their camera slate took multiple takes. As far as I was concerned, we were finished with them, but Nora keeps showing up. Somehow she knows when we're holding callbacks. I don't know how. But it has gotten easier to just run the boys through their paces and send them home than to fight it, so that's what I do. If you can discover how she's finding out about our calls, I'd appreciate it, because it's not me who's inviting her back."

"Have you specifically told her to stay away?" I asked.

"God knows I should, but in an audition situation, sometimes the path of least resistance is the easiest way."

"Couldn't you inform her through a letter?"

"I suppose so, but—" He stopped and regarded me with a narrow-eyed stare. "Are you accusing *me* of sending that threatening letter to her?"

"I'm just covering the bases, Mr. Holving," I said, as innocently as I could.

"Have you even seen this supposed letter?" he demanded. "Are you sure it exists, instead of being some figment of her demented imagination?"

I had not planned on showing him the actual letter, but now I pulled it out, unfolded it and set it down on the table. "As you can see, it specifically tells her to keep the kids away."

"Shit," he said, sliding the letter back to me after having read it. "I cannot state this emphatically enough. I had absolutely *nothing* to do with this. Threatening the boys would be a way of giving them attention, and I don't *want* to give them attention. I want Nora and the twins to go away, move to Arkansas, or somewhere."

As I refolded and returned the letter to my pocket, I heard a light tapping on the open door and a young woman came in holding a sheet of paper. It was the blonde who had smiled at us from the reception desk, now fully upright and visible. Usually I don't gawk at women, but it was hard not to stare at this one. Barely concealed under a painted-on tee shirt emblazoned with the logo for the game show *Brain Trust*, which I assumed Max Gelfan Productions produced, the young woman's bust thrust forth with the kind of 3-D effect of which James Cameron could only fantasize. Her lower half, though, was petite. If this woman ever tired of her job with Gelfan she could start a new career on *Sesame Street* by turning sideways and playing the letter P.

"Here's the number you asked for," she said, handing the paper to Holving.

"Thanks, Janelle," he said, barely looking at her. Either he couldn't have cared less about her figure, or had grown used to it, and although I had known him but a few minutes, my money was on the former.

Forcing myself to concentrate on her face, I saw that her upper lip was a little too large to be natural. Clearly she had undergone a collagen treatment, but the end result was to turn her lips into a parody of her body: heavy on top, light on the bottom. Maybe that was the point. She bounced out of the room, and I continued to gape at her with every step.

"She has a boyfriend, you know," Holving said, passing over the paper containing Leslie Brielle's information.

"Oh, yeah, well…she'd have to, wouldn't she?" I stammered, trying not to blush. "She kind of overdid the lip, though."

"I really don't like to gossip about my staff," he replied.

"Sorry."

"But you're right, she did. God knows why. She was cute

enough before doing it. The guys around here who care were dropping down and biting sticks in half just at the sight of her. When she first got the lip done, though, I thought she'd been assaulted in the parking lot."

"How much does a procedure like that cost?"

"Cost? I don't know. Why? Are you thinking of plumping your lips?"

"No, I'm just wondering where she got the money for it. Does Max Gelfan pay everyone so well that the assistants can afford cosmetic tweaks?"

His face darkened, and I could see him trying to follow my thoughts. "What are you suggesting?" he asked.

"You believe that someone in this office is passing information onto Nora Frost without your knowledge, someone with access to all the phone numbers. Someone who might be compensated under the table."

"Good god, you think Nora was paying her to be informed about callbacks?"

"Would you put it past Nora?"

"No, but I'd like to be able to put it past Janelle."

"There's one easy way to test her," I said, and then outlined a plan to him, to which he listened with a grim expression.

"All right," Holving said. "We'll walk out past her desk." Getting up, he led me down a different maze-like hallway, until we came to a reception desk at which Janelle was seated. Somehow, the affect of her torso was even more enhanced while seated. "So," Holving began, following my plan, "if you would tell Leslie that we'd really like to see her and Lexy on Friday, that would be great. Two in the afternoon. We'll call the others from here."

"Will do," I said. "Thank you for your time, Mr. Holving." As he headed back to his office, I turned to Janelle and smiled. "Nice meeting you," I said. "Um, could you tell me how to get out of here?"

"Sure," she said, standing up and shading the desk. "Go down here, turn left, and you'll come to the elevator. It will take you down to the lobby."

Thanking her, I set out into the labyrinth. Fortunately, her directions were correct, and hopefully, she did not realize she was being set up. I had no intention of telling Leslie Brielle anything about an audition on the twenty-fourth, but if Nora and the boys suddenly showed up at two o'clock on Friday we would know there was only one place she could have gotten the information. I hoped I was not getting Janelle fired. Then again, I doubted she would be out of work long, as she appeared to possess the natural attributes for getting ahead in Hollywood that have been in place since the days of Mack Sennett.

As I went back to my car, which I was glad to see was still there, and unticketed (the police in Hollywood materialized out of thin air to cite you and then disappeared in a puff of smoke, like Nightcrawler in *X-Men*). It was like a sauna inside the car, which is what happens when you leave your wheels out on warm day and forget to crack the windows open. I turned on the engine and blasted the air as I sat behind the wheel and thought. It was seeming less than likely that any of the other mothers had sent that letter since it was the boys who were the focus of the threat, while everyone's anger, at least those I had spoken with, seemed to be directed toward Nora herself. Despite his protestations, Terrence Holving, or perhaps someone on the staff I had not yet met, were higher on the suspect list. Holving, at least, had a reason for not wanting her to bring the twins back in.

Then another possibility entered my mind. It was one I didn't like much, but it was not impossible. And, as Holving had said, threatening the Alpha Brothers like that would have been a way of giving them publicity. It also explained why their names were spelled out in the letter. Pulling out my cell phone I poked in Nora's number, but got only her answering machine. I didn't bother leaving a message. Instead I decided to go over to her house. If she wasn't home, I'd wait. I would like to get my ominous suspicion cleared up as soon as possible.

It took almost as long to get to her house in Los Feliz from Gelfan Productions as it had to get to the Gelfan's from the valley, thanks to the omnipresent city work crews that were tearing up half of the streets in Hollywood. On the way I was nearly broadsided by another driver, who apparently thought the red light was an early Christmas decoration. That was the price for living in Los Angeles: a near death experience every time you went out on the streets, but the heat's dry.

Nora's Lexus was there, so she was home. I was not looking forward to this, but, as Bogie might have once said, I don't like being played for a chump.

If, as I was starting to suspect, Nora *herself* wrote that letter and hired me as part of a hoax to get publicity for the boys, I wanted to find out and then get out as soon as possible. I had no compunctions about keeping her money, either. Nora Faust had paid me handsomely to discover the source of the letter; if it turned out that *she* was the source of the letter, I had still fulfilled my duty.

Parking behind her car, I got out and went up to the front door, but saw that there was no need to hit the doorbell or knock. The door was half open. "Nora," I called, but received no reply. I went ahead and knocked loudly on the open door. "Nora, are you there?" Nothing.

I went inside the foyer. The house was dark and still as the proverbial tomb. "Nora?" I called. "The door was open, so I came in." There was no reply. Maybe she was in the bathroom, unaware that the front door was hanging open, and she was going to panic upon hearing me and pull a gun on me. "Is anyone here?" I called again. "Nora? Taylor? Burton?" What was the name of Nora's assistant? Elena, that was it...like Elena Verdugo, the teenaged star of *House of Frankenstein*. "Elena?" I called, and received no reply.

I carefully moved into the dining room, and then toward the kitchen, which was also dark and empty. The only sound coming from it was that of ice cubes being dropped into the ice dispenser. I called everyone's name again, but somehow knew that nobody was going to answer me.

That was when I smelled it. "Oh, sheez, no," I muttered.

You see, unlike all the books, plays and movies in which bodies are hidden indefinitely somewhere in a house, and nobody knows they are there until they happen to stumble upon them, in real life bodies have a definitive calling card: they stink. Immediately upon dying a person's bowels and bladder are released, a scent that is rather hard to miss. That latrine stench was what I smelled as I made my way through the Frost house. The kitchen was empty, and next to it was a breakfast nook, which was similarly empty. But on the other side of it was a bathroom, and the light was turned on. Steeling myself, I peered inside.

I wish I hadn't.

FIVE

Not very pleasant, is it? the voice of William Powell said inside my head. No, Bill, it isn't. And I'd be perfectly happy if you would just take the case over from here, with or without Myrna Loy.

Nora Frost was in the dry bathtub, fully clothed, but as dead as the Black Dahlia. Her eyes were open, staring in blind shock, and there were two holes in her blood-soaked blouse. Why she was lying in the tub was anyone's guess. Maybe her murderer had come upon her in the bathroom, shot her, and she'd fallen there. Maybe whoever it was forced her into the tub and then shot her there so the blood wouldn't get on the floor. A neat-freak murderer. Possibly the medical examiner could tell.

As I stared at the body part of me...oh, let's be honest...*all* of me, every fiber of my being, wanted to turn around and run as fast as I could, get out of here, and try and forget the scene I was viewing and smelling. But I knew I couldn't. Running wouldn't solve anything. Besides, my car was outside. If I were to turn tail and run, I figured I had about a fifty-fifty chance that there was at this very moment someone out there walking their dog, and they would happen to see me fleeing the house and wonder what was up, and then later, once they learned Nora had been murdered, would be only too happy to tell the police what they had witnessed.

Kind of a tough spot, kid, Bogie told me.

There was no real way around reporting the murder and then waiting for the cops to show up, but before I did that I steeled myself to go through the house, room by room, praying with each step that I would not also find the bodies of two twelve-year-olds. It only took about five minutes to canvas every room in the house, all of them empty. In what was clearly the twins' bedroom—there were matching beds on opposite sides of the room and a shelf containing enough video games to support a retail store—I took a peek inside the large, walk-in closet, and felt relieved that it contained only clothing. A lot of clothing. Some of it qualified as costume pieces: trench coats, police uniforms, even spacesuits. If I looked long enough, I would probably find superhero outfits complete with capes, but I was not interested in pursuing it.

I was satisfied the Alphas were not in the house, which hopefully meant they had not witnessed their mother's murder. But where were they?

Confident that this was somehow going to come back to haunt me, since like good deeds, no act of concerned citizenship goes unpunished, I pulled out my cell phone, held it in one unsteady hand, and with a shaking finger dialed 911. When the dispatcher answered I gave my name, Nora's address, and then reported the murder. "I'm a private investigator," I said, wanting to get as many facts as possible down onto the recording that I knew was being made, "and I came over to meet with my client, Nora Frost."

"That is the decedent?" the woman's voice at the other end asked.

"That's right. I found her house open and discovered Nora's body in the bathtub."

"In the bathtub. Did she drown?"

"No, the tub is dry. She was shot."

"Why was she shot in a dry bathtub?"

"If I knew that, I'd have to be the murderer, and since I'm not, I don't know."

After double checking the address, the dispatcher said the police would be on their way momentarily. "Are you going to stay there?"

"Yes, in case the victim's children show up."

"How old are the children, sir?"

"Twelve. Twin boys."

"Where are they now?"

"I don't know."

"Are they in danger?"

"I don't know."

"All right, the police will be there soon."

I'm sure there are less fun things in the world than wandering around a large, dark house with a dead body in one of the rooms, but I hope I don't experience one any time soon. If this were a movie, I'd go back into the bathroom and discover that Nora was no longer in the tub, that maybe she was still alive, though hopelessly insane, and after having staged her own death for some bizarre reason, would begin to chase me around with a butcher knife.

"Stop it," I told myself.

Oh, but why? Vincent Price's voice replied in my head. *We're having so much fun!*

"She's still going to be there, Vinnie," I said aloud, and then forced myself to go back and poke my head into the bathroom. I was right, she was still there. Still silent. Still dead.

It was nearly fifteen minutes before I heard the approaching siren, a period of time in which I began to get the feeling back in my body somewhat. That one was followed by several other sirens and before much longer the first black-and-white, all guns a-blazin', screeched to a stop out in front of the house. I casually strolled through the front door, holding my ID, in front of me. A phalanx of LAPD officers piled out and marched toward the porch, though once there they waited for an officer in plain clothes to take the lead. He was tall, lean, with salt-and-pepper hair, and the prominent, sharp features of a French New Wave movie star. He wore a dark suit with no tie. "Your name Beauchamp?" he asked me.

"Yes sir. I made the 911 call."

"I'm Detective Colfax out of Northeast station," he said.

"Show me the body, then we need to talk." I nodded. Re-entering the house, I led Colfax and three uniforms to the bathroom. "You didn't touch or move anything, did you, Mr. Beauchamp?"

"I touched only doors and knobs," I said. "I searched the house to see if Nora's sons are here, and they aren't."

"All right, wait out there somewhere." I went back into the Brothers Alpha shrine room and stood around while the various police officers covered the house with strips of yellow tape and started searching every surface and corner like bloodhounds. Eventually Colfax came back out, though on his way to me he was stopped by a young Hispanic officer also in plain clothes. "The M.E. can't make it here for at least an hour," he said.

Colfax jabbed a thumb toward the bathroom behind him. "I don't think she's going anywhere. Mr. Beauchamp, come outside with me." I followed the detective back out onto the front lawn. Colfax pulled a battered notepad from his hip pocket and took a pen from his jacket. "Okay, sir, so you're a rent-a-cop that the decedent hired."

"Um, I'm a private investigator, detective," I said, fishing out a business card and handing it to him. "Rent-a-cops are usually security guards."

"What were you supposed to be investigating?"

I filled him in on the case, so far as I knew it. There was no reason for me to hold anything back, since my client was lying dead in the other room.

"You saw her just last night," Colfax said.

"I left around six-ish, maybe."

"And the boys were here then?"

"Yes."

"Where are they now?"

"That's what's worrying me. I don't know where they are. Nora's car is out front, and they can't drive on their own."

"You think someone has them?"

"I don't know. It's not impossible."

"It's also not impossible that they ran to a neighbor's house when they saw someone coming in to kill their mother. Hey,

Hector," he called, and the young plain clothes officer I had noticed earlier came trotting up. "Mr. Beauchamp, this is my partner, Detective Mendoza." The younger man nodded in my direction. "Mr. Beauchamp is a private investigator," Colfax added, and instantly Mendoza's eyes widened and I got the distinct feeling that he was trying to will me to turn into stone. "Hector, take a couple men and check each house up and down the street. See if you can find two twelve-year-old boys." Turning back to me, Colfax asked: "What are their names again?"

"Taylor and Burton Frost. They're twins, but not identical. Dark blonde hair...why am I describing them? Just look anywhere. This place is practically wallpapered with their pictures."

"Okay, pick your men and get going," Colfax ordered, and Mendoza sprinted away. "A detective already," Colfax mused, watching him go. "They make 'em younger every year."

"Are you sure you shouldn't put out an Amber Alert?" I asked.

"Those come from the Highway Patrol, and you can only put one out once an abduction has officially been reported. Are you officially reporting an abduction?"

"No. I mean, I just don't know."

"Then let's see what the house checks turn up before getting the CHP involved."

Behind Colfax and the hubbub of activity at the house I could see Mendoza and two uniformed officers going up and down the street, knocking on the doors of neighboring houses. Colfax was saying something but I didn't get it. "I'm sorry, what was that?" I asked.

"You never told me why you came over here this afternoon," he said.

"I wanted to talk to Nora. Confront her, I guess you could say."

"Oh, confront her."

"Yes, confront her, detective, but not murder her. If I was the one responsible for this, do you really think I'd call 911 and then stay here until the police showed up?"

"Do you know how often I hear that excuse? What were you planning to confront her over?"

I took the threatening letter out of my pocket and handed it to him. "This."

Colfax read it, then turned it over and scanned the back. "This is the threat you mentioned? The reason she hired you?"

"Yes, and I followed some of the leads she gave me, but after a while I started to get a little suspicious."

"Of what?"

"That this letter might be nothing more than a hoax, one that Nora herself fabricated. That's what I wanted to confront her about."

"What would lead you to suspect that?" Colfax asked.

I told him how none of the "suspects" seemed to know the first names of the twins, and how adamant Nora was that her sons not find out about this letter. "She claimed she was protecting them from the knowledge of the threat, but I think she might have been protected them from the knowledge that she was pulling a cynical hoax."

"But why would she do such a thing? It doesn't make sense."

"It does if the driving force of life is turning your children into celebrities. Once word got out that the boys were being threatened, particularly if she could point the finger at another stage mother, the press would eat it up like starving wolves. The boys would go from obscurity to the lead story on *Access Hollywood* overnight. Within a week, everyone in the country would know the Brothers Alpha. At the same time, all the women named on this list, her competition, as it were, would all be put on the defensive, forced to protest their innocence."

Colfax checked his notepad. "Alpha?" he said. "I thought their name was Frost."

"It is, but their billing is the Brothers Alpha. It's a stage name."

"I take it you never found out if this letter was legit or not."

"No, I can't prove anything either way. At this point, the only way to prove or disprove its legitimacy is to wait and see it the boys' bodies turn up someplace dismembered."

"No, we can do better than that," Colfax said, flagging down another uniformed officer and handing him the letter. "Take this and see if you can find matching paper and a black sharpie somewhere in the house. Better yet, see if there are any handwriting samples that look like they're from the victim, and not the kids." When the officer was gone, he turned back to me. "Okay, let's say that you're right, and the woman did send this to herself to generate publicity. How does that square with the fact that she's dead in there and her two sons are missing?"

"I have no idea."

"I...have...no...idea," he repeated as he wrote on his pad, a move I strongly suspected was a sarcastic comment. He pounded the period onto the paper, then folded up the pad and replaced it in his pocket. "All right, Mr. Beauchamp, thank you for your help. Now, here's the way it is going to play from here. I have to wait for the M.E., which might take awhile. You, on the other hand, are free to go do whatever it is that you do. But I will need you to go down to the station to fill out and sign an official statement. Sooner, rather than later. In fact, as soon as you leave here would be good."

"Is that an order, detective?"

"A suggestion. You know where the Northwest division stationhouse is located?"

"Of course," I lied. The truth was, I hadn't a clue where it was, but having been unable to figure out that I could compare the writing on the letter to a sample of Nora's penmanship, I did not want to compound my incompetence in front of him.

"Good, be there within the hour. And I hope I don't really have to give you the usual rap about not leaving town and all that, do I?"

"I'm not going anywhere."

Detective Colfax smiled...sort of. "Let me offer you some professional advice, then," he said. "If I need anything further from you, I will come to you. I have your card, I know where to find you. But from here on out, that's the only time I want to see you. I don't want you interfering with our investigation. Got it?"

"I can't even contact you if I have new information?"

"Are you holding anything back from me?"

"No."

"Then there's no reason you would have new information, right?"

"Um, well—"

"Case closed, Beauchamp. We'll take it from here."

"I guess I don't have a client anymore, anyway," I shrugged.

"Exactly," he said, cheerfully. "Now get out of here and go file your report at the station."

I got out of there, grateful that Detective Colfax had not noticed that I hadn't actually agreed in so many words to stay out of the investigation. All I had said was I didn't have a client anymore, which I didn't. But I felt that I still had at least a few more thousand dollars worth of work to do before I could let the matter drop. If nothing else, I had to find out what had happened to the twins.

I walked over to my car, only to discover that it had been parked in by one of the black-and-whites. I strode back to find Colfax, to get the cruiser moved, but Mendez and the two uniforms that had been canvassing the block, looking for the boys, beat me to him. "Nobody on this side of the street has seen the kids," said one of the officers, a young African-American whose muscular arms could probably tear an iPad in half.

"No one on the other side, either," declared the other uniform, a fifty-ish guy with a graying moustache and the beginnings of a paunch. "But I'll tell you one thing. Nora Frost was not very popular with her neighbors."

"Swell. More suspects." Colfax then noticed me. "Mr. Beauchamp, why are you still here?"

"I'd like to leave, but I'm parked in," I said. "Can you get someone to move one of your cruisers?"

"Let him out," he instructed the two officers, then turned and walked away. It took a few minutes, but they finally cleared a path for me out of the driveway. I waved pleasantly at the officers as I pulled onto the street. Halfway down the block, though, I was nearly hit by an oncoming car that seemed to have suddenly lost control. I slammed on the brakes and the other driver did the same, screeching the rust-colored Taurus to a halt so violently the car turned sideways. A young, pretty woman jumped out of the driver's seat with a horrified look on her face. I likewise got out. "Excuse me, ma'am, but I need to—"

"My god, what are all these police cars doing here?" she demanded, ignoring the fact that she had nearly caused an accident. "Has something happened to Nora?"

I rushed over to her. "Are you a friend of Nora Frost's?" I asked.

"I'm Elena Cates, I work for her. Who are you?"

"I work for her too, sort of. My name is Dave Beauchamp, I'm a private investigator."

"What's happened?"

"You may have to brace yourself."

"Tell me what's happened!"

"Nora is dead," I said, quietly. "She's been murdered."

Immediately the woman became still. "Oh my god," she muttered, barely audibly. Another car was coming up behind her and tooting the horn. "What am I going to do now?" she asked.

"How about getting back into the car and pulling over so the street isn't blocked?" I offered. Of course, by now there was a car coming up behind me as well.

"I mean about them? What am I going to do with them?" She pointed into the back seat where, sitting perfectly placidly and oblivious to the armada of police cars just up ahead of them, sat the Brothers Alpha, both totally enrapt in their hand-held gaming consoles.

SIX

Twenty minutes later Elena Cates, the boys and me were all seated in a booth at The Pie Place, which was about a mile or so from Nora's house, on Vermont Avenue. I was having the banana crème, Elena was poking at a slice of strawberry, but shockingly, the twins said they weren't hungry. Maybe everything I'd been told about adolescent boys being bottomless pits was wrong, or maybe they were just too caught up in their palm-sized video games to worry about something as inconsequential as food.

Elena was the woman whose unavailability the night before had set Nora off. I learned that she had picked them up about ten this morning to take them to an art museum, at which time Nora Frost had been very much alive, and that was about all I was able to get out of her so far…that, and the fact that she did not do well under difficult or stressful situations. In fact, it was Elena's growing hysteria back on the street that caused me to take her by the shoulders and give her a mild shake, then instruct her to get back in her car and follow me to the pie restaurant.

So here we sat: she the color of paper, mechanically chewing a piece of pie, me wondering how much trouble I was going to be in if Colfax found out I had intercepted important witnesses, and the boys totally oblivious to everything except getting Deathmaster Bob to Level Six. We had not even told the twins about their mother yet.

The tense silence was all but drowning out the noise and activity of the busy restaurant, but then the boys broke it by announcing they had to go to the bathroom. Both said it in unison: I guess that's the sort of thing that happens at the same time for twins. Once they were gone from the booth, Elena said urgently: "We have to tell them."

"You're right," I said, "though I haven't yet come up with the best opening for saying, 'Oh, by the way, kids, your mom was shot to death.' How do you think they'll react?"

"Honestly, I don't know. I've been helping out with them for more than a year, and in that time I've never noticed much emotion of any kind. I think it might have something to do with the death of their dad. Nora turned him into a war hero to the point where Taylor and Burton are discouraged from thinking about him as a real person. Maybe this will make the dam break, or maybe they'll just retreat further into themselves."

"Or those games. But there's only one way to find out. Do you want to be the one to tell them?"

"Honestly, no." she said.

"I guess that leaves me, then," I said.

"You are the one who found Nora."

"Right."

Being relieved of the unpleasant duty of informing her charges that their mother was dead seemed to improve Elena's appetite. She shoveled a large piece of the strawberry pie into her mouth, and then said: "What will happen next, after you tell them?"

"I'll have to let the police know where they are. Otherwise they cops will keep searching for them."

"Maybe you should take them back to the house."

"No, because the police will still be there."

"So?"

"So I'd really rather not have to explain to them that I intercepted you and the boys not far from the crime scene and whisked you away."

"Couldn't you say we all ran into each other here at the restaurant?"

"That would be too radio show."

"Too what?"

Sometimes I forget that not everyone is into vintage movies, television and radio shows. In old radio shows of the 1940s, particularly the comedy shows, it was common to have script shortcuts in which two celebrities simply run into each other on the street, at the track, even on the moon, if that's where the show was set. *Why, look who's here…it's Sonny Tufts!* Bob Hope's voice echoed through my head. But real life—particularly that part of real life that involves policemen—hates those kinds of coincidences, and I could see how any attempt by me to tell Detective Colfax that, out of the entirety of greater Los Angeles, I *just happened* to go into a restaurant and run into Taylor and Burton Frost, would likely result in my arrest. But rather than try to explain all of that to Elena, I simply said: "What I mean is it's too contrived."

"What are you going to say, then?" she asked, not unreasonably.

"I don't know yet. I'll think of something."

Make it good, said the ever-helpful Bogie in my head.

I had a sudden flash. "How about this: we'll all go back to my office and I'll call Detective Colfax from there. I'll tell him you called me and that you had the boys the whole time, and that they're perfectly safe."

"Okay, but why would I call you?" she asked. "Until a half-hour ago, I didn't even know you."

"Right. Well…you called because Nora gave you my number and told you to call."

"Oh. Why?"

I leaned back in the booth and sighed. This was the same person who less than a minute ago was arguing that I should say I just ran into the missing twins in a pie shop. "How about this: Nora was angry that you weren't available to take the boys home last night, which meant I had to do it. So I'll say she forced you to call me and apologize for inconveniencing me."

She thought for a moment and then said, "Yeah, that sounds like something Nora would do."

"That's the story, then." I noticed that her face took on a worried expression. "Elena, trust me, the police will buy the story as long as we keep it consistent."

"That's not what's bothering me. The last time I ever spoke to Nora she was screaming at me for not being able to drop everything and come running anytime she snapped her fingers. At the time I was thinking how I never wanted to hear that voice again. Now I won't. I feel like this is my fault, somehow."

"Don't be silly, it's not your fault. Unless you're the one who killed her."

The worried expression morphed into one of shock. "Of course not!"

Across the restaurant I saw the twins emerging from the bathroom. "Remember, Elena, Nora gave you my number and told you to call."

Right as the boys arrived at the table, the waitress appeared to ask if there was anything else. "Can we just go home now?" Burton asked.

"Well, no," I said. "Not yet." To the waitress I added: "But we'll have the check, please." She pulled it out from her apron and dropped it on the table, with one of those practiced "tip-me-good-now" smiles and waited while I pulled out a twenty. Taking the money, she bustled away to get my change. Turning back to the twins, I said: "Taylor, Burton, I have something to tell you, something that's going to be very hard for you to accept. There's no good way to say it, I'm afraid."

"Has something happened to our mother?" Taylor asked.

"Yes, I'm afraid so."

"Is she hurt?"

"Guys, somebody…well, someone shot her."

"Dead?" Taylor whispered.

I nodded. "I'm very, very sorry."

The twins looked at each other, then looked back. "It was bound to happen one day," Burton said.

I picked up my glass from the table and took a large sip of ice water to see if it would warm up my blood. Maybe they were in shock. I've never actually seen anyone in shock, but from the stories I've heard, it turns you into a functioning automaton, which is how the boys were acting at present. Of course, that was not far removed from how they acted at most other times.

"Guys, do you understand what Mr. Beauchamp is saying?" Elena asked.

"We know what dead means," Taylor said.

"It means we're orphans now." Burton added.

"Boo hoo," Taylor sang, uncaringly.

"I think I need to go back to the bathroom again," Burton said.

"Come on," Taylor said, and the two of them ran through the restaurant.

"My god, those poor kids," Elena moaned, shaking her head. "They're probably going to fall apart in there."

"Maybe that's what they need," I said. "I'll give them a minute or so alone and then go check on them."

The waitress came back with my change and chirped her thanks as I laid out a few singles to cover the tip. The twins were now the only things holding us here. I was about to go into the bathroom after them when I finally saw the door open. Taylor came out first, followed by Burton. They both looked serious and glum, but I could not tell if they had been crying. "We want to go home," Taylor announced when he got to the table.

"You're home is still a crime scene," I told them. "We'll have to go somewhere else."

"Where?" Elena asked.

The best I could come up with on the spot was to go back to my office. Then I had another idea. Maybe its results would be catastrophic, or maybe it would result in a breakthrough of sorts with at least one of the boys, but I suggested that they split up, just like the police do with suspects, with one of them riding to my office in my car, and the other riding with Elena. The twins were not so much against the idea as puzzled at the notion that anyone would try to separate them. Finally, they agreed—if shrugs in unison can count as agreement—with Taylor coming with me and Burton with Elena. I had already given her my business card with the address, so I simply told her the best freeway exit to take and the nearest cross street to my building, and then headed out.

Buckled into the front seat, staring straight ahead, Taylor Frost remained still as a statue as I turned off of Vermont onto Los Feliz, heading for the 5 freeway North. "Again, Taylor," I said, "I'm really sorry about your mom." He said nothing. Finally, as we were transitioning to the 134 freeway, which would get us to the San Fernando Valley, he asked: "Did you, like, see her?"

"I'm afraid so. I found her in the bathroom."

He grimaced. "She must have hated dying there. She had a thing about the bathroom always being neat and spotless."

"Did you get along well with your mom?"

"Yeah, sorta," he said. "Sometimes she treated us like babies. She didn't want us to have friends. I think she was afraid we were going to grow up, and she didn't really want that." After that, he went back into his box.

The picture of Nora Frost was becoming clearer. Whatever names and terms might be used by others to describe her, only represented the symptoms. What fueled the cause was extreme control-freakery, a near mania to dictate the lives of her children, and everybody who came into contact with them. We rode on in silence for a bit longer, and then I tried once more to spark a conversation. "Do you and your brother like being in show business?"

"It's okay," Taylor said, unconvincingly. "It's what she wanted."

Okay, I'll admit I am not particularly skilled at talking to kids, but this was a situation that might have stymied Art Linkletter. The reason I wanted to split the boys up was in hopes that one of them might reveal information that could be useful in tracking Nora's killer: recent visitors, perhaps, or neighbors, or maybe the identity of someone the boys had overheard arguing with her on the telephone, anything that might give a lead. But the last thing I wanted was to push him for information in such a way that he backed off and closed up for good. I decided to change the subject. "You know, Taylor, your mom told me about your grandparents."

"What about them?" he asked.

"They were actors."

"Yeah."

"Well, I like old movies and TV shows, so I've seen your grandparents many times. It must be kind of cool to know that you're the grandson of Steve Cousins and Natalie Strange."

"I don't really remember them that much."

"Yeah, I guess you would have been pretty young when they died," I said, acknowledging another less than productive diversion. I glanced in the rearview mirror to see if Elena's car was in sight, and couldn't find it. Hopefully she was good at directions. If not, well, that was why God made the little green cell phones.

I did not try to get any more information from Taylor until I arrived at my office. Elena's car was already there, parked at the curb on the side street. Taylor and Burton waved at each other as I drove past to my assigned spot in the tiny parking area in back. The two of them were waiting for us at the front door of the building. "How did you manage to beat me?" I asked Elena.

"Well, for one thing I didn't take the Woodman exit like you said, I took the Van Nuys exit," she said.

"But that's back-tracking."

"And I also beat you."

She's got you there, sport, Errol Flynn commented in my head. How comforting it was to learn that after three years of coming to this building every day, I didn't know the best way to get there. I led everybody in and up the stairs to my office. The boys seemed happy to be reunited after twenty-five minutes apart, or at least as happy as they got. "All right," I began, taking my seat behind my desk, "the first thing we have to do is contact Detective Colfax of the police and let him know that the boys are okay. Where's my laptop?"

"Why are you asking us?" the twins said in unison.

"It was rhetorical, but I need it to look up the number of the Northwest police station."

"Can't you dial 411?" Elena asked.

"I'm still going to need my laptop eventually," I said. "I must have left it in my car. Everybody stay here, I'll be back in a minute." I got up and dashed into the hall and down the stairs, cautioning to the voices in my head: *The first one of you dead celebrity cutups who cracks wise about how smoothly I'm handling this is going to be banished*! Right; like I had control over who appeared inside my head and when. Still, the Hollywood Victory Tour remained blissfully quiet.

I ran out the building's back door and straight to my Toyota, expecting to find the laptop in the backseat, but not seeing it. I opened the trunk, which contained so much junk that I half expected someday to find Jimmy Hoffa hiding under it all. I rummaged through the junk—books, magazines, DVDs, grocery store cloth bags, a small suitcase with a change of clothes (you just never know), a package of toilet paper (you *really* never know), a miniature baseball bat that could double as a blackjack if I ever had occasion to press it into use (which, fortunately, I never had), and a bag of peanuts so old even Jumbo wouldn't have touched them. But no laptop. Sheez! Had I managed to leave it at the pie shop? No, I didn't have it there. But I did have it when I left for Nora's house, before all hell broke loose, and I had not used it since.

I checked the inside of the car again, and found it: it had managed to slide very neatly, and nearly invisibly, under the driver's seat. Grabbing the device, I headed back inside.

As I got back to the open door of my office, I called: "Everybody still there?"

"Oh yeah, the gang's all here," a voice answered. It did not belong to Elena Cates, or either of the twins. I stopped and watched as the form of a man appeared in the doorway. "Hello again, Mr. Beauchamp," Detective Colfax said, smiling like snake.

SEVEN

All right, I'll admit that I have never seen a snake smile, though some lawyers I've known have come close. The discomfiting grin on Colfax's face was the kind of sneer that should have been accompanied by a tympani roll, like the one that announces impending doom for Wile E. Coyote. I looked up, expecting to see an anvil.

"Come on in," Colfax said, inviting me into my own office. Detective Mendoza was there too, making the office a bit crowded.

"These policemen showed up right after you left," Elena whispered. Their presence was clearly bothering her.

"I went down to my car to get my laptop," I explained.

Colfax gestured toward the twins. "These two, I take it, are the ones you were so eager to have an Amber Alert issued for? You knew where they were the whole time, didn't you?"

"No sir, I did not," I protested.

"Then I suppose they showed up at the door selling magazine subscriptions and you invited them in," Mendoza sneered.

"Who sells magazines anymore?" Burton asked, guilelessly.

"That's just dumb," Taylor Frost added, never taking his eyes off his game console. Mendoza looked like he wanted to backhand the kid, but Colfax shot him a warning look.

"Look, Colfax," I began, "when I talked to you, I did not know where the boys were. Then I found out that Elena, whom I assume you've already met, had picked them up this morning and took them to a museum. Nora gave her my phone number at some point, so she called me."

"Is that true, ma'am?" Colfax asked, causing Elena to pale.

Come on, Elena; just like we rehearsed....

"Yes, of course," she said in a hushed voice. "Nora wanted me to apologize to Dave. He had to take the boys home last night in my place, because I couldn't get away, and that made Nora angry at me, so she made me call and apologize for not being available."

"Sounds like her," Taylor commented.

I picked up the story: "When she called I told her that something terrible had happened at the house. I suggested we... uh...."

Oh, what a tangled web we weave, a wry, jovial voice said in my head. It was Cary Grant.

"We, uh, what?" Colfax asked.

I stood there for what seemed like an eternity as the realization that it was not a cartoon anvil, but rather a serious flaw in the story I had fabricated, that was going to come crashing down on my head. I had gotten my story straight with Elena at the restaurant, but at that time the twins had been in the bathroom. If I gave the prevarication that I told everybody to meet me here, Taylor and Burton might wonder why I was omitting our trip to The Pie Place. And if I mentioned that we were all at The Pie Place, Colfax would well wonder why everybody so close to Nora's house made a special trip out here.

"Cat got your tongue, Beauchamp?" Mendoza prodded. I looked over at Elena, who simply looked back in confusion. Then I motioned for the detective to follow me out into the hallway, which he did.

"Detective Colfax, here's the thing," I said quietly. "The boys might be suffering from shock. You can see they're not acting normally."

"I had noticed something was wrong with them."

If he only knew.

"I don't want to keep talking about their mother's murder in front of them," I went on. "I'm afraid it might upset them even more. Isn't there a way we can let them go? They're safe, after all. Then I'll be happy to tell you everything."

Colfax thought for a moment, then walked back into the office. "Ma'am, do the boys have any place to go?"

"I can take them home with me," she replied. "They can stay there, at least temporarily."

"Isn't there any other family?"

"They have an aunt who lives in San Pedro. Nora's sister."

"*Nora's* sister?" I shouted, and all eyes turned toward me. "Um, I mean, how can that be? Nora told me she was adopted. Did the Cousins adopt two daughters?"

"Who's cousins?" Colfax asked.

"Nora's parents were the Cousins," I said.

"So she was inbred?" Mendoza asked.

"No, Nora was adopted by Steve Cousins and Natalie Strange, no relation," I said.

"To who?"

"To the aunt," Elena offered.

"I dunno, third base," Detective Colfax muttered, raising his arms in frustration, but also raising my estimation of him. Anyone who can quote Abbott and Costello can't be all bad. "So the vic, Nora Frost," he went on, "has a sister that was not raised by the cousins."

"Nora and her sister were orphaned as toddlers and then adopted by two different couples," Elena explained. "At least that's the story I got. A year or so back Nora hired a detective to try and track her sister down, and she found Marcella that way."

Congratulations to that detective. Whoever he was, he was better at this game than I was.

"That's the sister, Marcella?" Colfax asked.

"Marcella DeBanzi."

"Has anybody notified her yet?"

"I haven't spoken with her," Elena said.

"I only found out she existed a couple minutes ago," I added.

"All right, for the time being, you keep the kids, ma'am," Colfax said. "No sense getting the courts involved yet. But give the sister a call and let her know what's happened."

"Can we leave now?" Elena asked.

"Yeah, you can go. But leave me your contact information first, and contact info on the aunt, if you have it."

"I think I do," Elena said, pulling a small address book from her purse and flipping through it until she found the proper page. Then borrowing a pad of paper and pen from my desk, she wrote down her address and phone number, as well as those for the boys' Aunt Marcella. Ripping the page off of the pad, she handed it to the detective. "Okay?"

He examined the paper. "Okay. Thank you, Miss Cates."

Elena then she collected the boys, who only barely looked from their games, and started for the door. Before she had exited, though, Colfax said: "Oh, before you go, ma'am, what time did you pick the boys up this morning?"

"About nine-thirty," Elena said.

Colfax thought about that for a moment, then nodded, and said, "Fine, thanks. We'll be in touch."

"I'll call you, Elena," I said, as she exited the office with the boys. But at the door Burton stopped and turned back. "Is it true that they call you guys 'dicks'?" he asked.

"It's an old expression for a policeman or detective," I replied, stupidly.

"Hey, there's a bunch of real dicks in there!" Burton crowed, before Elena pulled him away and down the hall.

"Charming family, don't you think?" I said, once they had gone.

"If those two brats were mine, I'd sell them into slavery," Mendoza muttered, and while the young detective had offered me nothing much to like about him, I couldn't entirely disagree with his assessment of the Brothers Alpha.

"Okay, Mr. Beauchamp," Colfax said, "everybody else is gone, so we can talk freely. What was the point of bringing the boys here?"

Fortunately, the interval between the last time I attempted to answer that question had given me time to think. "When

Elena called me," I began, "I suggested that she bring them here instead of taking them to their house, and risk having them see the body of their mother, which I assumed would be a little traumatic for a couple of twelve-year-olds. I was just about to call you when you showed up."

"You weren't even here when we showed up," Mendoza spat.

"I told you, I was getting my laptop out of my car, so I could find the number for the Northeast station so I could call you. I gave you a business card, but you did not give me one."

"What I gave you, Beauchamp, was a request that you go down to the station and give an official statement."

"Right, but when Elena called, that seemed to take precedence."

He glared at me for a few seconds, and then said, "All right. But don't forget to do it." Fishing in his pocket, he pulled out a card and handed it to me. "Here. No excuses this time." I glanced down and read *Dane Colfax, Detective II*.

Dane Colfax? Was anybody other than a 1950s leading man using a studio-dictated stage name really called *Dane Colfax*?

"I'll go, I promise. Want me to do it right now?"

"I have a couple extra questions for you first," Colfax said. "One concerns an email we found on the victim's computer, which had been sent to you early this morning."

"Nora emailed me the names of certain people to question."

"When did you receive it?"

"Well, it was right after I booted up my laptop, and that was around eleven or so."

"That's when you received it, or when you read it?"

"When I read it. I didn't get into the office until then."

"Must be nice not to have to get up in the morning," Mendoza said.

"If you really want to know the truth, business is a little slow at present, so there's not much reason for me to come in at the crack of dawn. But if you want, I can check my computer and see when the email actually came into my system."

"Please do," Colfax said.

I went over to my desk and powered up the attaché-sized device, and checked the email. "It says eight-forty-seven," I said.

Mendoza referred to a notepad, and then said: "It was sent from the victim's computer at seven-forty-two. That's a discrepancy."

"I don't have the speediest email system," I said.

"That was the last time you had contact with Nora Frost?" Colfax asked.

"Yes."

"And Elena Cates picked up the kids at nine-thirty, so that's the last time we know Nora Frost was alive."

"That would follow logically."

"And you said earlier that you got over to her house and found her at eleven forty-five or so?"

"I think that's right. I found her a few minutes after I arrived. If you need to know the exact time, wouldn't the recording of the 911 call I made have it?"

Colfax turned to Mendoza. "Have you checked the 911 call yet?"

The younger detective shook his head.

"A rent-a-cop can figure out to check the call, and you can't? Do you want to make Detective Two or not?"

"What's to say he didn't arrive earlier in the morning and shoot her himself?" Mendoza spat.

"And then I called the police on myself? I said. "Hey, I have an idea, why don't you put me in a lineup and see if I can pick myself out?"

Mendoza took a step toward me, clearly intending to look intimidating, but Colfax put a hand out to stop him. "Just go check on that 911 call, okay, Hector?" he said.

"Fine," Mendoza said, pulling out his cell, and shooting me with a 9mm police special eye bullet before going out into the hall to make his call. *Good strategy*, Bogart's voice said, *hacking off a cop who already hates your guts*. Yep, that's me, always thinking. "Is there anything else I can help you with, Detective Colfax?" I asked.

"I think we're done. Go file that report, like I told you."

"I will. Scout's honor. But in return, can I take a look at that piece of paper that Elena wrote out for you? The information might come in handy."

"No, you cannot," Colfax said. "I told you once you're officially through on this case, unless I arrest you."

"I'm not responsible for Nora's death."

Colfax smiled, and somehow the expression was less than friendly. "You said you know where the Northeast Station is, right?"

"Well, it's...." I glanced down at the card he had given me, and saw it was on San Fernando Road. But San Fernando Road runs through at least three different cities. "Actually, I'm not sure I do know."

"It's just past Forest Lawn. You can't miss it. I'll expect you within the hour, but if for some reason I don't come out, ask for Mendoza, though you may want to hope that I come out. If you don't show up, though, I'll come back for you. See you, Beauchamp." Detective Colfax spun around and headed out the door, calling, "We're done here, Hector," on the way out.

After my shivering stopped, I went and sat at my desk. Pulling my notebook out of the bottom drawer, I opened it and jotted down: *What's the point of being helpful, agreeable and cooperative with the police if they are going to hate you on first sight anyway*? I wonder how many private investigators before me had made note of such an observation. Sticking the notebook back in the desk, I sat for a few minutes and thought. So Nora Frost had a sister. You learn something new every day. Maybe if I stayed on this case long enough, despite Detective Colfax's exhortations against it, I'd learn why those twins acted like they'd been built by Disneyland. But who knows? Maybe all twelve-year-olds act like robots these days and I was slow finding that out. In any event, I wanted to talk to Marcella DeBanzi. I also felt that remaining in touch with Elena Cates was probably a good idea. Sure, Colfax had taken the paper with her information, but he apparently had spent too little time watching mystery movies to know the oldest trick in the book: the imprint shtick.

I fished through my desk drawer for a number two pencil, and to my delight, also found a ten dollar bill hiding amidst the Post-It notes. The pencil wasn't sharp, but it did not need to be. I lightly rubbed the point over the page on top of the pad until the imprint of what Elena had written on the sheet above began to emerge. It was faint, only barely readable, but barely was good enough.

"Thank you, Mr. Moto," I muttered as I held the page up and read:

Elena Cates
619 Lemon Grove Ave.
Hollywood, CA 90029
(323) 853-1436

Under it was written:

Marcella DeBanzi
1707 Hanford Ave.
San Pedro, CA 90732

There was also phone number for her, but the digits were harder to make out. After transferring the information as best I could decipher onto a clean sheet of paper, I folded it up and stuck it into my pocket, and then headed out for my appointment with Colfax. On the way I sidetracked into the drive-thru at the local Burger Heaven to grab lunch. I could eat it in the car and still make it to the station within the insisted-upon hour.

Finding the LAPD's Northeast station turned out to be easy after all. I just went to Forest Lawn, like Colfax had recommended, and waved a ketchup-stained hand at Dick Powell, Alan Ladd, and George and Gracie as I passed, hoping they'd tell all the others I said hi, then headed down San Fernando. The plain-looking police station was about a half-mile away on the left.

Once inside the building I asked for Colfax, and was delighted when he came out, blissfully free of Detective Mendoza. "You know, detective, you came straight here, and I came straight here," I commented.

"So?"

"Why didn't you just bring me down with you instead of racing me back?"

"In the car, you mean?"

"Because it's Hector's car," he said, "and I wanted him to keep his mind on his driving, instead of getting distracted because you're in the backseat."

"You make it sound like he'd try to kill me if he got the chance."

"We're only here to protect and serve the community, Beauchamp."

Yeah, but what if Mendoza was convinced that murdering me and covering it up was a form of serving the community?

"Follow me," the detective said, and I tailed him back to his desk. Never having been inside a police station before, I couldn't help but notice that it looked dunkier than those in movies and on TV, and had far fewer extras. Once we were at his desk, which was in a large, crowded office area that contained several other desks and several other officers all talking, I sat down and made my statement. It was comprised of everything I had previously told him, but now was on the record.

"Do you know of anyone who might have wanted Mrs. Frost dead?" he asked when I was finished.

"I knew her only a few hours, but that was enough to conclude that everyone who ever met her at least wanted her in traction."

"Including you?"

"No. She was a client, and she paid up front. I like that in a person."

"Everybody else had it out for her, though?"

"Do you know what a stage mother is?" I asked, and he nodded. "By all accounts Nora Frost was the most extreme example of the breed anyone had ever encountered. She torqued everybody."

"Great. The only thing worse than not having any suspects is having too many."

"Am I free to go now?"

"One more thing." Colfax pulled something out of a cardboard box and handed it to me. It was a framed photo of a man in military uniform. "Who is that?" he asked.

"That's the boys' father," I replied, having seen the picture in Nora's house. "He was killed in Afghanistan."

"Okay." Now he reached back into the box and pulled out another picture. This one showed a guy of about thirty, whose hair and style of dress strongly implied that the photo had been taken sometime in the mid-1980s. "Tell me who that is."

I studied the photo, but came up blank. "I've no idea. Where did you find this?"

"In Mrs. Frost's house," Colfax said. "It was in her desk. Oh, by the way, Beauchamp, I'm afraid you're wrong about that letter."

"How so?"

"We found samples of Nora Frost's handwriting all over the house and even though we've called in a specialist, a blind man could see that the writing on the note is different."

That was something of a setback for my theory, though I did not let on to Colfax.

"Well, thanks for *finally* coming in," he said, punching the qualifier. "Now, there's something I'm going to tell you, and I want you to listen and listen good. Stay out of this investigation. I appreciate whatever help you offered up to this point, but this is it, David, you're out of it now. I'm serious."

That was the first time he had called me by my given name.

"You're client's dead," he went on, "so there's no reason for you to keep poking your nose in it and get in our way. If you do, I'll wash my hands of you. You may want to do the same, by the way. That isn't blood on your fingers, is it?"

"Ketchup," I said. "I grabbed a burger and fries on the way

here."

"So are we clear?"

"I understand what you said."

"Cause I'd hate to have to turn you over to Menendez and let him deal with you."

The voice of Fred Astaire suddenly popped into my head, singing: *You say a good cop, I say a bad cop; you say a hood cop, I say a mad cop....*

"You listening?" Colfax demanded.

"Yes, yes, I'm listening," I said, chasing Fred away and calling the whole thing off. "Am I free to go now?"

"I'd actually appreciate it if you did."

He was such a charmer. After muttering goodbye, I got up and weaved my way through the station, and ultimately out of the building.

So the letter was not a hoax and Nora had not been playing me for a chump. I should have felt relieved upon learning this, but instead I grew more concerned, since it strongly implied that the boys were still in danger. On the other hand, with Nora dead, their careers were effectively over, which is what the sender of the letter wanted. Maybe she or he would be happy now, and that would be that. But how could I be sure of it? And how could I just drop the entire matter without even trying to find out who had written the threat that had gotten me into this case in the first place? There was also Elena to consider. She seemed a little too vulnerable to simply leave fending for herself in the company of two strange kids and an army of inquisitive cops. Still, Colfax's admonition to do just that had been strongly delivered.

I mentally sized up both arguments. Either I took the money Nora had paid me and ran like Jesse Owens, or I kept at it until I found out who had threatened the twins and then killed Nora. No matter how I weighed it, the negatives of remaining on the case definitely outweighed the positives. Only an idiot would keep investigating.

So of course you're gonna do it, Bogie said in my head.

Of course I was.

EIGHT

Technically, San Pedro was a part of L.A., though you wouldn't know it. Located on the water about twenty-five miles from downtown, it looks like its own city, and houses the Port of Los Angeles. While I had been to the touristy parts of the town before, like the little harbor village, I had never ventured into the residential areas.

Marcella DeBanzi lived in a rather hilly neighborhood that might have been in any one of a dozen outlying areas of L.A., except that it was here. The lights were on in her smallish, Spanish-style house when I pulled up to the curb, so I got out of the car and went to her door. If the imprint of her phone number on the page under which Elena wrote had been clear enough, or had she been listed in the book, I would have called first, though simply showing up might be for the best, since it was much easier to get rid of someone over the phone than it was to slam the door in their face.

I had to ring the doorbell twice (and I hoped there wasn't an ordinance against impersonating a postman) before I heard any movement coming from inside the house. I was about to try a third time when a voice on the other side of the door asked, "Who is it?"

"Ms. DeBanzi, my name is Dave Beauchamp," I called through the wood. "I'm here in regards to your sister, Nora Frost."

The door was yanked open, almost violently.

I was not quite prepared for the woman on the other side.

If anyone in Nora's immediate family belonged in show business, it was Marcella DeBanzi. Whereas Nora had come close to being movie-star-photogenic, her sister was more than ready for her close-up. She was, not to put too fine a point on it, drop dead gorgeous: lustrous dark hair that cascaded down to her shoulders, a perfect cream complexion that was even more perfect because she appeared to be wearing no makeup, large hazel eyes, a naturally pert nose, full lips and the promise of dimples were she to smile. But she wasn't smiling. And she was holding a fireplace poker in her left hand. "Are you a lawyer?" she demanded.

"Well, yes, of sorts, but—"

"God, you people work fast! I learned that my sister died less than an hour ago, and you bottom-feeders are already showing up on my doorstep. Go away!"

She started to slam the door shut (okay, maybe it *was* easier than I thought), but I held it open with one hand. "Please, Ms. DeBanzi, hear me out," I said. "Yes, I'm a lawyer, at least technically. I used to work in a law firm, but now I'm a private detective. Your sister hired me to do a job right before she…well, I suppose I should really begin my saying that I'm very sorry for your loss."

She stared at me for a few seconds, and apparently it was long enough to decide that I wasn't an axe murderer. "What did you say your name was?"

"Dave Beauchamp."

"Are you the one Elena Cates told me about?" she asked.

"Well, I don't really know what Elena said to you."

"Of course you don't," she said, suddenly smiling. (Houston, we have dimples!) "Sorry. I'm a little scattered right now. Come in, Mr. Beauchamp." She stepped back and opened the door to allow me inside, then quickly closed the door again. I kept an eye on the hand with the fireplace poker, and she took notice of that. "Sorry," she said, replacing in the rack by the small fireplace. "Single women can't be too careful."

Especially single women who looked like Marcella DeBanzi,

I imagined. Inside my head, Errol Flynn was imagining a lot more, but I ignored him.

The house was plainly furnished, but looked comfortable. The walls were white plaster, there was a large curtained window in front, and the fireplace sat off to one side. There was one chair and a short sofa, a round coffee table with a few magazines spread on it, a floor lamp, and that was about it. There was not even a television. The place was incredibly neat, and unlike Nora's house, there were no photographs of any kind to be seen, only a small painting of a sunset over water on one wall. The lack of photos was something of a shame since my guess is that any camera on the planet would have taken Marcella DeBanzi as a lover, because not only was she beautiful, she had a near-perfect body: slender, but not thin; shapely, but in perfect proportion; high-breasted; low-waisted; and blessed with a delicate swan neck that curved down into a very soft looking brown sweater.

"Would you care to sit down?" she asked, motioning toward the small sofa.

"Thank you." I sat down on one end of the sofa, hoping she would take the other end, which given the size of the sofa would have made us virtually side-by-side, but she didn't. Instead she seated herself in the leather chair across from me. "I'm sure all of this must be difficult for you," I said.

"Unreal is what it is. How did you happen to become involved with my sister, Mr. Beauchamp?"

I gave a quick rundown of how I landed into the middle of this mess, including the fact that I was the one who found Nora's body in the bathtub.

"The bathtub?" she said. "Was she taking a bath?"

"No, she was dressed and the tub was dry."

"That's a little weird, isn't it?"

As opposed to the normal everyday way of finding a dead body? Bob Hope cracked.

"We're not yet sure what it, if anything, the location of her body means, Ms. DeBanzi. What can you tell me about your sister?"

"Up until last year I never knew I had a sister," she replied. "I knew I was adopted, but I never really thought about siblings. Then I was contacted by one of your ilk who informed me of Nora's existence. At first I thought it was a scam of some sort, you know, 'I'm you're long lost sister, and all I need is X number of dollars from you and we can reclaim our inheritance,' or some such. But upon seeing the paperwork they presented, I came to accept it as the truth. I was Nora's blood relation."

"Did she ever tell you why she sought you out?"

"Not in so many words, but I think it may have had to do with the death of her husband, who was killed in combat overseas. Maybe she felt alone in the world and wanted to find someone, anyone, around her, even if it was a virtual stranger. I'm sorry, would you like something to drink, Mr. Beauchamp?"

"Water would be terrific."

She rose and sashayed into the kitchen (and not everyone can sashay without looking like they mean it), returning moments later with ice water in a glass for me and a diet Dr. Pepper for herself. Then she sat back down again, curling her legs up in the seat of the chair.

"Mind if I ask how you got along with Nora?" I asked, after thanking her and taking a gulp.

She sipped the Dr. Pepper and set it down on a small table. "No, go ahead."

I had my mouth open to restate the question, when she laughed. "Sorry. Don't mind me. How did I get along with Nora? Hmmmm. Well, I tried to be as sisterly as I knew how, but I didn't have any experience in it. The truth is we didn't have much in common, so after a while I sort of stopped trying to be sisterly. The last time I spoke to her was six or seven months ago."

"What about Taylor and Burton?"

"What about them?"

"Did you have a good relationship with them?"

She sighed. "Does anybody? Look, I don't want to sound cold, but I could never find much there there with those two.

Nora wanted them to be celebrities, but I did a little bit of film work when I was young, mostly to earn money for school, and the one thing I learned is that if you haven't got a personality, you haven't got a prayer. Even if it's an antagonistic personality, there has to be something there that will project into the lens. Those boys are from a wax museum."

"I'm kind of surprised you quit, frankly," I said.

"Trying to be nice to them, you mean?"

"No, acting. You look like someone the camera would adore."

I meant to say *like*…someone the camera would *like*…but it was too late now to do anything about it. If Marcella DeBanzi thought it was an untoward comment, though, she did not show it.

She smiled. "At the risk of sounding immodest, I've been told that a time or two. But that whole environment simply isn't for me. It's boring, really, and a lot of the people are crazy. I'm happier in dermatology."

"You're kidding."

She regarded me with a strange, semi-dimpled expression. "What's wrong with dermatology?"

"Well, nothing, of course, it's just that, uh——

(*It's just that you're too gorgeous to do something so mundane*)

"——I guess I should be addressing you as Dr. DeBanzi, then," I said, trying to make it sound planned.

"I'm not a doctor. I'm a licensed dermatological physician's assistant. As for addressing me, just call me Marcy."

"All right, and please call me Dave." She smiled, which I took to be an indicator that maybe I had flunked my *Who Wants to Be a Real Jerk?* audition after all. The next moment, though, I heard myself asking: "So, Marcy, you mentioned you were single, but have you ever been married?"

Her face took on a subtle expression of disapproval. "Why are you asking that?" she said.

"I don't want to appear to be prying," I stammered, "but——"

"But it's what you do for a living."

She had me there. "I guess so."

"For what it's worth, I was married once, but both of us were too young. Or maybe I was too young and he was too immature. Or maybe he was just a horse's ass. Anyway, that ended about fifteen years ago."

"So you're living here alone?"

Her eyes narrowed once more and she leaned forward. "Are you sure you're here about Nora, or is there some other reason you're asking these questions?"

"There's a very good reason I'm asking these questions," I said.

Okay, kid, what is it? Bogie wanted to know. So did I. Then it came to me.

"Your personal status might be of relevance to the court if it turns out that you have to take in Burton and Taylor, now that both of their parents are dead," I told her.

That appeared to startle her. "Oh, good god," Marcy said, "I hadn't even stopped to consider that." She got up and started to pace back and forth. "I still think of myself as kind of an outsider as far as Nora is concerned, but I probably am the only relation the boys have now." She laughed grimly and without humor. "I've heard of women becoming first-time moms at thirty-seven, but usually they start with babies."

She did not look thirty-seven, or even thirty, but I kept that to myself.

"Well," she went on, "there's not much use stressing about it right now. Whatever happens will happen." She settled back into her chair. "Anything else?"

"Yes, and I apologize for asking, but do you know of anyone who might have wanted to harm Nora?"

"Dave, I know you're trying to be thoughtful and considerate," she said, "but I'm sure you know as well as I do that the Dalai Lama would try to harm Nora if forced to spend time with her. Her philosophy of life was 'Walk a mile on the toes of others.'"

At that moment a thought occurred to me, and it must have

shown on my face, because Marcy said, "What? Did I say something?"

"You said that you speculate Nora started the search for you because her husband died, but her mother, her adoptive mother, also died a few years before that."

"I think that's right."

"Nora's mother was an actress, and so were you."

"I was not an actress. Dave, I was somebody who did a few parts to earn money for college."

"The point is," I said, "you were in the business. What if Nora somehow found that you had done some acting work and that's why she tracked you down, because she thought you could help the boys' careers? Sort of a replacement for their grandmother."

"I could clear up their zits," she said, with a light laugh. "Honestly, that's the only help I can offer."

But maybe Nora realized that only after she had found Marcy. And once she had realized it, maybe she dropped her sister from her life like unwanted poundage. I was about to explain into this theory, for whatever it was worth (and chiefly what it was worth was the chance to keep me here around her a little while longer), when Marcy's head suddenly bobbed up, as though alerted to a sound. "Did you hear that?" she asked.

"No."

"I think someone's on my porch."

"It might be the police," I cautioned. "A detective named Colfax is probably to show up at some point to talk to you."

"Did you send him?"

"No, he got your address from Elena Cates, too."

"I'm glad Elena doesn't know my social security number," she muttered.

As though on cue, the doorbell rang. She walked to it and as she had done with me called out: "Who is it?"

"It's us," a voice called back. "Your nephews."

Marcy and I exchanged looks and then she opened the door. Burton and Taylor Frost were standing on the small porch, facing the street behind them, each clutching a small duffel bag with one hand, while waving at someone with the other. Then in unison they turned and took a step in. When they saw me standing behind Marcy, they both registered an expression of surprise. "Crap, *you're* here, too?" Taylor said.

"Good to see you again, as well," I deadpanned.

"Boys, what are you doing here?" Marcy asked.

"Elena just dropped us off," Taylor said.

"She couldn't come in," Burton added. "She had to go somewhere."

Probably celebrating the felicitous riddance of Charlie and Mortimer, the voice of W. C. Fields drawled inside my head.

"I need to speak with Ms. Cates," Marcy said. "To say I wasn't expecting you two is a bit of an understatement."

The boys shuffled in and dumped their duffels on the floor. "We're just here for the night," Taylor said. "Elena's going to pick us up on the morning."

"She's kinda freaking out," Burton asked.

"And she's got this boyfriend," Taylor went on.

"Who's a real dick," Burton finished.

"I see," Marcy said. "Well, I guess I'd better go make sure I have enough bedding." She disappeared into the hallway of the house.

Once she was out of sight, Taylor turned to me and said, "So, are you gonna stay here all night, too?"

"Of course not," I told the little brat. "I came to talk to your aunt, but I was just about to leave."

"Door's right there," Burton said.

"Smell ya later," Taylor added.

I was still hashing over in my mind whether any jury would convict me for giving these two a Three Stooges head bonk when Marcy re-emerged from the bedroom.

"Okay, I think we're set," she said. "Have you guys eaten?"

"We stopped for a hamburger with Elena on the way over," Taylor answered.

"It was really crappy, too," Burton said. "Some place called Burger Heaven."

Okay, that was it. One can insult me, but you better not tread on my favorite fast food joint. "Look, junior," I started to say, but Marcy cut me off.

"I'd better check to see if I have anything on hand for breakfast," she said, dashing into the kitchen.

Now that I was alone with Frick and Frack, I thought about telling them exactly what I thought of them, but then figured it would be wasted energy. Instead I called into the kitchen: "Marcy, I'm going to take off. You have my card if you need me."

"All right, Dave, thanks," she called back.

"If she *needs* him," Burton muttered, snickering. Taylor jabbed him in the side, but he was snickering too.

"You know, fellas," I said, forcing myself to smile, "you really need to be nice to your aunt while you're here."

"Yeah? Why?" Taylor asked.

"Because if she gets sick of you, the only place left for you to go is an orphanage, and I don't think they computer games there."

I did not get the reaction I was expecting. Instead of showing alarm, the turned to look at each other, and then back at me. Now Burton's face was wearing a smug, knowing grin. It was the most expression I had ever seen him display.

"Man, you are such a loser," he said. "You don't even know what you're—"

A sudden sharp elbow jab from his brother silenced him. "We will be nice to her, Mr. Beauchamp," Taylor said. "Goodbye."

I left Marcy DeBanzi's house wondering what that had been all about, but even at that, happy to know that the Brothers Alpha were not going to be my immediate problem from now on.

NINE

It was dark by the time I got home. I was hungry, but not sure I had anything in the fridge to eat. But I could always order a pizza (Burger Heaven didn't deliver).

It was almost impossible to get Marcella DeBanzi out of my mind. Even as I examined the mail for the day—more bills and grocery store fliers, to which I should probably pay attention now that I could afford food again—all I could think of was Marcy walking out of my bedroom in black-and-white, a cigarette dangling from her lips, her hair in a 1940s flip, asking me if I knew how to whistle. For her, I'd play a kazoo.

I closed my eyes and tried to shake her out of my head, wondering...not for the first time...whether Bonnie at my old law firm had been right, and that I needed to seek out some professional help.

Bullshit, Robert Mitchum told me. *Anybody who wants to go to a shrink should have his head examined.*

"I'll try to remember that," I said aloud, then went to the phone and ordered a pizza from Domino's. While waiting for it to arrive, I went to my stash of comfort film DVDs and grabbed *Armored Car Robbery*, a tight little heist picture starring three of the four horsemen of postwar crime dramas, Charles McGraw, William Tallman and Steve Brodie (the fourth was Raymond Burr), and popped it into the player. It was about, well, an armored car robbery. That's one of the things I loved about film noir movies: you knew what you were going to get from the title. Had *Citizen Kane* been made as a classic noir it would have been called *I'll Never Forget My Sled.*

Of course, when the doorbell finally rang, announcing the arrival of the Domino's guy, I was taking a bathroom break. As quickly as I could I finished up and ran to the door. "Domino's," the kid said, a bit redundantly, given that he was wearing a Domino's shirt and held a pizza box in his hands. I settled up, leaving him a decent tip, and then sat back down in front of the television. Were I the introspective type, I probably would worry that sitting at home at night in front of the television, eating a pizza by myself, earned me a solid 9.5 on the Dork Scale. But I had just slightly over twelve-grand in the bank, most of which came from Nora Frost, so I could cut myself some slack. I was sitting here eating a delivery pizza, watching an old movie, because I wanted to. Sure, it would have been nice if Marcella DeBanzi were snuggled next to me, munching on a slice of sausage and green pepper, but one can't have everything.

When my cell phone rang I figured it would be a wrong number, or Detective Dane Colfax calling to harass me about something else. I was wrong on both counts. "Dave, it's Marcy DeBanzi," I heard on the other end. "Sorry to bother you."

"Oh, it's no bother," I said, tossing down the crust in my hand in order to grab the remote and freeze the film.

"Is this a good time to talk?"

"Yes, fine, what's up?"

"I didn't know who else to call," she said. "There's someone hanging around outside my house."

"Who?"

"If I knew, I wouldn't be frightened and calling you."

"Is it a man or a woman?"

"Man, I think. I saw him earlier."

"Have you called the police?"

"No, I wanted to talk to you first."

"The police might be better equipped to handle this."

"I'm sure you're right, but I don't want the frighten the boys."

"All right, take a deep breath." I imagined her breasts rising and falling with it, which did not help my focus. "Were you able to see anything about the person, anything identifiable?"

"No, I only saw a shape. But he appeared to be casing the house."

"Lock all your doors and windows. You have a cell phone, right?

"Yes."

"Keep it with you. Try not to spook the twins, just go about your business, but if anything funny happens, dial 911. Don't be afraid to. Okay?"

"Okay," she said. "Thanks. I feel better just talking to you."

I didn't need anyone here with me, or even the evidence of a mirror, to let me know that I was grinning like an idiot. I could feel it. "Call me again later if you want."

After she said goodbye and hung up, I had a hard time concentrating on anything else but Marcy, and the thought that someone was snooping around her house. Maybe I should call Colfax myself. No, that would be interference in the name of protection, or overprotection. Worst case scenario: if Marcy knew I had called him and no longer trusted me.

Not quite, my friend, an oddly formal voice said in my head. *The real worst case scenario would be to have harm...or even death...come to the lovely young woman.* It took me a minute to figure out who was taunting me now. At first I thought it might be Bela Lugosi, but the accent was wrong. Finally I got it: Ricardo Montalban.

When had Ricardo Montalban joined my mental Friars Club?

"I'll trust you know what you're doing, Marcy," I whispered to the empty, quiet room. "And Ricardo, go back to the island."

After polishing off another slice of the pizza (leaving two slices for breakfast), I watched the rest of *Armored Car Robbery*, and then got ready for bed and stretched out, wondering if I was really going to be able to get to sleep.

Apparently I did, because I awoke the next morning at the usual time, with vague memories of a dream in which I was being chased through the streets at night by somebody who wanted to kill me. I like chase dreams, since those I remember after awakening give me the feeling of having exercised, when I know I haven't. Today was Thursday, and in just about any other given week, Thursday promised to be a lot like Wednesday. But I had every expectation of breaking that rule since I was not planning on stumbling across another murder victim today.

After shaving and showering, I set out for the office a little before ten. Traffic was light, for some reason, so I made in a bit earlier than usual. I was there for only five minutes when my cell rang. "This is Dave," I said into it.

"Hi, Dave, it's Marcy again."

"Oh, hi," I said, trying to sound casual, when the truth of the matter was I had spent the entire drive in trying to come up with a reason to call her. "Is there another problem?"

"Well, sort of. It's the boys."

"What did they do?"

"Nothing, they didn't do anything." She was still speaking in hushed tones. "It's just that they're still here. Elena hasn't come to pick them up."

"Did you try calling her?"

"Yes, but there was no answer."

"She must be on her way, then."

"I've been trying her for almost two hours. Taylor said she'd be here by eight-thirty. I even tried her cell phone."

Maybe Elena had gotten the flip side of the light traffic I had enjoyed earlier, but even if that were the case, a couple hours to get from Hollywood to San Pedro was pretty excessive, unless there was a major accident on the 110 South. And given what I knew about Elena Cates, if she were truly tied up in traffic, she would have called on her cell to let Marcy know.

"I was supposed to be at work ninety minutes ago," Marcy was saying, "and I can't leave the boys on their own. I've managed to reschedule my morning appointments, but there are a few this afternoon that I don't think I could cancel."

"Do you want me to come down and babysit until she arrives?" I asked her.

"Could you get here by noon?"

"Yeah, I'm pretty sure I could."

"You're a lifesaver, thanks."

"How are the boys doing?"

"They playing with those gizmos of theirs," Marcy said in hushed tones. "They were up half the night playing them, too. Honestly, I'm not sure that the reality of their mother's death has fully hit them yet."

Either that or they haven't figured out how to distinguish the fun, exciting death that is everywhere in the gaming world with the real thing.

"Maybe I'm overreacting, Dave, but I'm thinking of calling social services to see if they need a psychiatric test. They simply aren't acting normal."

"Do what you think is best," I advised, "but let me ask this: how many twelve-year-old boys do you know?"

"None, other than Taylor and Burton. Why, do you think I'm that far out of touch with the younger generation?"

"I think the universe in general is that far out of touch with the younger generation." I also had a feeling that people have been saying that for five-thousand years or so. "Right now, Marcy, your primary job is to keep them safe, which you are doing. I'll be down as soon as I'm able."

"I love you," she said, and my heart stopped. Then she hung up. But I sat there, holding the phone against my ear until the unnamed, ubiquitous female voice chimed in to tell me that if I wished to make a call, please dial again. Marcy was expressing her appreciation, that's all, I told myself. She didn't mean *I love you* in the literal sense; I'm not so dumb or naïve as to believe that.

Says who? Bogart asked, menacingly.

Thanks, Bogie. I can always count on you.

I glanced at my watch and saw I had about an hour-and-a-half in which to get there. I could leave now and speed my way down, showing up pathetically early, or I could use the extra forty-five minutes I had at my disposal to try and turn up Elena

Cates myself. I fished out the piece of paper with the imprint of her number and dialed it, getting nothing but a machine. Okay, since Laurel Canyon, which is where she lived, was not that far away, and was between here and San Pedro, maybe I should just swing by on the way to Marcy's. Locking up, I headed out.

Laurel Canyon was an old community in the hills above the western edge of Hollywood. In the twenties it had been an elite area, with mansions dotting its winding pass boulevard, including those owned by Tom Mix and Harry Houdini. In the 1960s it became rock musician acres, with the old houses and cabins transformed into smoke-filled pads and hangouts. Today it was somewhere in between, but not the likeliest area of the city in which to find a personal assistant living, unless she was independently wealthy. Or, unless her employer overpaid her as much as she had me.

Elena lived on a street called Turcott Way, which was not easy to find, given the area's net of curvy, spider web streets and lanes. After stopping twice to recheck the Thomas Guide, I finally found the tiny street and wove my way to Elena's house, which was a small, one-story domicile that looked like the love child of a log cabin and an American Craftsman bungalow. It was dark brown in color, which made it blend in nicely with the woodsy foliage surrounding it. Double checking the address to make certain that I was not about to bother a total stranger, I wedged my car along the curb of the steep street, making sure the emergency brake was on, got out, went up to the small porch, and pushed the doorbell. When after a minute no one came to the door, I bypassed the doorbell altogether and knocked. Then I rattled the knob and discovered the door was unlocked.

That was when I had the most horrible feeling of *déjà vu*.

"Elena, it's Dave Beauchamp," I called, going inside the house. The tiny living room was dark and empty, and I didn't even have to move into the kitchen to see most of it. I went in anyway, and similarly found it empty. The bathroom was off of a short hallway, its door wide open, revealing it to be unoccupied. At the end of the hall was another room, this one with its door closed. It had to be the bedroom. If Elena was still in bed, she was probably not alone, based on what Taylor Frost had said about her having a boyfriend who thwarted her efforts to keep the boys. I only hoped whoever he was, he had a sense of humor.

Then again, the front door *was* unlocked, which implied that Elena might be gone, but only for a minute. Had she forgotten about the promise to retrieve the boys? Or was she so forgetful as to not lock the front door behind her? Or had the boyfriend left, forgetting to lock the door, leaving her asleep in bed alone?

I stepped to the closed door and said in a loud voice, "Elena, if you're in there, don't be alarmed. It's Dave Beauchamp, from yesterday. I need to talk to you." There was no reply, so I tried knocking on the door.

Nothing.

"Well, here goes," I said, pushing the door open.

Elena Cates was in bed. Alone. But she wasn't asleep.

"Oh, sheez!" I cried, reaching for my handkerchief to cover my mouth and nose. Like Nora, she had been shot twice in the chest, and the holes were easier to see since, unlike Nora, Elena was naked. The white sheets on which she lay were sodden with her blood.

I already had my cell phone out and had dialed 9 and the first 1 when I stopped to think. Was I really going to call the police and report my second body in as many days? Was I really going to wait for a detective to arrive and tell him how, once again, I had just stumbled into an empty house containing the body of a woman who had been shot? A woman who had worked for the first victim? At that moment it did not seem like a wise thing to do. But if I didn't report it, that might make things even worse for me, particularly if Colfax or Mendoza came to learn that I was here.

My only chance of not ending up in a holding tank, as near as I could see, was to capitalize on the fact that nobody knew I was here.

Taking my handkerchief, I wiped the doorknob to the bedroom door, pulled it closed, and then crept back through the house. I hadn't touched anything else inside, I was sure of that. Peeping through the curtains in the window of the front door, I stood and waited, heart racing, until a jogger passed on the street. Once they were gone, I quickly opened the door, wiped the front doorknob for prints, closed it again and then walked as casually as I could, as though nothing was wrong (just in case a neighbor was watching), to my car.

As I was getting in, I heard the siren behind me. "Shit!" I muttered, fumbling the key into the ignition. The siren was coming closer now, but I managed to get the car started and tried to pull away, only to go nowhere! Then I remembered that I had put the emergency brake on. Disengaging it, I lurched noisily away from the curb and headed down the road, vowing to take the first turn in any direction, no matter where it led. I'd find my way out of here eventually; right now I just had to get away from the house.

The siren was coming closer, though by this point I couldn't tell from which direction. Nor could I be certain that it had anything to do with Elena Cates lying dead in her bed. All I knew is that I felt that overwhelming, smothering sense of guilt, the kind I had only experienced in dreams. Why I have vivid nightmares in which I know that I've killed someone and their body is about to be discovered is another lifelong mystery of mine, but I didn't have time to worry about that right now.

Up ahead there was a stop sign, and the chance to turn right onto a driveway-sized street that I hoped would take me some-place. I followed it to another street, turned left, and spent the next five minutes weaving around like an ant in an ant farm until I somehow dumped back out onto Laurel Canyon Boulevard. Since the boulevard was elevating to the right, I took that direction as North and headed that way. I was all the way to the top of the mountain when I became aware that I was still breathing, which was a good sign. A low-flying helicopter suddenly appeared out of nowhere and zoomed overhead in the direction from which I was coming. Again, I had no idea if that was related to the discovery of Elena's body, but it did not seem impossible. Though if somebody *had* been there to her house just before I arrived, left the front door unlocked, and then rushed away to contact the police, though, *who was it*? Elena's mysterious "kinda" boyfriend, whoever he was, was a possibility, though an even bigger possibility was that he was the killer. As I fled like a rat, another irrational thought shattered what little sense of security I had at present: what if a voice-activated tape recorder had been place somewhere in the house, its tape now imprinted with variations on *Elena, it's Dave Beauchamp*? I decided that was just silly, but even so, a sense of security was not exactly flooding back into my mind.

I needed to warn Marcy, but when I pulled out my cell, I saw that the battery had run down. *Sheez*! I had no choice but to head back to my office, as quickly as I could. When I got there I parked the car in my usual spot but stayed there for a few minutes. I wasn't sure if my legs would support my weight enough to climb the stairs in the building. It was a delayed-reaction panic that immediately reminded me of the scene from *The Maltese Falcon* in which Spade pulls a dangerous bluff on the collected bad guys, and then goes out into the hallway and reveals how badly his hand is shaking. I hoped I was playing the scene as well as Bogie.

Fat chance.

Don't you ever go on break, Humphrey?

When it felt like I might be able to navigate my way inside without looking like I was having a seizure, I got out of the car and went to my office. Going to my desk, I picked up the phone, but not to call the police. Not yet. Maybe not ever. Instead I jabbed in Marcy's number.

She answered on the first ring.

"Marcy, it's Dave," I said.

"Dave, thank heavens. There's something I have to tell you!"

"Me first," I said. "Marcy, I've just come back from Elena's house. I think you'd better cancel your afternoon appointments."

TEN

There was a long silence at the other end of the line. Then Marcy's voice whispered, "What's wrong?"

"Elena's dead," I told her.

"God, no," she moaned.

"I'm afraid so. She's been shot, just like Nora."

"Oh my god, Dave, what's going on?"

"I wish I knew."

Let's just hope she doesn't think you're the one committing these murders, a soft voice said, pronouncing *murders* as *meaudeaus*. Peter Lorre, ladies and gentlemen.

"I'm sorry I don't have more information, Marcy, but you said you had something to tell me."

"I saw that man again," she said.

"The one casing the house?"

"Yes. This morning, when the boys finally got up, I told them to go outside and play their games because I was getting tired of the repetitious noise. I looked out the window and saw a man standing across the street, staring at them."

"And it was the same man?" I asked.

"I don't know. I didn't see him clearly last night. But he definitely gave the impression that he was keeping an eye on Taylor and Burton."

"Have you called the police?"

"Yes, but they didn't seem to take it very seriously."

"And you've never seen this guy before?"

"No. Dave, I'm frightened. I don't know what to do. I think

I'm going to have to call social services and ask them to take the boys after all."

"That may be for the best," I advised. Truth was, I was pretty much thinking only of her at this moment. The boys were so disconnected from the real world as to be adaptable to just about anything. "I'm going to come down, like I said, but you keep them inside for the rest of the day, and keep the doors locked until I get there, no matter what time it is. You understand, Marcy? Cancel all your appointments if you have to."

"All right."

"And if you see that guy again, call 911 again. Force the cops to take you seriously."

"Dave, whoever it is that's doing this, whoever it is that killed Nora and Elena, are they going to come after me now?"

"I don't think you have to worry," I told her. "I think it's the boys who are in danger, not you."

"Why them?"

"I don't know. Call it a gut feeling. But I think you need to keep them inside and out of sight."

"As long as they have those digital things of theirs, I don't think it will be a problem. But hurry, please."

"I'll be there as soon as I can."

After hanging up I glanced at the clock; it was 11:29. Time sure flies when you're tripping over dead bodies. There was no way I could make it to Pedro by noon, but I don't think that mattered anymore. I could head out now and maybe even have time to drive through a Burger Heaven on the way, since I was getting hungry. Locking up the office, I headed back out to my car, but before I got there, I saw an all-too familiar, all-too uninvited face. "Can I help you, detective," I called to Dane Colfax, who appeared to be snooping around my building's parking area.

"Hi, Beauchamp," he called back, continuing to snoop.

"Did you lose something?"

"I didn't, no. But someone else did."

"Okay, fine. I have nineteen questions left," I said. "This

thing that's lost, is it bigger than a breadbox?"

He stopped what he was doing and looked up at me with that *I'm-holding-all-the-cards-shithead* expression. "Elena Cates," he said, and I worked overtime to not let the panic I was suddenly feeling show. "She lost a car."

"I'm sorry to hear that," I said.

"Thought it might be here."

Careful! "Why would Elena Cates' car be here?"

"You tell me."

"I haven't a clue."

"You have seen her car, though."

"Yesterday, yeah." Had it been at her house earlier today? I now realized that I had not even noticed if her rust-colored Taurus was anywhere in sight when I was there. "Has she reported it missing?" I asked, cautiously.

He examined me as thoroughly as an airport screener. "No, because she can't, because she's dead."

"Elena? Oh, god." I don't pretend to be an actor, but I've watched enough good performances to be able to affect surprise. The key is to not overdo it. "What happened to her?"

"She was shot, just like the Frost woman."

"You're joking."

"Do I look like Jay Leno?"

"But I just saw her yesterday."

"I know. Do you have a gun, Beauchamp?"

"Yeah, though I've never used it."

"Where is it?"

"My office."

"What caliber is it?"

"Thirty eight."

"Nora Frost was shot with a .32. Ballistics report on the Cates woman is still pending."

"Like I said, mine's a .38."

"You could have two of them, one a .32 and the other a .38."

"I could be George Clooney, too. But I'm not. Come on, detective, why would I kill Elena? Or Nora, for that matter?"

"David, I don't know," he said, and there was a ring of honesty to his voice. "I just don't know. This is a weird one."

"What's the deal with her car, then?"

"It was missing from its usual spot in front of her house."

Probably the spot where I parked.

"So you think somebody killed her and then took her car?" I asked.

"Possibly." He looked around the parking area. "That's your car, right?"

"Yes, just like it was yesterday when you saw it."

"Has it been here all morning?"

Don't choke on this one, pal, Jackie Gleason said in my head. *Jackie Gleason?*

"Since I got in, yes," I said, not specifying as to which time I got in, before or after I visited Elena's house. "Why?"

"Neighbor said he thought he saw someone go into Cates' house, but he couldn't be sure. Thought he saw a car, too."

"Could be your murderer."

"Yeah, but nobody reported gunshots."

"Can't help you there."

"When was the last time you saw the Cates woman?"

"Yesterday, like I said. Last night, actually. She dropped the Alpha Twins off at their aunt's house."

"The one in San Pedro?"

"Yeah."

"When?"

"About 7:30, I think."

"And you know this because…."

"Because I was there."

"At the aunt's house?"

"Yes."

There was another long, stare-filled pause, and then Detective Colfax said: "Okay, Beauchamp, I think you're too dumb to lie to me. That's the difference between me and Hector regarding you."

"Not that I'm complaining, but why isn't the charming

Detective Mendoza with you?"

"He's got paperwork to fill out back at the station, something you should probably be thankful for."

"What did I do to him that makes him hate me so much?" I asked.

"Well, I don't know that he hates you for yourself, really," Colfax said. "He hates the profession you're in."

Okay, I get it; yet another LAPD officer with P.I. baggage. I suppose that made the fact that he hated me easier to take, since it wasn't me, per se, that he wished would fall down a well. "What about you, Colfax?" I asked.

"What about me?"

"Do you hate PIs too?"

"Beauchamp, I try not to hate anybody. Doesn't always work, but I try. I do tend to dislike guilty people, though. You're not a guilty person, are you?"

"I'm not guilty for any of this death, if that's what you mean."

"Stay out of trouble, and we'll get along fine. See you." Colfax walked over to his unmarked car, got in, and drove away. I guessed that he was likely on his way down to see Marcy. I ran to my car and tore out of the parking spot, then zoomed onto Ventura Boulevard, where I sat in traffic and waited for a long succession of lights to all agree with each other. Since I didn't know any secret shortcuts down to San Pedro, Colfax was likely to get there first. Maybe I should bypass Marcy's place and head for the port, and then charter a boat to Mexico. Then again, a friend in the D.A.'s office once told me that they had evidence that was where O.J. was heading while on the infamous White Bronco freeway chase, and that did not exactly pan out for him.

The drive down to San Pedro was the longest fifty minutes of my life, made longer by the fact that I was not able to call Marcy, my phone being dead. How did we survive before cell phones? I confess that I sped through the residential area in which Marcy lived, and when her house came into view, I was gratified to see that it was not surrounded by police cars. I slowed down and parked on the street, and then trotted to her porch and jabbed the doorbell.

There was no answer.

"Oh, no, *please*!" This was the third time in two days that I was standing outside a woman's house, ringing the bell to no avail. *Please don't let me find her dead*! I tried the door and found it unlocked. Bursting in, I called Marcy's name and heard a moan coming from the kitchen! There I found Marcy DeBanzi lying on the floor, her hair disheveled, her face streaked with tears, seemingly too weak to stand! "Marcy!" I cried, rushing to her.

"Dave…issat you?" she drawled.

"What happened?"

"Someone hit me…back of head…I passed out."

I gently brought her to an upright seated position, leaning her against the refrigerator. "Did you see who did it?"

"No…came up from behind…are the boys all right?"

"I don't know, I just got here."

She tried to get up, but could not. Falling back down to the floor, she started to cry. I tried to pick her up, which looks a lot easier in the movies than it is in real life, but somehow I managed to get her up and onto a chair without doing too much damage. "I'll look for them," I said, leaving her leaning over the kitchen table with her head in her arms.

It did not take long to search the house, but the Brothers Alpha were nowhere to be seen. "I can't find the boys," I said, rushing back to her. "Where were they the last time you saw them?"

"In the bedroom," she said. "Please…get me some water."

I rushed to the sink and started opening cabinets around it until I found a supply of glasses, and filled one up for her. She took the glass and tried to gulp it down, but the very act of drinking water seemed to cause her pain.

"You have to go to the hospital," I told her.

"What about the boys?"

"They aren't here. I'll go look around outside, but when I come back, I'm calling 911 for an ambulance for you." Dashing out of the house, I started called the twins' names and then ran around to the back yard looking for them. The yard was not so big that anyone could hide, even a small child. Marcy did not have a garage either, only a driveway. I peered inside the car parked in the back, and saw it was empty, then circled back around front and called their names one more time.

The boys were nowhere to be found.

I was about to go back inside the house when a couple objects caught my eye, on the grassy parkway by the curb. They looked like things that had been dropped, and as I got closer to them, near enough to see what they were, a sick feeling began to form in my stomach. They were identical and about the size of an open wallet. I started to reach for one but then stopped, procuring a handkerchief from my back pocket and using it to shield my hand…and any prints that might be on the thing… before picking it up. Letters stenciled on it read "Sony PSP," but I didn't need the branding to tell me what it was, I had seen it often enough over the last few days. These were the handheld game consoles that the Alphas were never seen without, but now they were dropped on the ground like they'd been discarded or lost. While hanging onto the one, I carefully picked up its brother with hanky-wrapped fingers and then rushed back in the house.

"Did you find them?" I heard Marcy call even before I got to the kitchen. Once there, I saw that she was not able to stand up on her own, and she was refilling her glass from the sink.

"No, but these were out there." I laid the game consoles down on the table.

"I don't think I ever saw those out of their hands. Why would they be left lying around?"

"They wouldn't, not of the boys had anything to say about it."

"I don't understand this, Dave."

"Marcy, I think they've been abducted."

ELEVEN

"Oh, Jesus God!" Marcy moaned, holding her head. "Abducted by who? And why?"

"I don't know, but I think that the only reason they would leave these things behind was because someone forced them out of their hands. If they had simply gone for a walk, they would have carried them with them. We have to call Colfax, and this time he'd better get an Amber alert out."

"I have kids for only one day...one freaking day...and they disappear."

"This isn't your fault," I said, going to her. In the movies, whenever a man is trying to calm a hysterically sobbing woman, there are certain moves he invariably makes: caressing her face, wiping away her tears, holding her head in his masculine hands——

"*OW*! Shit!" Marcy cried in my ear as I held her head, remembering only after she screamed that she had been clubbed over the cranium.

Smoooooooooooth, said the howling voice of Red Skelton, pretending to sell "Guzzler's Gin," inside my own damaged head.

"Sorry! Sorry!" I cried, to both of them. "Sheez, you've really got a lump."

"Damn!" she said, feeling it herself. "Maybe I should go to the ER."

"I agree, but let's call the police first." Fishing out my cell, I dialed 911 and reported an assault and apparent abduction, and gave Marcy's address. But even before I had finished, a car pulled up in front of her house, and through the window I saw Detectives Dane Colfax and Hector Mendoza get out and head for the house. Colfax either retrieved him from the station, or Mendoza had been there at my house the whole time, but stayed hidden. Could he have been inside my apartment while Colfax was keeping me busy? I didn't even want to think about it.

"Who's out there?" Marcy asked.

"It's the detective I told you might be coming," I said, "and the trained pit-bull he travels with. He's here to interview you as a witness to Nora's death, not because of the assault."

"Witness? I didn't see anything."

"Not eyewitness, Marcy, just a witness. A concerned party who might have information."

She put her arms around me. In a different, far more preferable, situation, it might have been called an embrace, but now I understood she was hanging on for dear life. "You'll help me get through this, won't you Dave?"

"I'll help you get through anything you want," I said, perhaps not too wisely, but too well. The doorbell rang and Marcy gave me a look that I could not interpret, although I managed to project into it something like: *I love you and I want to massage your feet every night and cook for you and spend each weekend in a hot tub with you and—*

She pulled away suddenly. "Are you getting a hard-on?" she demanded.

"What? Oh, no, that's, uh, my phone."

She broke away and went to answer the door, while I fought down an adolescent blush and forced my iPenis to stop ringing.

Detective Dane Colfax introduced himself and Mendoza, and after ascertaining that she was Marcella DeBanzi, asked to come in. Then he looked up and saw me. "Jesus Christ," he groaned. "Are you sure you're not twins, too, Beauchamp? No one person could get in our way this much. What the hell are you doing here?"

"Helping Marcy, who was coshed on the head," I said. "The

boys are missing, too. The local police are on their way here."

"You trying to go over our heads?" Mendoza growled.

Wouldn't calling the locals be going under *your head*? I heard Groucho say, and repeated it aloud for him.

I could see Mendoza desperately trying to come up with a retort, but for whatever reason, words failed him. Maybe his anger short-circuited his tongue.

"Hopefully the locals will call for an Amber alert," I added.

"I seem to recall you trying to convince me to put out an Amber on those two once before, and it turned out they were safely with their nanny the whole time," Colfax said. "Why should I give you any credence this time?"

"Because I think we can rule the nanny off the suspect list this time," I said. "Whoever the boys are with took them against their wills."

"How do you know that?" Mendoza shot back.

"Because their game players were discarded on the street."

"What game players?"

"The ones you never saw the boys without. Even when they ate, they took bites in between plays. They probably slept with them."

"They took them into the bedroom with them last night," Marcy said.

"So," I went on, "I'm having a hard time imagining that they would simply put them down on the sidewalk for safekeeping. Either they dropped them while being abducted, or whoever it was that took them tossed the gizmos aside." As I was speaking, the first police siren was heard.

"Where are these things?" Colfax asked.

"Right here," I said, pointing them out.

"You picked them up and *moved* them?" Mendoza shouted.

"I used a handkerchief, so if there are any prints on them, they're still there and uncorrupted."

"But you might have destroyed other evidence by taking them from their original location," Colfax said, more calmly.

"What kind of amateur asshole are you?" Mendoza queried.

"One who's planning on taking the test to be a professional asshole, so I can join the LAPD." *Sheez*! Where did *that* come from?

Mendoza took a step toward me but Colfax reached out and grabbed his arm. "He's not worth it, Hector," he said.

"Look fellows," I said, "you can slam me against a wall all you want, but this lady needs to go to the hospital and get checked out, and the boys have to be found."

The sirens were getting louder.

"Ma'am," Colfax said, "are you able to answer a couple questions before you go?"

"I think so," Marcy said.

His questions turned out to be the fairly generic: did you see anybody, hear anything, anyone want to hurt you, yada yada yada, though there was one that I had not anticipated. "Has Mr. Beauchamp done anything to you, or has he coerced you to do or say anything?"

Marcy looked shocked. "Dave? No, of course not! He found me unconscious. He's helped me. He has tried to help the boys."

"Detective, get serious," I said. "Why would I have called the police each time if I were responsible for any of this?"

"I'm not talking to you now, I'm talking to her," Colfax snapped. "Ma'am, what do you think happened to the boys?"

"I just don't know. I agree with Dave, though. They wouldn't leave their palm pilots, or whatever those things are called, just lying around on the ground if their absence was innocent."

The ambulance was now pulling up in front of the house.

"Who would want to abduct or harm them?"

"I don't know," Marcy moaned. "There was a strange man hanging around last night. Maybe he had something to do with it."

"A strange man?" said Mendoza, who had that ability to make every sentence he uttered sound like an accusation. "What strange man?"

"I don't know! There was someone hanging around outside."

At that moment a voice hollered into the house: "Paramedics."

"In here," Colfax said, and two uniformed EMTs rushed inside. Upon ascertaining that Marcy did not need to be strapped onto a gurney, they walked her to the front door. But at the door she turned back. "Can you come to the hospital with me, Dave?"

"Not yet," Colfax shot back. Then to the EMTs he asked, "Where are you fellows taking her?"

"Peninsula," one of them called back.

Assuming *Peninsula* to be a hospital or medical center, as opposed to a finger of land sticking out into the ocean, I told Marcy that I would be there as soon as possible. Then I watched as the paramedics walked her out and helped her inside the back of the ambulance. Before it could speed away, though, a police car arrived and joined the collection of city vehicles out front. Two uniformed officers, a man and a woman, knocked on the open door and were asked in by Detective Colfax, who flashed his badge at them.

"So what's going on?" one of the cops asked.

"I made the 911 call," I announced, and then did my best to try and fill them in on what had happened…at least what I believe to have happened…to the Brothers Alpha.

"Are you two already on the case?" the uniform asked Colfax and Mendoza. He looked a bit confused.

"We're out of Northeast," Colfax explained. "We're investigating the murder of the sister of the woman who was just taken to the hospital. The sister had two kids, twins, who appear to have disappeared, and those kids had a nanny who was also murdered."

"You keep characterizing her that way, but Elena wasn't really a nanny," I said. "She was Nora's assistant."

One of the uniforms, a thickset, steely-eyed guy with a Marine haircut, who reeked of cigarette smoke, and whose nametag identified him as Officer Fillmore, looked at me and asked, "Who did you say you are?"

"I'm a private investigator who…you know, officer, this is going to take a couple minutes or so to explain."

Turning to the uniforms, Colfax said, "You two go ahead and

take his statement about the presumed abduction. We'll stay out of your way, but let us know when you're done. We still have business with him." He led Mendoza outside.

The other uniform was young African-American woman named Baker, who must not have been long out of the Academy, because she appeared to do everything as though following a checklist. "May I see some ID, sir?" she asked politely, and I handed over my driver's license, which he quickly scrutinized. "Thank you. Now, sir, could you tell us what you know about this."

Fillmore remained silent but menacing as I once more recounted the events leading up to my discovery of Marcy. My earlier estimation was wrong; it did not take a couple minutes. It took ten. When I was done and there were no more questions, Fillmore chimed in. "What about this strange man the lady said was hanging around?" he asked. "Any idea who it might be?"

Elena Cates' boyfriend? I thought, but had no evidence of that one way or the other. "I did not see anyone first hand, so I have no idea who it might have been, if anyone."

"Are you saying you don't believe there was a strange man?"

"I saw no one, that's all I know."

"There no way it was you, is there?"

"Me? Officer, if I had seen myself lurking around the house in the dark I would have recognized me."

"A comedian," Fillmore sighed, glaring at me. "Swell."

"No, I was not the man Marcy saw. I was not here at the times she reported seeing him. Before she was assaulted, I was willing to believe there was no man at all, only her imagination acting up. But now...."

"Now what, sir?" Officer Baker asked.

"Look, *someone* had to hit her! She couldn't have done it herself. And the boys are missing. They're only twelve so they can't drive, and I don't think they have bikes, at least not here. Maybe they're just walking around, but I think somebody snatched them."

"Have you got a picture of them?"

"Not on me, no, and I don't think there are any here, because the boys only showed up last night. Maybe there's something in their backpacks in the bedroom, but if that doesn't pan out, you'll have to go to their mother's house, or possibly the Internet."

"Go check out the backpacks, Rebecca," Fillmore said his Baker immediately headed to the bedroom. Then turning to me, he said: "I'm going to have a chat with the detectives. You stay here." It was very difficult not to reply, *Sir, yes, sir*! as he strode out of the house.

Fillmore may have told me to stay put, but he did not specify that I had to remain in place at attention. Since I was interested in learning as much as I could about Marcy DeBanzi, albeit for different reasons than those of the police, I started looking around. The front room contained no clues as to her life and history, save for the fact that she appeared to like medical thrillers. Several such novels lined a built-in bookshelf. Making certain that I was still unobserved by any of the policemen, I moved into the kitchen to carry out my refrigerator theory of research, the one that says you can learn more about a person from their fridge than any other source.

The outside of Marcy's fridge had only a couple things stuck to it with plain round magnets, chiefly a fading Sunday *Zitz* comic strip referencing a dermatologist, and more than a dozen coupons for restaurants. On the side against the wall was a postcard. Fishing it out, I saw it was a reminder for a dentist appointment dated late last year. Obviously Marcy had lost track of it. I stuck it back in its hiding place. Taking a quick look inside the fridge, I discovered very little: a loaf of bread (and only people who don't eat very much bread keep it in the fridge), some coffee creamer, margarine, little tubs of pudding, and three cans of diet Dr. Pepper. The overall impression was that, like me, Marcy did not like to cook or eat at home much. In a perfect world we'd be eating beautiful take-out together.

Closing the fridge I went over to the sink to get a glass of water. I'd been talking to the cops for several minutes on end and was a bit dry. Glancing out the window as I drank, I saw something that caused me to inhale a drop of water and begin choking.

Dropping the glass, which shattered in the sink, I tried calling for Officer Baker, or anyone, but couldn't summon up the wind power. Instead I continued to gasp and kept looking out the window and the dark figure peering over the wall at the back of Marcy's property.

A strange man, who was looking directly at me.

TWELVE

Officer Baker was the first to arrive in the kitchen. "I heard something break," she said. Fillmore came next, followed by Colfax and Mendoza. I was still choking.

"Somebody try to kill you, too?" Mendoza asked, a note of hopefulness in his voice. I was tempted to flip him off, but under the circumstances it didn't seem wise.

"Out there," I managed to get out, gesturing to the window.

"What's out there?" Colfax asked.

"Strange...man."

Fillmore was the first one through the back door, with Baker in tow, while the detectives stayed with me and peered through the window. Of course, whoever had been there was now gone. When I recovered enough of my voice to speak, I said: "Someone was out there by the fence, looking this way."

"Describe him," Colfax ordered.

"Dark hair, bearded, nondescript clothes."

"It could have been somebody who lives there, you know," Mendoza said, "somebody who actually belongs in the neighborhood." The continuation of that thought, *Unlike you*, hovered silently in the air around us.

"You're right, it could have been," I said. "But he was looking straight at me. It startled me. That's why I choked."

Baker came back into the house. "No sign of anyone. If someone was out there, he's vanished."

"Or ran inside his own house," Mendoza said.

"What's wrong with all of you?" I shouted, a little more

forcefully than I had intended to. As a rule I'm not the kind of person who loses his temper, but I had been pushed nearly to the limit. "Look, we can stand here and argue over whether there really is a peeping tom out there somewhere or whether it is just a neighbor, but that isn't going to find the boys. Now are you going to call in their disappearance or not?"

"Officer Fillmore already did that, sir," Baker firmly announced.

"Oh, okay, all right," I said, giving her my best Larry Fine capitulation wheedle.

Now Fillmore arrived back in the kitchen. "I talked to a woman from the house next door and she confirmed that someone has been loitering around the property. She described him as tall, dark haired, bearded, and wearing a long military style coat."

"Thank you," I said.

"Don't think you're off the hook," Mendoza sneered.

"Hector," Colfax said, "take those game consoles out to the car, and be careful with them."

Pulling a pair of rubber gloves from his jacket pocket and stretching them on, Mendoza went in the other room, picked up the Alphas' gaming devices and dutifully carried them outside and to Colfax's car.

"What do you want us to do, detective?" Fillmore asked.

"You two concentrate on figuring out who our prowler is and keep your eyes and ears open regarding the two boys," the detective answered. "If we find anything pertinent on those gaming things, I'll let you know, but you keep me in the loop, too." Colfax pulled out business cards and handed them to the officers, who then left the house, leaving me alone in the kitchen with the detective. "We need to have a little talk, Beauchamp."

"If it's about the facts of life, detective, I already know," I said, hoping to lighten the tone.

It didn't.

"Okay, you want to know why I'm here," I speculated. "Marcy DeBanzi called me this morning to say that Elena Cates hadn't come back to pick the boys up. She dropped them off last night."

"And what did you do when she told you that?"

Careful. "I tried calling Elena but she didn't answer. I guess we know why, now."

Colfax continued to look at me. "You didn't go to her house, did you?"

"Why would I do that?"

"I don't know."

"Like I said, detective, I called her, I got no answer, then I came down to see Marcy because she had mentioned seeing someone who looked like he was casing the joint. Then when I got here, I found her on the floor, injured and the twins gone. I called the locals, and you and Mendoza arrived almost immediately afterwards. God's honest truth." It was, too, since I had done all of that. I simply wasn't including that I had also gone over to Elena's house and found her body.

"Are you being one-hundred percent straight with me, Beauchamp?"

"About what?"

"About everything?"

"Of course. What would I be lying about?"

"I don't know, that's why I'm asking," Colfax said.

"Everything I have told you, detective, is the absolute truth."

"Uh-huh. But it's what you haven't told me that makes me question you."

I sighed. "Do I need to go all through it again?"

"No. Forget it."

"Can I leave, then?"

"Yeah, get out of here. We know where to find you if we need you. But I'm only going to say this once more. I don't want to see you again unless it's by my choice."

"Just so you know, I'm going to go to the hospital now to check in on Marcy. I don't consider that to be part of an investigation into Nora's murder. I'm simply a concerned friend." I started to leave but was stopped by Colfax's voice.

"Is that your car out there?" he asked.

"I'm parked out front, yes. Why?"

"Oh, no reason. It's just that one of Elena Cates' neighbors saw a car pull away from her house this morning, before her body was found. The description she gave kind of matches your car."

So someone *had* seen me, and Colfax *was* playing cat and mouse. I forced myself to smile at him. "So you think I was there?" I asked.

"What I think takes second chair to what I can prove, and if I could prove you were there, you'd be in custody already. Now beat it."

I did not have to be asked twice. Walking out, I passed Mendoza, who seemed disappointed that I was not in cuffs, and the two uniforms, then jumped in my car and took off. I had no idea where Peninsula Hospital was, but that's why God gave us cell phones (though He gives GPS to those He likes more). But since my cell was out of juice, I had to stop at a gas station and ask for directions. Even at that it took me a half hour to find the place. Once I had made there, I parked and rushed into the ER to ask after Marcy. She was still in X-ray, I was told, so I waited…and waited…and waited.…

About two hours later she came back out in a wheelchair, which is the standard way people leave a hospital, whether they are able to walk or not. It has to do with liability.

"Sheez, they kept you long enough," I said upon seeing her. "Are you all right?"

"They took x-rays," she said. "I hate x-rays."

"They had to find out what was wrong."

"Fortunately, nothing much is wrong. There are no signs of fracture or concussion, just a bump."

"You're lucky."

"Yeah, that's me, Miss Fortunate of 2013," she said grimly. "Any news on the boys?"

"Nothing yet. At least the cops are taking me seriously this time. They put out an alert. Are you ready to go home?"

She nodded, and then winced. "Ow, I have to be careful

about doing that. I'm still a little sore."

The orderly who was pushing her offered to take her all the way out to the curb, while I pulled my car up, but Marcy refused, opting instead to walk. Even so, I took her by the arm, and she did nothing to dissuade me. It felt good, like the warmth of the sun shining down on us. "I have some other news, but I don't know whether it's good or bad," I said.

"Now what?"

"You were right about seeing someone hanging around the house. I saw him, too."

"I wasn't lying about it."

"I believed you, but now the police are convinced as well."

"Did you get enough of a look at the guy to describe him?"

"Not conclusively, no. He might be a street guy, and possibly a veteran, since he was wearing what looked like a military coat. He had a dark hair and a beard. He was looking over the brick wall in your backyard, looking into the kitchen."

"Damn it, Dave. That doesn't make me feel very comfortable about returning home."

We were at my car now. "The police are looking for him," I said. "Neighbors have seen him, too." Fishing out my keys, I opened the passenger door and helped her in. Once I was behind the wheel, I started the ignition and pulled out of the lot.

"Do you think he's the one who did this to me?" Marcy asked. "Is he the one who took the boys?"

"If he is, he'd be pretty dumb to loiter around afterwards."

"Who *does* have them, then?"

"I don't know." There was one wild card in this mysterious deck, however, and that was Elena Cates' gentleman friend. "Did either of the boys happen to say anything about Elena's boyfriend?"

"No. You think that's who's behind this?"

"I don't know, but it can't be discounted."

"God, I feel so helpless," she moaned.

Please let me help, I begged silently.

I drove her back home, though I almost missed her street, my mind being so preoccupied with fantasies of what might happen once I got her inside her house. "Would you like me to stay for a while?" I asked, hopefully.

"No thanks," she answered. "You've been really sweet, Dave, but I need to rest. You'd be doing me a bigger favor if you found out what happened to Burton and Taylor."

"It's my top priority," I said, not adding that I didn't have any other cases at present to distract me. With cash in the bank and Marcy needing my help, I might actually turn down any come in.

I showed myself out and went back the car, the plate of which may or may not been written down by Elena's snoop sister neighbor, though the fact that Colfax had not arrested me argued that the Gladys Kravitz of Turcott Way had not been able to find a pen. Getting behind the wheel, I realized that, despite what I had told Marcy, I didn't have a clue as to how to find the trail of the boys. Missing persons, particularly missing children, was not exactly my province, especially when the children in question would delight most of civilization by remaining missing. No, I shouldn't say things like that. Still, they were only kids… rude, annoying kids…who did not deserve to be terrorized. I needed to think, to try and figure this whole mess out, because I knew whoever had abducted the twins was not going to be so accommodating as to jump out in front of the car.

That knowledge was why I nearly lost control of my Toyota when the man suddenly stepped out into the street a half-block in front of me, holding out his hands as though ordering me to stop. He was tall, dark haired and bearded, and wearing a long military-style coat, and unless I had suddenly gone nuts, it was the man I had seen through Marcy's window. He showed no signs of moving, so I had little recourse but to comply, screeching to a halt mere yards in front of him. I got out of the car but stayed behind the opened door, in case I needed to use it as a shield. "Who are you? What do you want?" I shouted.

"Could ask you the same questions," the man said. He did not appear crazed or even particularly angry.

"Okay, I'll go first. My name is Dave Beauchamp. I'm a private investigator."

"Really? Like Magnum?"

"Sort of. Now, who are you? Elena's boyfriend?"

"Elena? I don't know any Elena. I'm Alan Kleinbach."

"Okay. What have you to do with Marcy DeBanzi?"

"I don't know any Marcy DeBanzi. All I know is there were two boys who came to live around here. Twins."

"That's right," I said. "And what do you know about them?"

"Turns out, I don't know anything about them."

"Okay, but who are you?"

"I'm Nora Frost's husband."

I had not been expecting that one. "You're saying she married again after her husband died in Afghanistan?"

"No, I'm saying we were married and divorced before she ever took up with G.I. Joe."

"Who was the father of the twins," I said.

"Like hell."

"Mr. Kleinbach, you're not making a lot of sense."

"Nora had twin boys," he said. "G.I. Joe was killed in Afghanistan. But the father of Nora's twins is alive and kicking."

"Randall Frost was not their father?"

"Nope."

"Then who is?" I asked.

"You're looking at him," Alan Kleinbach said, sticking a dirty hand out for me to come and shake.

THIRTEEN

That was when it hit me: Alan Kleinbach was an older, much more street-hardened version of the mysterious man in the photo that Colfax had shown me, the one found in Nora's house. Seeing that his hand was empty of any kind of weapon except dirt, I walked up and shook it. Kleinbach had a strong grip and clear, non-wino eyes. But what he was telling me made no sense. How could he claim to be the father of the twins and yet not know anything about them? Maybe he and Nora had divorced when the boys were tiny. "You know, Mr. Kleinbach, the cops are looking for you," I told him.

"Why?"

"You were spotted prowling around the house and peeking in the windows. I saw you myself out back."

"That's easy to explain."

Somewhere in the distance, a siren whined. "We really shouldn't be seen talking to each other out here," I suggested.

"Why not?"

"You know that Nora's sister was assaulted, don't you?"

His face darkened. "Nora didn't have a sister. She was adopted."

"So was her sister. Nora tracked her down. That's who's living here."

"You mean that hot babe who lives in that house is Nora's *sister?*"

"Yes. Her name is Marcy DeBanzi."

"Shit! Wish I'd found her instead of Nora."

The siren was getting louder. "Look, Mr. Kleinbach, whether it's easy to explain or difficult, I think you need to tell me why you have been snooping around this house."

"I wanted to see Ricky and Bobby?"

"Who are Ricky and Bobby?"

"The twins. My sons."

"You mean Burton and Taylor, don't you?"

"Those are their middle names. They were born Richard Burton Kleinbach and Robert Taylor Kleinbach. To me they're Ricky and Bobby. Nora probably started calling them by their middle names because I called them Ricky and Bobby, and she couldn't bring herself to do anything in agreement with me. So where are they?"

"I'm sorry, but they've disappeared."

His face darkened even further, Meanwhile, the siren was only a couple blocks away.

"We need to talk, Mr. Kleinbach, but it might be best if we do it somewhere else. If the police come back here right now and find us here just a block away from Marcy's house, we might both end up in a holding tank for the night."

"Cops," he said, disgustedly.

"Do you have a car?"

"No, a motorcycle. It's over there."

"Do you feel safe leaving it behind for a bit?"

"Got a chain lock on it."

"Okay, get in my car. I'll bring you back to get the cycle."

"Where are we going?"

"Restaurant, coffee shop, somewhere we can talk more freely."

"Awesome! I haven't eaten today. Didn't eat much yesterday, either. Your treat, right?"

The siren was very close now.

"Yes, yes, just get in the car, please."

Alan Kleinbach hopped into the shotgun seat and I pulled out. "Cops really got you spooked, huh?" he said. "What did you do?"

"I'm a serial stumbler," I told him. "I repeatedly stumble over bodies right before the police show up, and they find that interesting."

"Like Jessica Fletcher?"

I had to smile. "I suppose so. But without a hundred years' worth of residuals."

I would have felt a lot more comfortable getting out of San Pedro before stopping for a bite, but circumstances mandated that we pull into the first place that didn't look like a cop hangout, which was a Mexican restaurant called Gilhooley's on Gaffney Street (and why so many Mexican restaurants in L.A. have Irish names is something that perhaps only Anthony Quinn could have answered). Kleinbach ordered a combo plate and a beer called Negra Modelo, and when his meal came he regarded it as though it was the first hot food he had seen in a year. "Shit howdy," he said. "Don't get chow like this very often."

Since I was not particularly hungry for anything except information, I ordered a taco and a Coke, and then tried to open up the man seated across from me. "How can I be sure that you're really the father of the boys?" I asked.

"I knew their real names, didn't I?"

"Yes, but I didn't. You could be making it up and I'd have no way of knowing."

In between ravenously-consumed mouthfuls he pulled a tattered wallet from his back pocket and withdrew an equally tattered photograph. It showed a clean shaven, slender, widely-grinning man with two blonde toddlers sitting on his lap in front of a Christmas tree. It took a little bit of imagination to see that the man was the same one who sat across the table from me now. "That was their second Christmas," Kleinbach said. "Ten years ago."

"What happened?" I asked, handing the photo back.

"Nora wasn't easy to live with, God knows, but I have to share the blame. I fucked up. Nora wanted only one thing out of life: stardom. Her folks were actors."

"I know, but I got the impression she didn't personally want to follow them into the business."

Kleinbach chewed and swallowed, and then took a long swig of beer. "That's almost right," he said, wiping his mouth with the napkin. "She didn't want to do what it took to be an actress, she didn't want to put in the long years of study and work, she just wanted to be famous. When she decided it was too hard for her, she turned to our sons, figuring she'd get her taste of fame through them."

"'Mama Rose' syndrome," I said. "You know, from *Gypsy*?"

"I know," he said. "I was in *Gypsy* in high school. But Nora made Mama Rose look like a Geisha. But it's not like she had to force it, because if you live in Los Angeles and you have twins, it's almost guaranteed that they're going into showbiz, because they use twins all the time on film sets. You cast them in the same part, and each one works only half of the time. That way you don't have to work any one kid more than the law allows. For babies, you almost have to use twins, because if one kid gets fussy on the set, you just swap him out for the other one and keep shooting."

"Did the boys work much?"

"A little. Not enough for Nora, of course."

I finished off my taco and slurped the last of the soda while Kleinbach attacked his chile relleno, which was the last thing on his combo plate. "I take you grew weary of that situation," I then said.

"What I grew weary of was Nora," he said. "Then I fucked up."

"How so?"

"I started drinking a little too much, staying out, gambling, I had an affair...I guess you could say I wasn't the ideal family man. But I loved my boys. I always came back to them, and Nora couldn't tolerate that."

"Okay, Mr. Kleinbach—"

"The name's Alan. Mr. Kleinbach's my dad, who's still respectable enough to be called 'mister.'"

"Okay, Alan, and I'm Dave. But I'm afraid you just lost me.

You're saying that Nora couldn't tolerate you coming back to your family?"

Finished eating now, except for the few remaining tortilla chips in the bowl between us, he looked at me with an expression of infinite regret. "Do you know what the vast majority of child stars have in common?"

I shook my head.

"An idiot for a father. You can go right down the list starting with Jackie Coogan in the silents, through Robert Blake, to Michael Jackson, Drew Barrymore, Macaulay Culkin, and this new one...what's her name...the one who keeps ending up in jail. The one with the knockers. You name 'em, they all had problems with their fathers." He paused before adding: "And they were all, in their times, the hottest things in show business."

"Are you saying that Nora believed your being a failed father was a prerequisite to the boys' success?"

"I wasn't a *failed* father, all right?" Kleinbach snapped. "I just wasn't a great one. But yeah, Nora thought if I became a total asshole, somehow it would somehow temper Ricky and Bobby and make them stronger in their careers." Kleinbach sucked out what little was left in his beer bottle and then held it up to me. "Could I squeeze another one of these out of you?" I signaled for the smiling, mustachioed waiter from whom Kleinbach ordered another Negra Modelo before going on. "I honestly believe that if Nora had found an ancient book that said you had to sacrifice a virgin at midnight to guarantee success, she would have done it. If she could have found a virgin in Los Angeles. I remember exactly when she decided that my being a problem was good for the cause. She came to me and instead of being angry that I'd spent all night out somewhere, she said: 'Fine! Great! Perfect! Be a fucking moron! That's just what the boys need to put them over the top!' I think she'd been reading *People Magazine* or something, and had an inspiration. It didn't take a genius to see that a split was coming, either legally in court, or with her just throwing me out. The thing was, I wanted to straighten up. I didn't want to be cut out of my sons' lives."

His beer arrived and he took a long drink before continuing. "What I really wanted was to get the boys away from her, get custody of them. I was probably fooling myself that any court anywhere would go for it, but that's where my head was at the time. The thing was, legal battles take money, and I didn't have any. Nora controlled the finances, mostly through her inheritance. So I turned to gambling to build up a pot, and of course that didn't work. All I that got me was into hot water with a bookie. I was desperate, didn't have any other choice, near as I could see, so...."

"So you turned to crime," I guessed.

Kleinbach sighed. "Just one job, robbing a woman at an ATM. I was hoping to get her cards so maybe I could use them to clean out her bank account, and yes I know how awful that sounds. I was desperate, and a little stupid, too. Maybe more than a little. Anyway, all I got was a couple hundred bucks in cash, no cards, which was nowhere near enough to hire a lawyer or pay off my debts. Worse, there was a security camera and I was glimpsed on the tape, though not clearly enough for a positive ID, but enough to be tagged as a suspect. I got lucky, though, and the woman couldn't pick me out in a lineup."

"So you got away scot free."

"Oh, no. I paid, believe me. Nora knew I had done it, and she made me an offer. She would alibi me to the police, so the investigation would go somewhere else, and settle my debts with the bookie. In return, I would give her a quickie Vegas divorce, and then leave, and never make any claim of any kind on the boys. I couldn't even see them. That was the deal. If I tried to get back in their lives, she'd go straight to the police."

"What did you do after that?"

"Dropped out. I did whatever I could just to stay alive. Took odd jobs when I could find them, went to soup kitchens when I couldn't. I even did extra work in a film shooting downtown, which is pretty fucking funny when you think about it. They needed authentic looking street guys, so I got a hundred bucks and two hot meals. Then I started working in a shelter down-town, trying to help others. It's regular money, though not much, but honest work. I'm hoping maybe I can go back to school at some point, get a degree in something."

"Did you ever try to contact Nora in the time you were gone?" I asked.

Kleinbach shook his head. "She got remarried, and apparently the boys were in a stable home, so...."

"Forgive me for saying this, Alan, but I'm not sure I believe you."

"Yeah? Okay, how about this? I believed what Nora told me, that if she ever saw me again, she'd turn my ass over to the police."

"But isn't there a statute of limitations on purse-snatching?"

"I don't know." He took another pull on the beer. "I didn't feel like taking the chance."

"What do you know about her second marriage?" I asked.

"Not much. It's not like I was invited to the wedding. For a while I kept in contact with a friend from the days when Nora and I were together, and he said my replacement was a real straight arrow, a National Guardsman. That's part of the scenario, too, see? The baby daddy's an asshole but the second husband is the honorable one, raising the kids as though they were his own. From what I hear, he tried his best to do just that, too, until he got deployed and ended up becoming a casualty."

"Couldn't you have come back into the twins' lives after the lieutenant died?"

"I told you, already."

"Sorry, Alan, but it's not adding up. You would steal for the sake of your boys, but not even take the chance to see them again?"

He slammed the beer bottle down on the table, which caused me to jump in the padded faux-leather seat. It silenced the chatter at the next table, too. "What the fuck would I have told them when they asked why I ran away, huh?" he shouted. "You tell me how I was supposed to look them in the eyes and argue that

I had any claim on them as a parent when I ran the fuck away, scared off by their mother!" He quieted and bowed his head, shaking it back and forth. "You were right when you used the words 'failed father.' I did fail them. How, then, was I supposed to face them and make everything right?"

A man in a shirt and tie, whom I took to be the manager of the restaurant, appeared at our table. "Is there a problem here, señor?" he asked.

"No, we're fine," I said. "Sorry if it got a little loud."

"Can I get anything for you?"

Kleinbach was sitting there, staring at his hands, one of which clutched the Negra Modelo bottle. "Do you want another one of those?" I asked him.

"Want? Sure. But I probably shouldn't have it. Nora always reminded me that it was the third drink that was the first one too many."

In spite of everything the man had told me, I could not help but wonder if there was not still some tiny little wind-blown torch for Nora in his heart. Turning to the manager, I said: "We're good, thank you," and he nodded and stepped away.

"Try to stay calm, Alan," I admonished. "Do you mind if I ask why you started showing up to try and get a look at the boys, after staying away so long?" *Since you're asking questions*, the voice of Jimmy Stewart drawled in my head, *why doncha ask him how he was able to figure out the boys'd be down here at Nora's sister's house, when he didn't even know Nora had a...a...a sister*? It was a great question; I wish I'd thought of it.

Our waiter, now grinning broadly, as though afraid that he would set Kleinbach off again if he didn't, hustled over to take our plates away, and promised to return with the check.

"Nora's death was reported on the television news," he said. "She wasn't identified, they just said a woman had been killed, but I recognized the house. I headed on over as soon as I saw it. All hell was breaking loose, with police cars and everything. I stayed hidden and watched, but I didn't see Ricky or Bobby anywhere."

"How did you know to come to San Pedro, then?" I asked, on behalf of Jimmy.

"Oh, that was easy. I followed you." My surprise at this must have shown on my face, because he smiled and started to explain himself slowly, as though he was taking to a kid. Or an idiot.

"While I was outside Nora's house," Kleinbach began, "I saw a car drive up with a couple kids in the back, but I couldn't see them clearly. Then I saw you appear and talk to the woman who was driving, and then the both of you drove away. I followed you to a restaurant, and then to building in the valley."

"On a motorcycle?"

"That's the easiest way. Bikers don't have to pay attention to traffic rules, since no one expects us to in the first place."

I would have to remember that for future investigations.

He went on: "I lost track of the woman's car after that, but I kept following you, and you led me down here. I took a chance that the boys would eventually show up at that house, so I kept watch. Finally they did. I was able to get a little better look at them, and that's when I saw it."

"Saw what?"

"Christ," Kleinbach muttered, shaking his head again. "Is that offer for another beer still on the table?"

As the waiter approached with the check, I informed him that we weren't quite done after all. He took the news with equanimity, and dashed away, returning almost immediately with the Negra Modelo, which he set down in front of Kleinbach.

"Thanks, man," Kleinbach said, acknowledging the waiter for the first time since we'd been seated. That was probably as close as he was going to come to offering an apology for his earlier outburst, but the waiter seemed to accept it, nodding and smiling. Kleinbach took a long pull on the beer.

"Will you be all right to drive your cycle?" I asked.

"Oh, yeah, I'll be fine. Takes a helluva lot more than this to put me under, no matter what Nora said."

"You never answered my question, Alan. What was it you saw regarding the boys?"

Before Kleinbach could answer, the waiter reappeared, this time with the revised check, which he set in front of me. Then he scurried away. I glanced at the check: just under thirty bucks, thanks to the refreshment. As I pulled out my wallet, I said: "You are going to tell me, aren't you?"

He drained about half of the bottle and then set it down, offered a quiet burp, and then said: "Dave, do I come off as crazy to you?"

I sighed. "No, Alan, you do not come off as crazy. The worst I can say about you is that you have a maddening habit of not finishing your thoughts."

He smiled. "I don't think I'm crazy, either."

"Good, we agree."

"So if I'm not crazy, that means there really is something going on that's not right."

"Yeah, I think we can also agree that murder, kidnapping and assault is not right."

"That's not what I mean. I'm talking about my boys."

I was practically ready to slide out of the booth and get down on my knees to *beg* him to fill me in on what he had noticed about the Alphas. Instead I calmly stated: "What is it about them. Please, Alan, tell me."

He drained the beer bottle and set it down on the table. "I was there, this morning, out behind the house, and I saw the boys come outside. I finally was able to get a good look at them. I was standing behind a wall, so they didn't see me, but I saw them."

"And?"

"They aren't my sons."

I shook my head, and said, "I'm afraid I'm not following you."

"Earlier I asked you where Ricky and Bobby were, remember?"

I nodded.

"I meant that literally. I want to know where my Ricky and Bobby are, because the two kids I saw at that house are not them."

It took me a few seconds to figure out how to respond to that one, especially since Kleinbach had already announced that his consumption of three beers was the beginning of a potential danger zone. "Could you elaborate on that?" I asked.

"Don't start looking at me like I'm nuts," he pleaded. "I'm not nuts, and I'm not drunk, either. Slightly buzzed maybe, but still okay. I know what I'm saying. I may not have seen Ricky and Bobby for years, but a father knows his own kids, particularly if they're twins." He once more produced the photo of him and the boys that he had shown me earlier, plopping it down on the table. "Look at those faces," he commanded. "What do you see?"

"Children," I said.

"Look more closely."

I studied, I looked…and then I saw what he wanted me to see. "These two are identical, aren't they?"

Alan Kleinbach nodded. "They're identical. I never saw two living creatures so identical. They even made the same sounds. But the two boys you've been dragging around, they're not identical, are they? From what I've seen of them, they could easily pass as non-twins. If those two kids are my sons, the ones in this photo, I'll eat this bottle."

I glanced up to see him staring with laser intensity at the upside-down photo of happier times involving his children. Then he looked up at me with tired eyes set in a worried face. "So where *are* Ricky and Bobby?" he asked, softly. "Where are my sons? What did Nora do with my boys?"

FOURTEEN

I could have rejected the idea as simply the paranoiac mutterings of a lightly-oiled man with an ex to grind, but Alan Kleinbach did not strike me as paranoiac, nor could the evidence in that photo of the two kids be blown away like so much smoke. Granted, kids always change in looks as they grow, in large part because all babies tend to resemble one another. While the two infants in the picture certainly did not look much like Taylor and Burton Frost, I could not prove that it wasn't them. "What do you propose to do about this?" I asked Kleinbach.

"What I'm doing," he said, "telling you. You're the P.I., so you find out what happened to them."

"Are you offering to hire me?"

Kleinbach snorted. "Oh, sure, I'll cash in one of my CDs and hire you. It's a Billy Joel CD, should be worth about seven-fifty." He laughed and then rested his head in his hands. "Sorry, man," he said. "Didn't mean to dump on you. It's just that of late, things have kind of sucked. By late, I mean the last several years."

"Don't stress it. As for finding out what happened to your sons, once I finally locate the twins that I know, I'll look into your claim. You ready to go?"

Kleinbach nodded and slid out of the booth, and we left the restaurant. Mr. Necktied Manager seemed happy to see us go.

Out in the parking lot I fished out a business card and handed it to Kleinbach. "Bow-champ?" he said, looking at the card. "I thought your name was Beachum."

"It's pronounced Beachum. I have thought about changing the spelling at time or two."

"Why not change your whole name?"

"To what?"

"How about Dave Jones, P.I.?"

It didn't have quite the same ring as Philip Marlowe or Sam Spade, or even Joe Friday or Richard Diamond, but I didn't press the issue. Once we were inside my Toyota, I said: "By the way, how can I get in touch with you?"

"I live at the Kirkwood Arms downtown. We call it the Broken Arms, given the way the manager twists us for the rent every month. But it has a roof, hot water, a bed, and no twenty-eight day shuffle."

The twenty-eight day shuffle, I knew, was the practice among slum or near-slum landlords of evicting tenants before thirty days had passed, thirty days being the minimum requirement for legal residency and the rights that come with it. The fact that Kleinbach had experienced the shuffle implied that he had been stationed at Fort Hardknox for some time now.

As I pulled the car onto the street, he suddenly said: "Dave Davies!"

I looked around, assuming he had seen someone he knew. "Who?"

"You. Dave Davies, P.I. Kinda has a ring to it."

For a sportscaster, maybe, or the kind of low comedian that used the diminutive of his last name as a first name, like Rags Ragland. "I'll think about it," I said.

"How about Dave Danger? That's pretty cool. Or Dave Derringer, P.I.? Like Magnum, you know?"

I remained silent, and fortunately, Kleinbach did, too, until we arrived back at the spot where he had parked his cycle, and which point he asked: "Don't suppose you could float me a little until the next time we run into each other, could you?"

Sighing, I pulled a twenty out of my wallet and handed it to him, proud to be pioneering the latest innovation in investigations: the detective paying the client. He smiled, jumped out of the car, and headed for his cycle. "Watch out for the police," I called after him, but I don't think he heard me. Once he had peeled out on the bike (which sounded a bit like a 787 taking off), I pulled away from the curb. Part of me...no, most of me... wanted to turn around and go right back to Marcy's house, but I respected her need for peace and quiet. Later I'd give her a call just to let her know that the mystery man was Nora's ex, and that she shouldn't be frightened by him. I should probably give Colfax a heads up as well, but doing so would put Alan Kleinbach at the very top of the suspect list for Nora's murder... since spouses invariably are...and would virtually guarantee that his claims the two missing boys were not really his children would either be ignored or taken as laying the groundwork for an insanity defense.

Sheez, what a mess.

It was nearly four before I finally pulled into my parking area, which was blissfully free of police officers. Once inside my office, I noticed the light on my phone machine was blinking (which reminded me to plug my cell into the charger), indicating a message, and hoped it might be Marcy. No such luck, though: it was some woman named Nellie Marsh who found my ad in the phone book and was calling to see if I would take on a missing person case. It seemed her pet Pekingese, Cha-Cha, had disappeared. She lived in Glendale, many neighborhoods of which are tucked against the Verdugo foothills, which is the natural habitat for bobcats and coyotes. Under different circumstances I might have agreed to take the job, walked around the neighborhood, broken it to her that Cha-Cha was probably the daily special at the Prairie Wolf Café, and billed for a day's work. But I had other things to worry. Then again, it was gainful employment, and Nora's retainer, generous though it was, would not last forever, particularly if I wanted to keep indulging my eating and housing habits. "I'll think about it," I muttered to myself.

There wasn't much I was able to do at the moment, about anything, at least not without crossing paths with the police and becoming a person of interest myself. I would have liked to have gone and talked to the Nora's and Elena's neighbors, to see what they knew, but both of their homes were active crime scenes, which meant my snooping would be spotted by the police that were still on site. I had no leads on the disappearance of the boys, and certainly no leads on what might have happened to Nora's original children...if indeed Kleinbach's claim was true. In short, I had nothing. At times like this in the past I had learned that there was but one logical course of action, so I closed up the office and set out for Edendale Video and Poster.

Edendale is a place that any real film buff in the L.A. area knows about, because in addition to the usual stuff, they have a private reserve for connoisseurs, "under the table" goods, if you like; films that aren't commercially available. Somehow Edendale has managed not only to find them but to get them onto DVD. These they loan out for free, thereby skirting any rights issues, as long as you pay to rent something else. Even the store's name has significance for buffs, *Edendale* being the old name for the stretch of Los Angeles real estate that was the place where the first movies in California were shot, several miles away from subsequent production centers, Hollywood, Burbank and Culver City. Edendale is part of Echo Park now, and every day thousands of downtown commuters blindly drive past a torn-up vacant lot where once stood the West Coast's very first motion picture studio. Los Angeles has always been the kind of place that backs up its history onto film and then deletes it.

But despite its name, Edendale Video wasn't located in the former Edendale. That was simply a nod to buffs like me. Instead it was in North Hollywood, which was not far from my home, which made it handy. Even if it were further away, though, I would make the effort. When I got down to my car, I saw that someone had stuck a flier under my windshield wiper. Hopefully it was not from the cult religion that was well on its way to owning more real estate in L.A. than Bob Hope ever dreamt of. Picking it up, I was relieved to see it was the take-out menu from a pizza joint. It was good to know—one can never have too many pizza joints nearby.

I was about to open the door when I heard a pop and a ping just over my head. I looked around to see what it was. The answer came a second later when I heard another pop and my side rearview mirror exploded in a cascade of glass. Someone was shooting at me!

I hit the asphalt painfully, not simply because it was asphalt, but because I had body-slammed down on broken glass fragments, a few of which entered the palm of my left hand. I heard another shot, and this one pinged off my fender. Whoever was trying to kill me, for whatever reason, had three shots left, if they were using a normal gun. I didn't feel like hanging around and waiting for them. I crawled backwards on my hands and knees, leaving a trail of blood from my hand, until I was hidden behind my car. If my assailant felt like approaching the car I was probably a sitting duck, but I did not have a lot of other options. After an eternity of three or four seconds, one more shot came, again pinging off the car, followed by the screeching sound of a vehicle peeling out. I raised up high enough to see through the windows of my Toyota, but the speeding car was already out of sight. Since, I had not paid any attention to other cars parked or stopped on the street, I had no way of identifying it.

Now the shakes were starting to set in. I'd never been shot at before. Slumping back down I remained seated, leaning against a tire for support, for about five quiet minutes, and then attempted to stand. My legs were watery, but they worked. I looked at my left palm, which was blue and red and dotted with glass punctures. Less than a mile away was a walk-in clinic that I had used once before when I sprained an ankle, and I decided to visit it now. It was not easy to drive with only one hand and no side rearview, but I made it.

Because of the blood, I was taken in almost immediately. The good news was that most of the puncture wounds were superficial; the bad, that there were quite a few of them. "What did you do, put your hand through a window?" the unsmiling nurse asked.

"Fell on a broken mirror," I said.

"Try not to do it again, okay?"

I did not bother to explain that I had not been trying to do it this time, that some idiot was shooting at me, because it seemed pointless. After picking out the glass and slathering disinfectant on my palm, which was bruised, she told me to be careful…and to pay at the desk on my way out.

I went straight back to the office and called Colfax.

"What do you want, Mr. Beauchamp?" he asked. "Are you calling to confess?"

"I'm calling because someone attempted to kill me about a half-hour ago."

"Oh. You sure about that?"

"I may not be Sam Spade, but I know when someone is firing bullets in my direction."

"Did any hit you?"

"No, but the experience didn't exactly make my day. How about coming out and checking the crime scene?"

"Out of my jurisdiction. You need to call your local precinct."

"But this could have something to do with Nora and Elena's murders, and the disappearance of the boys."

"You think it does?"

"I kind of hope it does, otherwise somebody's trying to kill me just for kicks."

I could hear Colfax sigh. "Okay, fine, I'll come by. Where did it happen?"

"My office," I told him. "I know you know where it is. I'm here now. I just got back from the medical clinic."

"I thought you said you weren't hit."

"Not by a bullet. I cut my hand on some shattered mirror glass."

"One of the bullets shattered the mirror?"

"Yes, obviously."

"Is the slug still there?"

"Uh, I didn't think to look."

"You're right, Beauchamp, you're no Sam Spade. As a detective, you're not even David Spade."

"Look, Colfax, my usual purview is tracking cheating spouses," I protested. "I'm not used to getting shot at."

"Okay, I'll get there as soon as I can." The detective hung up.

While waiting for him to arrive, I went back down to the small parking garage in my building. Pulling out the tiny but powerful penlight I carry on my key chain, I examined the broken mirror for a bullet fragment. Finding nothing, I tried the garage itself, but could not find anything resembling a slug, or even a shell casing. The best I could turn up were the rubber marks where the car—presumably belonging to the shooter—had peeled away from the curb, but I knew from taking a community college class in forensics that it took one complete revolution of a tire—covering twenty feet—in order to get an accurate, identifiable tire print. There was nowhere near twenty feet of lain rubber against the curb.

Going back inside, I picked up the phone and dialed Marcy, but it went to her machine. Hopefully, she was still asleep. When I got the beep, I said: "Marcy, it's Dave. I still don't have any information on the boys but I found out who the strange man hanging around your place is. His name is Alan Kleinbach, and Nora's first husband, and the boys' real father. I think he's harmless, but I can't swear to it. If you see him again and feel like calling the cops, go ahead. And be careful, okay? I'll talk to you later. Bye." I cut off the call. Should I have told her that someone had taken shots at me? Perhaps I should have, but leaving something like that on the machine might also have spooked her even further. The next time I see or talk to her in person I will tell her.

After forty minutes Colfax had still not arrived, so I popped a disk of *Dead Men Don't Wear Plaid* into my laptop. It's the Steve Martin parody of film noir, in which he is optically inserted *Zelig*-like into a host of old film clips and appeared to act alongside Golden Age Hollywood legends. It's the perfect time-killing film since there really isn't a plot anyway, so you just watch the gags and marvel at how well they were able to recreate sets and lighting, until it's time to stop.

It was dusk by the point it was time to stop. Detective Colfax arrived at seven thirty-five—sans Mendoza, thankfully. "Where's Tonto this time?" I asked.

"Better watch it, Beauchamp," the detective cautioned. "That could be construed as a racist remark."

"I didn't mean it that way," I said. "I just meant to be mildly insulting."

"You do everything mildly, don't you?"

He had me there.

"I told you not to take what Hector says personally," Colfax went on. "He's hated all private dicks since one was hired by his mother to get the goods on his father, who was sleeping around on her. That broke up the marriage. Hector was pretty young at the time…well, he's still pretty young. But he's a good cop."

"I see. Pardon me for pointing out the obvious, but it wasn't it the actions of his father that destroyed the marriage, and not the private eye who followed his father?"

"You want to tell him that?"

"Uh, no."

"Didn't think so. Anyway, I'm here, so show me where you were when you got shot at."

I took him down to the parking area and stood approximately where I was standing when I heard the first ping, and then pointed across the street where the sound of the car peeling out had come from. I showed him the tire marks on the road. Since it was getting dark, Colfax pulled out a much more powerful flashlight than mine to examine the site. Then he walked across the street and crouched to the approximate height of someone sitting in a car seat. Pulling a laser pointer out of his pocket, he then shined it onto the side of my building. "Look above your head," he called out. "Is that a hole?" I looked, and danged if it wasn't.

"Think there's a slug in there?" I asked.

"Short answer, yes," he said, waiting for a car to drive by so he could cross the street. "The question is whether it will be of any use." The laser pointer was an attachment to a Swiss Army knife, from which Colfax now flipped out an awl spike and began digging into the wall. Before long he uncovered a small ball of lead. Holding it up in the nearly vanquished light, he said: "Might be too damaged for ballistics."

"But at least you believe me," I said. "Someone really was shooting at me."

"If I didn't believe you, I wouldn't have shown up." He produced a small baggie from his pocket and put the slug into it, then returned it to his pocket. "Can you describe the car?"

"I never saw it, I just heard it. I guess we don't have a lot to go on, huh?"

"*We?*" Colfax said, pointedly.

"You know what I mean."

"I have something to go on, Beauchamp. Whoever shot at you was either a terrible shot, because otherwise you'd be dead, or they didn't really want you dead, just frightened."

"Do I need to go down to the station and fill out a report?" I asked.

"Oh, now you volunteer to fill out a report. Before, I had to threaten you."

"Let's say I learned my lesson."

"Then it wouldn't hurt. Do it at West Valley, though. That's the precinct covering this neighborhood. As for me, I'm done," Detective Colfax said, turning to leave. "Watch your back, David."

"Detective, there's something else you might want to know." He stopped and turned back. "That mysterious figure I saw at Marcy DeBanzi's place? The tall, bearded guy in the military coat?"

"What about him?"

"His name is Alan Kleinbach, and he's the father of the twins."

Colfax approached me and gave me an Eastwood squint. "I thought the late soldier was the twins' father."

"So did I, but it turns out the soldier was their step-father."

I gave him the *USA Today* version of what I had learned from Kleinbach, but omitted his suspicion that the missing twins were not really his natural sons.

"What's your gut say about this guy?" Colfax asked.

"He didn't strike me as dangerous if that's what you mean, at least not as long as he's sober."

"Oh?"

"Look, I don't want to incriminate the guy, but he gets a little testy and sarcastic after three beers. If you're asking whether I think he killed Nora and Elena...."

"Well?"

So tell him, Robert Mitchum ordered.

"No, I don't think so," I said. "My gut's telling me he's not involved."

"Could he be the one who took the shots at you?"

"No, that I'm pretty sure of. Kleinbach rides a motorcycle, and I know I didn't hear a chopper roaring away."

"Still, it won't hurt to talk with him. Where does he live?"

I gave Colfax the name of his apartment building, which he wrote down, and after recommending once more that I not get murdered (the man was nothing if not considerate) he ambled to his car and drove away. Since there was nothing more I could do here except stand around and perfect my impersonation of a clay pigeon, I got in my car and left, too. I was getting more used to driving without a side mirror; angling the rearview to the left helped a bit. By the time I got to Edendale Video and Poster, hours after I had intended to, the sun was long gone and L.A. was floating in darkness. Los Angeles always looks so much better in the dark than it does in the daylight. Thousands of multi-colored lights come on like so many jewels bedraping the buildings and dressing the place up. Maybe that's what the noir filmmakers of the 1940s figured out.

The interior of Edendale Video and Poster lived up to its name: just about every surface was covered either with shelves of DVDs or old movie posters (though these days, the 1980s counted as "old"). The place still had an ample supply of old-fashioned, non-digital, VHS tapes, but they had been relegated to the back room and were available by request only. I heard the cry, "Hey, Dave, what's up?" as I walked in. It was the proprietor, a middle-aged, balding guy named Brian McLiamore, who everyone called "Mac," and who appeared to know everything there was to know about old movies and Hollywood. As far as I knew, he did not use this knowledge to write books or articles or even blogs. Instead she shared it, person-to-person, with everyone who came into his store.

"Hi, Mac," I said.

"What did you do to your hand?"

"Oh, got shot at today. You know, private eye stuff."

Mac laughed. "Right. Broke a mirror and cut yourself, is what you mean."

He meant it as a bantering joke at my expense, obviously, since like everyone else he knew my normal daily routine involved nothing more exciting than photographing an insurance cheat or following a husband to his secretary's house, but what he said was close enough to the truth that I wasn't able to laugh. I muttered something about bad luck, and started looking at titles until Mac called out, "Hey, come see what I just got in."

I went up to the counter as he carefully slid a rolled poster out of a cardboard tube, and almost reverently uncurled it. It was vibrantly colored, but yellowed enough with age as to announce its authenticity. Much of the one-sheet was taken up with a ghastly green shriveled head, belonging to Boris Karloff. This was a poster for *The Mummy*, and there was only one such poster known to exist. That one, I heard, held the record for the highest price ever paid for a movie poster at auction. "Good God, Mac, don't tell me you bought that!" I said. "Did you win the lottery or something?"

"No, another one turned up in a garage out in the Pasadena, can you believe it?" he said, grinning like a kid on Christmas. "But that's just the start. There's a whole story behind it."

I wasn't really up for a long-winded story, but knowing I was going to get one anyway, I leaned against the counter and tried to make myself comfortable.

"So," Mac began, "a few days ago this fellow comes in and tells me that he's the great nephew of Willy Lipton. You know who Willy Lipton is, right?"

"The voice actor," I replied. "The guy who always did little kid characters, even at the end of his career."

"Right, because he had some glandular thing and his stones never dropped, or some such. Well, before he went into cartoons and radio, he did movies, playing kids. You know, like Billy Barty, who played babies in the 1930s, even though he was a teenager?"

"Yeah, I know, Mac. What does Willy Lipton have to do with this poster?"

"It turns out he appeared as a Saxon child in *The Mummy* in one of the flashback reincarnation scenes that were cut out before the release. Somehow Lipton got hold of a poster when it first came out, even though he was cut out of the movie, and after he died this poster ended up with a bunch of his stuff in the garage of his sister, who lived in Pasadena. The sister died last year, she was like ninety-five, or something, and her grandson, the guy who came in, found the poster while cleaning out her garage. So now I've got a double treasure!"

"A double treasure?" I asked.

"Not only do I have the poster, in pristine condition, but I'm the only one who knows that Willy Lipton, the voice of Sheldrake in *Colonel Dogbody's Time Machine*, was in *The Mummy*!"

"But since you just told me, you're no longer the only one."

"Okay, the *first* one, then."

"What did you have to pay for that poster?"

"I offered the guy five grand and I thought he was going to collapse."

"Five grand?" I cried. "That's only ten percent of what the thing's worth, isn't it?"

"One percent is closer, but it didn't matter to him. I didn't diddle him, Dave. I told him I'd give him that much right now or he could take it somewhere else and get it appraised. But I sized him up as a guy who wanted a sure bet, and I was right. I also told him that if I ever decide to sell it, and there's a profit from it, I'd give him half."

If Mac was right about the value of the poster, that would still leave him with a quarter-million in return for a five-thousand-dollar investment. "Are you going to sell it?" I asked him.

"Not any time soon," he replied. "This may be my retirement plan." He carefully rolled the one-sheet back up and replaced it in the tube. "I'm not going to display it either, at least not here."

"And if the guy finds out what it's really worth, comes back with a lawyer, and demands you sell it back to him?"

"I deal with things like 'ifs' on an as need basis," he said. "Now, what can we do you for this evening?"

That was a good question. I looked over his classic noir shelf, but it was largely the same as the last time I'd been in. He had one or two new DVDs of 1950s and '60s crime dramas from Hammer, the British studio that brought back *Dracula* and *Frankenstein* with stunning Technicolor success, but there was something about Brit Noir that wasn't quite…real. Oh, hell; maybe after what I'd been through today I should just go for a comfort film. I picked out *The Big Sleep* with Bogie and Bacall. I never get tired of it. I probably should buy a copy of my own.

"Ah, going for the good stuff," Mac said as I laid it down on the counter. "Have you seen the 1945 pre-release version?"

"Yeah, but I like the official one better."

"Me too." He opened the box up and examined the disc, then said, "Okay."

"Okay what?" I asked.

"Oh, I had a problem a month or so back, where someone came in to rent this and it turned out to be the wrong disc inside."

"What did they get?"

"*The Big Sleepover.*"

"Sounds like an eighties teen sex comedy."

"It's a hardcore porn film."

"Oh."

"You know how it is with porn producers. They can't come up with an original idea so they parody what someone else has done and slap a pun title on it. The worst I've seen is a spoof of *Gladiator* called *Glad He Ate Her*. Anyway, someone came in and ordered the real *Big Sleep* and *Big Sleepover* at the same time but they returned them in the wrong cases, and I didn't catch it. Then a teacher came in to rent the Bogart film to show to her class on the last day of school."

"I went to the wrong school," I commented.

"Well, it was for the last day, or something, the classes had ended. But the point is, instead of Bogie and Baby, what she got was the skin parody. When she brought it back in here I wasn't sure I was going to escape with my life."

"It almost makes me want to see what they did to Raymond Chandler," I said, and before I could add the second *almost*, Mac reached down under the counter.

"Have a look," he said, pulling up a DVD. "I haven't seen it all the way through, so you can give me a review."

"Why do you even carry stuff like this, Mac?"

"Edendale Video not only caters to every taste, but every lack thereof," he said, proudly.

I glanced down at the cover of the DVD and saw a young man in a fedora and trench coat, which he was opening in flashing fashion toward a woman, while looking back over his shoulder toward the camera. While not unhandsome, the guy looked stoned, drugged, or maybe just naturally stupid. But it was the woman who drew my attention. She was young and clearly nude (though a streamer reading *Starring Philup Marlo…and it took a lot to Philup her!* had been matted across the nipples of her very large breasts), and she was reacting with shock at the detective's exposure. The woman looked familiar for some reason. Could it be an actress who had since made it in the mainstream? I turned the box over to see if there were any photos on the back, and found that there were. "Oh no, oh my god!" I moaned.

"You okay, Dave?"

I didn't reply. My attention was riveted on the photos, until it slid down to the company logo in the bottom of the box, "Triex Distribution." *Triex Distribution*...the name of the porn company that had been operating, unbeknownst to me, downstairs at my office building! Then my eyes slid back to the photographs. They weren't good photos, but they were clear enough to recognize the two "actresses" pictured. One of them was the same woman as on the front of the box, and in this shot I easily recognized her: it was Janelle, the busty young lady who worked at Max Gelfan Productions. But it was the sight of the other woman, who must be playing the Bacall role, that really caused me to gasp for air.

It was Elena Cates.

FIFTEEN

Mac was surprised by my decision to rent six different Triex discs and leave the real *Big Sleep* behind, until I told him the reason for my interest, which was that I had only recently found out that the films were shot in a makeshift studio below my office. "Can I come over for lunch sometime?" he asked.

"They aren't there anymore."

"Damn."

"It wasn't exactly run like a sports arena, where you could buy a ticket and watch. I didn't even know what was going on down there." I kept to myself the fact that I had personally met two of the "actresses" involved in the films, and that one of them had been murdered.

"Let me know if you like any of those," Mac said.

I was particularly careful driving home, in part because of my broken mirror, in part because my sore hand still made turning the wheel difficult, but also because I did not want to be stopped for any reason and have the police officer spot the porn in the passenger seat. Even though porn was perfectly legal, I could read the headlines in the *Valley Voice*, the little toy newspaper that covered my small section of the sprawl: *Local investigator stopped for traffic violation with rented skin flicks. "He's an asshole," says Hollywood Detective Hector Mendoza*. I did not completely relax until the engine and lights were off in the parking garage for my apartment building. First thing tomorrow, I'd run the car into the shop and get a new side mirror.

Once inside, I headed straight for the fridge to see if there was anything to munch on. I should have eaten more at the Mexican restaurant. Further search turned up a can of chunky beef soup whose label was not in Latin, meaning it was probably not too old to eat. After heating it up, I didn't even bother pouring it in a bowl. I just carried the pan into the living room, and then took *The Big Sleepover* and stuck it in the DVD player. In addition to *The Big Sleepover* I had *Abraham Lickin: Vagina Hunter*, *Pussy in Boots*, *Breasts of the Southern Wild*, *'Ave a Tart* ("He'll shag you blue!" the tagline promised), and perhaps most cringe-inducing of all, *No Cuntry for Old Men*. I could only imagine what a porn version of *The Big Clock*, the film that had gotten me in trouble with Hot Ticket Home Video, would be titled. With more than a bit of trepidation, I sat down to watch, hoping the film wouldn't adversely affect my eating.

Since I'm not an aficionado of porn (or even Sharon Stone movies) I don't know if this one was any better or worse than other examples of the genre, but by any standards of filmmaking, it was voyage to the bottom of the barrel. The best thing that could be said about it was that most of it was in focus. Not all of it, but most. Whoever it was playing Philup Marlo looked even more stoned and dopey than he appeared in the cover art, though I had to admit that Janelle, as the wild sister, proved to have a modicum of acting ability, though that was not why she had been hired. Not by a long shot. It was her bared, spectacular chest that stole the movie. The very sight of her breasts might have turned Charles Nelson Reilly straight. When Elena came on—not, as I had guessed, in the Lauren Bacall role, which was handled by an anonymous blonde whose attempts to talk in a sexy baritone was funnier than anything on Comedy Central—but as the wife of the gangster, patterned after the original's "Eddie Mars," I fought the urge to close my eyes. As it turned out, all Elena did was push up her breasts while talking dirty to Marlo, showing a lot less flesh than many mainstream actresses displayed in their successful quests for the Oscar. The epic ended with the drugged-out-but-well endowed leading man saying to the anonymous blonde, "Here's licking out you, kid," which offended me on a half-dozen different levels.

I went on to the next movie, and then the next, until I had watched five of them. Janelle appeared in two more, and Elena was in four of the five, though as before, her performances teased far more than she actually showed. A scene in panties and a sheer bra, which could probably be shown on network TV these days, was about the height of her nudity.

It was now nearly three in the morning, and I had been right earlier: Thursday had not been a repeat of Wednesday. It had been a lot worse; maybe the longest, strangest day of my life. I was exhausted, and not so much aroused as numb. I can't say I found anything in these films particularly appealing (even the sight of Janelle's boobs began to pall after a while) but at least the answer to one lingering question seemed evident: that was how Nora Faust had known the Triex offices had been a make-shift porn studio. There were two points of connection between her and Triex, Janelle and Elena, either of whom, or both, could have informed her of the facility.

But where did that leave me in regards to the murders? Did Triex have anything to do with Nora's death, or Elena's? Perhaps it was time to talk once again to Janelle.

Tomorrow.

* * * * * * *

It was nearly ten in the morning when I woke up. Even though there was nothing in particular I had to be awake for, I disliked sleeping late. Who knows…maybe I'll miss something?

Before heading to the office, I had to do something about my car mirror. Jumping online I found a place in Encino that specialized in auto glass, and after getting cleaned up and wolfing down the last of a box of Lucky Charms, I set out for it. The place was staffed by a group of guys who looked like extras from a prison movie. The supervisor was a bald, tattooed man roughly the size of a manatee. He knew his business, though, and within an hour I had a new mirror. The problem was that they took cash only; I had the seventy-five they asked for on me, but only just. I had never developed the going-to-the-ATM habit because I had rarely enjoyed the having-money-in-the-bank condition required to maintain it. I had a small stack of Nora's bills stashed away in my work desk, though.

There was nothing awaiting me at the office except another call from Mrs. Marsh, the woman who had called yesterday, informing me that my services would not be needed after all. Cha-Cha the Peke had made his way home on his own, little the worse for wear. I could only assume he was out kibbling it up with the boys. Fishing out the envelope I had hastily stuck in the bottom drawer of my desk, the one containing money, I grabbed another C-note and then close up shop again and headed out for Max Gelfan Productions. The whole way to Hollywood, I glanced every five seconds or so in my beautiful new side mirror. I paid for it; I was going to use it.

Parking at Gelfan's was a little harder on this day, but I managed to snare a spot on the street about three blocks away. Once inside the building, I signed in at front and then went straight to the elevator and up to the fourth floor, where Janelle's desk was, and then made the mistake of trying to find my own way around without a guide. In this particular building, I might have needed a Sherpa. I finally spotted a reception area that I believed to be Janelle's workspace, but it was inhabited by a striking young woman of East Indian heritage. "Hi, can I help you?" she asked, her voice betraying an English accent. She had a kilowatt smile and dark, deep eyes. Had I simply never noticed so many beautiful women around before, or was I just going to all the right places this week?

Not that it's going to do you any good, I heard in my head. Thanks, Mitch, now please go away.

"Hi, I think I'm in the wrong place," I said. "I'm looking for Janelle."

"You're in the right place," she told me, "but Janelle is no longer her. I'm her replacement." Her voice was musical.

"Oh. Do you have any idea how I could get in touch with

her?"

The smile faltered a bit. "May I ask what is this regarding?"

"My name is Dave Beauchamp and I'm a private investigator, and I need to speak with Janelle. If you can't help me I'd be happy to talk with Terrence Holving."

"Mr. Holving is busy right now—"

"Then I'll wait." I took a seat in the reception area and picked up a *Hollywood Reporter*, which was only about eight pages thick. Apparently not much was happening in Hollywood these days. Every few seconds I looked up at her and smiled, a technique that stood Jack Nicholson well in *Chinatown*, and danged if it didn't work in real life, too.

"Look, you're making me nervous," she said.

Olivia Hussey; that's who she sounds like.

"If I tell you where Janelle is, will you please leave?"

"I don't want to make you nervous. All I want to do is talk to Janelle."

"Fine, but I'm not supposed to do this." She opened a rolodex on her desk and wrote something down on a slip of paper, then held it out to me. When I took it I saw an address.

"Thank you," I said. "Are you an actress, too?"

"I hope to be," she said. "Right now I'm just doing some loop group stuff, because of my accent, but there is a trend for young Brindians right now, so I'm hopeful."

"Brindians?"

"British people of Indian heritage. Like Parminder Nagra."

"Oh, right, and Merle Oberon."

"Who?" she asked.

"Yes, well, I'll be looking for you," I said, leaving the office. It would be a shame for her not to be able to get her face on camera, but hopefully she wouldn't end up in the same kind of films as Janelle.

The address on the paper was for Kings Road, which is in West Hollywood, which meant my trusty, shot-at Toyota was getting a far greater workout than usual. It was an apartment, which I figured, so I hoped that there was a buzzer directory out front. As it turned out there was, though it only listed the last names of the tenants. I did not know what Janelle's last name was. I punched the "manager" button and a second later a voice said: "Manager."

Awareness of oneself is a wonderful thing.

"Hi, I'm here to see Janelle, but I think I have the wrong apartment number," I said. "I wrote down one-oh-seven, but the person who answers isn't Janelle."

"Hold on," the voice said, and a moment later came back and said, "Janelle Wynn is in two-oh-five. I don't know how you got one-oh-seven."

"I don't either. Thanks." I heard the line click off and prayed the manager wasn't of a suspicious nature as I punched the button for *Wynn*, 205. A second later a voice answered: "Got something for me?"

"Um, no, Janelle, it's Dave Beauchamp. We met at Max Gelfan Productions."

"You! You're a fucking asshole, you know that?" she cried, and I opted to treat the question as a rhetorical one. "It's because of you I got fired, you fucking piece of dogshit!" I could tell her after-hours manner was considerably different than her office etiquette.

"Um, I'm sorry about that, but I need to talk to you."

"You can bite me, is what you can do!"

It vill be...a pleasure, the voice of Bela Lugosi said in my head. I ignored him.

"Janelle, don't hang up," I said. "All I need is a couple minutes of your time."

There was a pause, and then she said: "How do I even know you're who you say you are?"

"Janelle, why would anyone lie about being Dave Beauchamp?"

She laughed, and then said: "You got me there. I'll be right down, and you've got exactly one minute." A few seconds later, Janelle appeared, her Olympic-sized bust threatening to burst through the boundaries of the tee shirt she was wearing. She opened the door but refused to step back so I could enter the lobby. "Okay, what is it?" she demanded. "You here to get me thrown out of my apartment, too?"

"No, I…Janelle, I know you act in porn," I said. It wasn't the greatest conversation opener I've ever used, but I figured I had limited time for small talk.

"And what? You figured if I'd do it for the camera, I'd do it for you? Get the fuck out of here or I'll call the cops." She turned and started to walk away, but I was able to catch the door before it closed, so I invited myself in.

"Wait, that's not why I'm here," I called after her. "It's about the Brothers Alpha."

"Those little shits? Why should I care about them now?"

"They were watched by Elena Cates."

She stopped and turned back to me. "So?"

"Elena was in some of the films you did."

"So?"

"Elena Cates is dead," I told her. "She was murdered."

Her face suddenly drained of insouciance. "Mother Mary."

"Nora's dead, too, and the Alphas are missing."

"Motherfuck! When did all this happen?"

"Last couple of days."

She walked over to the cushioned bench in the lobby and sank down. "Are you here because you think I know something about all this?"

"Do you?"

"Hell no! I got canned at Gelfan's thanks to your telling Terry I was taking money from Nora for getting the twins into auditions. That's the last contact I've had with anybody."

"I never told Holving you were taking Nora's money," I protested. "I didn't know you were taking Nora's money, but I suspected it, so—"

"So you set up a goddamned sting, and I walked right into it! Terry started checking my emails when I was on break and he found the one I sent to Nora about that crap callback you talked about. When I came back, he shitcanned me right then and there."

"I'm sorry about that. Really."

"Oh, fuck you, you're sorry. But I'm not through with Holving yet."

"What do you mean?"

"I know things…oh, why am I even talking with you?" She spun around and started to leave again.

"What about Elena?" I said.

She stopped and turned back again. "What about her?"

"When was the last time you saw her?"

"It's been a while. It's not like we were particularly close. Elena was kind of high-handed. She wouldn't do sex scenes, she'd only do dialogue, like she was Julia Roberts, or something."

"How did Elena make the transition from sex films to helping out the stage mother of a couple of twelve-year-olds?"

Janelle Wynn appeared to deflate…most of her, anyway. "I put Elena in contact with Nora. She wanted out while getting out was still possible."

"I'm not following you," I said.

"Look, doing these kinds of films always seems like a good idea for a while, particularly if you've got the goods." She bounced her boobs for emphasis. "The pay is incredible. At least it used to be. The fucking recession has hit the porn industry, too. And it's kind of exciting at first. But after a while…I'm not sure how to describe it, really…it just gets meaningless. Maybe it's not that way for the guys, all those zonked-out retards with cocks the size of baguettes who want to fuck every woman in the world that doesn't look like Seabiscuit. But for us, you show up each day and someone new is sticking it into you, and you have to pretend like it's the best you've ever had, you know? And not simply for the camera, either. You literally have to pretend that every one of these losers is the best fuck you ever had, or else they get mad. And then there's the guys in charge, who are all pretty scummy. Half of them are connected to the mob, so on any given day Jilly from Philly can show up on the set and want a personal sample of the goods he's investing in. Then you have the constant AIDS testing, which gets to be a drag, and you start to wonder if you really want all this hanging around in your past."

"Sounds like you regret ever doing it."

"Maybe I do," she said, pointing a finger in my face, "but you're not allowed to judge me, you got that? Only I'm allowed to judge me. I don't need any crap from you or anyone else."

"Okay, no crap intended. It just sounds like you hate it."

"I like the money, and if you dare use the 'P' word on me, I'll drive your balls into your throat."

I held my hands over my crotch defensively and said: "Let's talk about Elena instead. You said she wanted out while it was still possible. What did you mean?"

"You don't know how seductive this business can be," Janelle replied, "but there comes a point of no return, when there's no getting out of it voluntarily. Maybe the money's become too comfortable, or you're too hooked on drugs, or your self-esteem has spent too long on its back to think of anything else to do, there's lots of reasons. It was easier for Elena because she wasn't as in demand, because she'd only do come-ons instead of coming. Most ladies hang around long enough to get their sag card."

"I didn't think SAG covered porn," I said.

"It's an industry joke. A sag card is a pink slip. It means you're so old that your tits sag down to your knees, so they can't get them in the same camera shot as your face. That means you're out. You're replaced by newer, higher tits, which may good for the producers and the bastards watching this stuff, but it's the end of the line for the women. That's why a lot of us want to get out before we get our sag cards."

"Could someone have wanted to kill her because she got out? Jealousy, perhaps?"

"I really don't know. Like I said, I wasn't that close to her on a personal level, and this is getting kind of boring. So unless you have any other questions—"

"Just one," I said. "Look me in the eyes and swear to me that you have no idea where Burton and Taylor Frost are."

I had never really looked into her eyes…I suspected most men didn't…but now that I was I saw they were very large, hazel and warm.

"I have no fucking idea where the little spawns of Satan are," she said, meeting my gaze. "I'm sorry if they're in trouble, but I just don't know. I'm sorry Nora's dead, sort of, but I also wish I'd never met the lot of them. I wish I'd never met you, for that matter. If I hadn't, I'd still have a day job."

"Janelle, have you ever tried getting acting work in real films?"

She looked at me with a mixed expression that conveyed both frustration and a good measure of pity because of my naïveté, and got up off the bench. "What kind of roles do you think I would get with a rack like this?" she asked, bouncing her breasts so violently that it must have hurt. "You know good and fucking well what kind of roles I'd get! I'd be the pole dancer in the background at the Bada Bing Club, or I'd be Whore Number Three in the brothel scene of a Steven Segal film, or I'd be the naked punchline in a teen comedy. I'd be showing just as much tit, bush and ass as I do in porn, and I'd be blowing just as many producers to get the gig, but I'd be earning scale for it instead of three-grand a fucking day. Why don't I try acting in real films? Bite me!" She stormed away and headed up a staircase.

While I've not done many things right in my life, I silently gave thanks that I never had any interest in the film industry, except as a consumer. Had Jean Harlow gone through what Janelle Wynn had? Probably, though that was a depressing thought. Jean was long gone, of course, but I took a moment to pray that Janelle Wynn would come out of this all right. Then I showed myself out of her apartment building. I went straight to my car and noticed something sticking under the windshield wiper. "Aw, sheez," I moaned, recognizing the paper as a ticket. I had not noticed any parking restriction signs anywhere on the block, and it turned out the ticket was not for a parking viola-

tion, but for not turning my wheels into the curb. This was L.A.:
you want to take a shot at someone, go ahead. No one will ever
see you. But fail to turn your wheels to the curb and the cops
will get you.

Or maybe my good friend Detective Hector Mendoza had
managed to put out a harassment order on me.

I didn't bother going back to the office; I went home instead.
When I arrived there was little for me to do except check the
mail, which consisted of more bills, real estate ads, grocery
store fliers and something from a politician. Apparently there
was an election coming up; in California, elections were practically a weekly event. I needed to return the stellar films I'd
rented from Edendale and thought about scooping them all up
and doing just that, but there was one I had not yet watched, *No
Cuntry for Old Men.* I was looking forward to it as much as I
was looking forward to orthodontic surgery, but I had paid for
it, so I was going to get my money's worth.

Popping it in, I paid particular attention to the credits, trying
to discern if Janelle was in this one, too. Her real name never
appeared in the credits, of course, but all the other films in
which she appeared listed "Bo Dacious" and "Tia Ney" in the
credits. My money was on Janelle being Bo Dacious, but that
name did not appear here (though there was a credit for "Liz
Behan"). The plot—if that word could actually be applied to
this kind of film—involved two aging Western policemen, one
of whom was played by a clearly young man with very bad
shoe-polish hair whitening and a moustache that looked like it
was made from hair from a cat comb, chasing a robotic killer
who clubs his victims, all women, on the head with a gigantic
dildo, after which he used the murder weapon in a different
way. Once again, the result was about as erotic as a WWF title
bout. Janelle finally turned up as the chief detective in charge of
the case, who was first seen seated behind her desk completely
nude, while a male officer shouted, "Shit, lieutenant, you're out
of uniform!" She assigned a new officer to track the dildo-blud-
geoner, an equally buxom blonde in a rhinestone cowboy hat

and a halter top made of gauze, after which the male officer rushed back in and announced he had a 69 in progress, and the scene turned into a threesome.

Of course, Officer Sexpot managed to capture the crazed murderer (after having an encounter in a swimming pool with the suspect's equally stunning landlady, presumably played by "Liz Behan"), and her reward was to be "sent to the showers"… literally. The last scene was the actress (for lack of a better word), in what was supposed to be the police locker room shower, with a couple of naked male friends, their backs to the camera. "This is no cunt…[pregnant pause]…tree for old men," she said into the camera, fingering herself as her companions started soaping her up. Then they turned to the camera.

"Oh, God, *no!*" I shouted aloud as I watched the two rub themselves all over the woman, who was rubbing them back.

It was Burton and Taylor Frost.

SIXTEEN

I probably broke every speed limit getting over to Edendale Video and Poster. I did not want to risk telling Mac what I needed to tell him over the phone. After carelessly parking, I rushed in, bearing the DVD's. Upon seeing me, Mac said: "Boy, you plowed through all those in only one night?"

"Back room, Mac, we need to talk," I said.

"Hell, Dave, what's—"

"Back room!"

Calling to his employee, a middle-aged, very gay guy named Bonn, who was restocking the shelves, he said: "Can you watch the register for a minute?"

"Sure," Bonn replied. "Hey, Dave."

"Hi, Bonn," I said, practically pulling Mac back to his small, cluttered office.

"Man, what's got you so exercised?" he enquired as I closed the door.

I held up *No Cuntry for Old Men.* "Is this the only copy you have of this?" I asked.

"I think there's another one, why?"

"Get rid of them. Now."

"That bad, huh?"

"That illegal. There's a sex scene in this with two twelve-year-old boys."

"Holy shit. Are you sure?"

"I know the boys in question, and I know they are twelve. I'd hate to see you get shut down and have to register as a sex offender."

"Fuck, man," he said. "That's nuts! Why would any producer do that? That's practically begging to be arrested and sentenced."

"I can't figure it out, either," I told him. I did not bother trying to fill him in on the case, nor tell him that the fact that the boys were involved in child pornography suggested at least a reason, if not an actual motive, for some of the carnage that had been going on the last few days. "Man, you hear about things like this, but you never really expect to see an example of it," Mac said. "But thanks for tipping me off. I'll get rid of the disks right now."

"Actually, I might need to keep one, if that's all right."

Mac cocked his head and squinted at me. "What for?"

"Because it might turn into evidence."

"Won't that put you at risk to having to register as a sex offender, if you're caught with it?"

"If I turn it straight over the police, I should be fine."

"All right, Dave, but if you get caught, the secretary will disavow any knowledge of your actions."

"You don't have a secretary," I said.

"Then I'll do it myself."

"I'll be careful, Mac. I'm going to have to go, now." Sticking the copy of the illegal porno in my pocket, I went back out into the store, where Bonn was ringing up a woman's order. As I started to leave, he said: "You're not getting anything today, Dave?"

"No, not today."

I heard him comment, "Must be sick," under his breath as I walked outside and made a beeline to my car, and then spend away. Halfway home I managed to convince myself that there was no reason to be nervous. The photos of the boys were not on the packaging, nor was there a banner reading, *See naked adolescent boys soaped up in the shower with a hot babe*! You had to watch the film to find that out. The only positive thing I could project onto having seen this heap of sleaze was that Elena Cates was nowhere to be seen in the film. It must have been made after she decided to get out.

When I got back home I placed a call to Marcy, to make sure nothing else had happened to her.

And to hear her voice, Bogie said.

Okay, yeah, to hear her voice. This time she answered. "Dave, do you have news about the boys?"

"Unfortunately not," I said. *At least not the kind of news you want to hear.*

"I'm really getting worried."

"I know. You haven't received a ransom call or anything?"

"Nothing."

"Until we hear otherwise, let's try to assume the best case scenario. They're fine, and who knows? Maybe they're playing someone else's video games. How are you feeling?"

"Better. My head is still a little sore, as I'm sure you can imagine. Oh, and thanks for letting me know that the strange figure is really their father. I had no idea the soldier wasn't. If I see him again, I'm not planning on letting him in or anything, but at least I won't be terrified."

After some more chitchat, I hung up and let her go back to whatever it was she was doing…probably worrying. Then I tried to get back to what I should be doing, which is trying to figure out just what the hell is going on all around me. I wasn't getting very far, because nothing really seemed to fit together. Nora and Elena were dead, but Marcy wasn't. Someone shot at me but missed. The twins were gone, their presumptive father was a combat fatality, but a strange homeless, or near-homeless, guy who was really their dad suddenly appears, and he's convinced the boys are not really his kids. Even Howard Hawks couldn't direct this into any semblance of coherence.

Then I had a brainstorm. Last year I had been contacted by a mystery writer, a guy named, believe it or not, Jack Daniels (though he wrote under a pseudonym), who phoned out of the blue to ask if he could pump me for information about private investigating to use in his books. He said he found me through the Yellow Pages, and once we had established a cordial relationship, he confessed that the first three investigators he had contacted had rudely hung up on him. Since then we had casually stayed in touch, but I hadn't talked to him for quite some time. Digging his card out of an old shoebox that I laughingly refer to as my rolodex, I dialed his number, and he answered on the fourth ring. I could hear the sound of a vacuum cleaner in the background. "Hi, Jack? This is Dave Beauchamp."

"Who?" he asked.

"Dave Beauchamp. The private investigator."

"Oh, shit, hi, Dave, how the heck are you? I can't hear you too well, because the cleaning woman is here."

"Oh, I can call back later—"

"No, no, it's fine. What can I do for you?"

"If you have a minute or two, I'd like to run something past you."

"Please don't tell me you're thinking about writing a book," he said. "Don't bother. Writing crime fiction is a lot like crime itself. It doesn't pay."

Maybe not, but he could still afford a cleaning woman. "It's nothing like that. I'm working on a case and nothing about it makes any sense. Since I'm trying to approach it from inside my own peculiar box, and getting bogged down, it just struck me that if I could get a fictional mind working on it, that mind might see something that I'm missing."

"Oh, cool! That's different." The vacuuming behind him was getting louder now. "Tell you what," Jack said, nearly shouting. "Buy me a beer, and we'll talk."

"When?"

"Now. I can't get much work done anyway with Sarah here."

Sarah I took to be the cleaning woman. We agreed to meet in an hour at the Hound & Badger in Santa Monica, which is where Jack lived. (Santa Monica; not the Hound & Badger.)

To me, a joint called "Hound & Badger" sounded like a place you went to in order to get nagged, but Jack swore by it. It was, obviously, a British pub. There were several such pubs in Santa Monica, since there was a high percentage of Brits living there, and the cool, often foggy coastal weather reminded them of home, but without the VAT. I had probably put seventy miles on my Toyota today alone, and a round trip to the Santa Monica would likely push it to one hundred, but what the hey? Philip Marlowe never complained about the gas.

That's 'cause I charged for expenses, junior, Bogie's voice said to me. Thanks for reminding me.

It took only about forty minutes to get to Santa Monica, but a good portion of the rest of the allotted hour was spent looking for parking. I finally swallowed the pill and pulled into a lot. After paying the parking attendant, I understood out why a place like this was called "a lot." I walked the few blocks down to the Hound & Badger, which was within a stone's throw of the palisades overlooking the ocean. Jack was already there waiting for me.

Jack Daniels was a big, open, friendly, rumpled guy with uncontrollably thick hair and a crooked grin. He looked like anything but a man who spent his waking hours trying to figure out new and better ways to kill people. After shaking my hand forcefully, we took a table in the bar area of the Hound & Badger. "How's Kim?" I asked. Kim was Jack's wife.

"Great, great," he said. "She's got a business function this evening, so she'll be out late."

Terrific. I hope Jack wasn't under the impression that I was going to entertain him until last call. After a few more minutes of catching up with each other, during which time a British barmaid appeared to take our order—something called an ESB and a sausage roll for Jack, and a glass of ice tea and a bowl of clam chowder for me—Jack said: "So, Dave, why don't you tell me what your problem is."

As concisely as I could I outlined the various events of the past couple days, while Jack listened in silence, interrupting only to thank the barmaid when she brought his beer, which was a dark amber, and sausage roll, and my soup and tea. He took a sip of the brew and savored it. "Oh, that's good," he whispered. "Okay, now that I have my thinking juice, tell me the rest."

"That's about all there is," I said, taking a spoonful of the excellent chowder. "Where would you take this story if you were writing it as a book?"

After taking a chomp out of the sausage roll, he said, "Let's see...the two kids are doing porn, probably because the woman looking after them is doing porn. But did the mother know about this?"

"My best guess is that she knew of Elena's past in porn, but I doubt she knew her sons were involved. No matter how desperate Nora was to get them into showbiz, there still had to be a line she wouldn't cross."

"Maybe, maybe not."

"I don't know. I think Nora regularly left the kids in her assistant's care for the entire day. Elena could have been doing anything with them, other than taking them to the zoo."

"Maybe this Elena person was simply fulfilling every twelve-year-old-boy's fantasy, that a hot older woman wants them."

"That's too creepy to contemplate."

"But isn't that why you're talking to me? Because I can come up with ideas too creepy for you to contemplate?"

He's got you there, sport, said Errol Flynn, a man reputed to have known a thing or two about underage sex.

"Okay," Jack went on, "what if the boys somehow found out what their caretaker's day job was, and, being twelve year old boys, they tell her she'd better take them to watch a filming or else they'll squeal about her to their mom."

"But their mom may already know about her past."

"Maybe the boys tell Elena that if she doesn't do what they say, they'll tell their mother she abused them."

"That's pretty cold."

Jack took a long swig from his beer. "It is pretty cold," he said, "but your description of these two doesn't make them sound like models of warmth."

"True."

"Well, let's just cut to the chase and start with the boys being on the set of the porno, however they got there. We know they were on the set, because you saw them in the movie. So they're there, one thing leads to another, and the director or producer decides to put them in the film. Maybe he didn't realize how young they were."

"Boy, that's a tough one to accept," I said, wiping my mouth with a real, cloth napkin. "I mean, one would have to be blind to not realize they're underage. But let's say for a moment that the director was either blind or just stupid. Elena still knew they were only twelve."

"Right, which is a potential motive for her murder."

"How so?"

"Mom finds out that her kids have been sexually exploited and realizes it has to be the fault of the assistant. So she flies into a rage and kills her."

"Doesn't wash, I'm afraid," I said. "The mother was killed before the assistant."

"Oh, right." There was a pause of about four seconds, and then Jack said: "Ooh! Ooh, I got it! The killer is the twins' *father*, and *he's* the one who finds out how his boys are being exploited. He confronts the mother who tries to put the blame on the assistant, but Dad doesn't care, because the kids are still her responsibility. He's loses control and kills her. *Then* he goes after the assistant, since she was in on it too. Then he tries to get you because he thinks that you might have realized that he's the killer."

"Well, that one makes sense," I said. "But there's still the aunt, who wasn't killed, and the missing boys."

"Dad could be the one who took the boys. As for the aunt… what if Dad goes after the aunt with the intent of killing her, but when he gets to her house, the boys are there. He's already killed two people in order to protect his sons, but they don't know that, and he doesn't want them to find out. Most of all, he doesn't want them to see him murder someone right in front of their eyes, particularly someone they know. So he subdues the aunt just enough to take the kids and run, but doesn't kill her."

"That's not bad, Jack, but there's a wrinkle."

"I hate wrinkles."

"And you'll hate this one. Alan, the father, told me he doesn't believe the boys are really his kids."

"He told you what?"

I repeated myself, then went back to my chowder.

"Hmmm, that's a good one. Why would someone believe his kids are not his kids? Maybe he really is bughouse crazy."

"I haven't ruled that out completely," I admitted.

Jack drained his glass and then held it up. "This, my dear Watson, promises to be a two-pint problem."

I laughed and flagged down the barmaid, so Jack could order another ESB. When it arrived he went through the same ritual of sipping it, savoring it, and commenting on it, and then said, "All right, where were we?"

"We both agreed it's possible for the dad to be insane."

"Right, he's nuts. Or...oh, I like this...he's nuts like a fox. What if he's only telling you that the boys aren't really his in order to deflect his real motive, which is to get rid of the mom and regain custody of his children?"

"It's possible. The thing is, Jack, I've seen pictures of the boys when they were babies, and they looked different. They were a lot more identical than they are now."

"My two nieces looked like identical twins when they were babies, and they were born three years apart."

"Point taken. But could there be any other explanation for the guy's claim, outside of insanity or deviousness?"

"Well, sure," Jack said, finishing off his sausage roll. "He could be telling the truth. Maybe they really aren't his kids. Hey, wait a minute.…" I could practically hear the sound of the engine in Jack's mind shifting into high gear. "Maybe all this has nothing to do with that porno movie. Maybe the father is pissed because he's discovered that the mother got rid of their real kids and substituted two other ones, and that's why he killed her! The assistant knows about it, maybe she was even in on it, so she has to go, too. The aunt, though, she doesn't know anything about the switch, so she's spared." He took a swig, set the glass down, and sat back triumphantly.

"Okay," I said, "but how does one go about discarding their twin children and replacing them with others? Last time I was in Target, I didn't see a twins section."

"And if this story were set anywhere other than Hollywood, I'd agree with you," Jack said. "But you know that twins are always in demand here because of the film industry."

"Yeah, I know all that."

"So does everybody else. If you live in Enid, Oklahoma, and the doctor says you're going to have twins, you start thinking about moving to L.A. and get the kids working."

"Okay, let's say you're right. But how would one go about finding another set of twins? Craig's List?"

"Ha ha. Were it me, theoretically, I'd start with a casting director."

"Oh."

"Dave, that was an awfully meaningful 'oh.'"

"There's somebody else who's kind of involved in this, another porn actress who worked on the side in the casting office of a television company. She used to call the twins in to audition for TV shows."

"You've been holding out on me. You didn't mention her."

"She didn't fit into any of the scenarios until now," I said. I had to admit that a lot of what Jack was saying made sense in an odd sort of way, which is why I called him in the first place. *Never underestimate the value of writers, kid, no matter what Jack Warner tells you*, Bogie said, helpfully.

"You still there?" Jack was asking.

"Hmm? Oh, yeah, I'm here, I'm just thinking. You've come up with a couple great theories, Jack, but the problem is I don't know how to conform them. It has to be one or the other, either the twin substitution or the porno movie, because there are too many puzzle pieces to make only one picture."

"If this were a story of mine, I'd go with the one where the dad kills everybody because the kids have been put into X-rated movies."

"And the bit about the boys not really being his?"

"Either misdirection or delusion, in my opinion."

I ran my hand through my hair. "Okay, Jack, you've given me a lot to think about. Thanks."

"This was kind of fun, you know? Any time you've got another problem, give me a—" His face took on a faraway expression that had nothing to do with the alcohol he'd consumed. "Oooh, you've given me an idea," he said. "Of course...damn! That's how I can fix that problem I've been having with my new book!" He looked at his watch. "Dave, I don't want to appear rude, but I need to get back and get this idea down before it flies away."

"Not a problem," I said, "but won't you still be interrupted by the cleaning woman?"

He drained the rest of his second pint and said, "If she's still vacuuming, I'll tell her to stop. Thanks, Dave, I'll talk to you later." Then he got up and lumbered out of the pub.

As I watched him through the window of the bar practically running down the street, I felt glad that *somebody* was getting a useful idea. The barmaid came back and asked if I was ready for the check. Instead, because the chowder had only whetted my appetite, I ordered a fish sandwich. I needed to think, and this place seemed as conducive to it as anywhere. Maybe I'd get a brainstorm, too. Besides, at what I had to pay for parking, I wanted to get my money's worth. I sat and thought, but no matter how I turned or twisted the facts of this case around, they didn't all add up to a cohesive whole.

When the sandwich arrived, I was delighted to find that it was every bit as good as the chowder had been, but while my stomach was being satisfied, my brain was still wandering through the desert. If only cases were more like movies, where going over and over something would reveal a new insight. Maybe they were for better investigators. Maybe a more experienced detective could see through the choose-your-own-adventure structure of this case and figure out how all the dead ends tied together.

Don't beat yourself up, kid, Bogie's voice said encouragingly.

After all this time I still don't know who killed Taylor.

I had to smile. Bogie was not referring to Taylor Frost (or Kleinbach), but rather Owen Taylor, the Sternwood's chauffeur, whose limo was pushed off an unnamed pier in *The Big Sleep* with Taylor still in it. In one of classic Hollywood's most famous anecdotes, director Howard Hawks and screenwriters William Faulkner and Leigh Brackett could not figure out who offed Taylor, so Hawks contacted source novelist Raymond Chandler, who didn't know either. It's the kind of story that has been told so many times it might even be true, though the recently discovered print of the film's original cut revealed that the killing had, in fact, been attributed to a secondary character, rightly or wrongly, which served to refute the legend. Increasingly, classic Hollywood lore was being rewritten through the discovery of previously lost footage, or even artifacts, like Mac's poster for *The Mummy*. Who knew? Maybe all those sequences cut out of *The Mummy* would turn up, including the one featuring Willy Lipton.

The barmaid reappeared at my table and said, "Luv, I'm about to go on break, so if there's anything else I can get for you, let me know."

"Yeah, you can tell me the identity of a murderer."

"Are you reading a mystery novel?" She grinned broadly. "I like Lee Child, you ever read him?"

"No, I'm afraid not."

"He's British, you know."

"No, I didn't."

"He's the best. Not mystery, really, more thriller. But do you want anything else to eat?"

"No, I'm good, thanks."

She snaked away through the growing crowd and quickly returned with my check. It was a good thing the food was so enjoyable, given the prices. I left the money, got up and left, vowing on the way home not to, as Bogie so eloquently put it, beat myself up any more over this case, at least for the rest of the day.

Tomorrow is another day, a voice said in my head, so vividly that I looked behind me to see if someone had actually spoken. But there was no one within earshot. The voice that had spoken was not the expected one, Vivien Leigh. It was a man's voice, an ominous voice, even a menacing voice.

It was the voice of Detective Hector Mendoza.

SEVENTEEN

Even though I had become used to hearing the voices of classic Hollywood in my head (knowing, deep down inside, that they were simply manifestations of some part of my own mind, which, in addition to the fact that I could not afford it, is why I haven't had myself committed), I have to confess that it spooked me to hear the voice of Mendoza so clear, so vivid, and so threatening. I worried about it all the way home. Once there, however, a combination of the food in my stomach, which was starting to slow me down, and the fact that TCM was airing *Lady in the Lake* pushed it out of my mind. *Lady in the Lake* isn't a great movie—it's the one where Robert Montgomery plays Philip Marlowe, but he's seen only a few fleeting times in mirror reflections because the film is shot in subjective camera POV—but it's better than a network reality show. Unreality is always more interesting (and less dangerous) than reality in my book.

Before the movie came on, I was tempted to call Marcy, but I really had no reason to do so. I did not have any new information about the twins, except for the fact that they appeared in a porno, which I did not think would make her day. I should probably have phoned Colfax with this information, but decided it could wait until later. The movie started, played and ended the same way it had the last time I'd seen it, but I managed to notice a few new things along the way, notably that the set department had misspelled the name "Philip Marlowe" on the door of the detective's office, giving an extra "l" to Philip.

Next time they should get the "l" out of there, a raspy voice drawled. Thank you John Huston. I'll forward your message to Mr. Montgomery, who also directed the picture.

I was also somewhat amused by the fact that part of the action is set in "Bay City," which was Raymond Chandler's disguised version of Santa Monica, where I'd been earlier with Jack Daniels. No one ever disguises Los Angeles for a book or a movie. I guess it's just too big to be offended by what anyone might say about it.

The film ended, and I decided to turn in early. There was no reason not to.

I arose the next morning early as well, which was okay. I got up and put the coffee pot on, then went into the bathroom to shave, and got in the shower. I treated myself to a particularly long, hot shower this morning, since I was now able to afford the water bills for the near future, thanks to Nora Frost. When I finally shut off the water and slid the shower curtain open, though, my heart nearly stopped when I saw the figure standing in my bathroom.

"Jesus, where did you come from?" I screamed, reaching for the towel to cover myself.

"San Bernardino, originally," Alan Kleinbach said. "Hey, sorry if I startled you, man."

"Startled me? You nearly gave me a heart attack! You don't sneak up on a man in the shower! Haven't you ever seen *Psycho*?"

"Hitchcock, right?"

"Yes, Hitchcock. Why are you here? How did you even get in?"

"Your door was unlocked."

"Okay, so I left my door unlocked. How did you get inside the building? It's supposed to have a security door."

"I waited for someone to come out and then went in."

"Who?"

"Older woman who didn't seem to speak English."

I sighed. I must have been Mrs. Zarakanian, who lives at the end of the hall. In my experience she has never spoken in any language, communicating instead by giving the stink-eye to anyone who walks by. Somehow I was going to have to try and convince her not to let strangers in the door when she leaves, since the next time it might not be Kleinbach, but someone with a gun. "Fine, Alan, but how did you even know where I live? Did you follow me here as well?"

"Naw. I looked in the phone book."

"Really?"

"You don't even know that you're in the phone book?"

"I don't call myself all that often," I said. The truth was, I didn't realize that my address was listed in the phone book. *You have to pay not to be,* Jack Benny in my head said, and after a pause added: *I'm still listed in Waukegan.* To Kleinbach, I said: "Would you mind if I finished drying myself and got dressed?"

"Go for it."

"Would you mind *leaving* the bathroom while I dried off?"

"Oh. Okay."

He shuffled out while I quickly toweled off and, wrapping the damp towel around my waist, ran to the bedroom where I pulled out the first clean clothes I found, a pair of green slacks and a purple polo shirt, and put them on. When I went back out, he was standing in my kitchen, drinking my milk out of the container.

"Alan, why are you here?" I asked.

He wiped the white residue off his moustache. "Did you tell the police where to find me?"

"Yes. I was trying to clear you."

"Some guy came to see me, asked me questions."

"That would have been Detective Colfax."

"Didn't get his name, but he looked like Lyle Lovett, sort of. He looked around my apartment to see if I was hiding someone there."

"You weren't were you?"

"Of course I wasn't. There isn't enough room to hide anyone."

"I imagine he was looking to see if you had the boys."

"I don't. They aren't even mine, remember?"

"Did you tell Colfax that?"

Kleinbach remained silent for a second or two, and then shook his head. "Sounds kinda crazy," he said, softly.

"Yeah, well, I've stumbled on something that's even crazier," I told him. Then I outlined the fact that the twins...at least the twins that I had met...had turned up in a porno film.

"Isn't that against the law?" he asked.

"It's against every law. But there they were. I saw them myself."

Kleinbach shook his head as though he was trying to rattle a gnat out of his ear. "Man, if this is really what normal life is like, I'm kinda glad I went a different route."

"Alan, I know you didn't take the time and trouble to come here just to say hello and drink my milk," I said. "So why did you come here?"

He sighed heavily, and put the milk carton down on the counter. "Either I'm nuts, or I'm being followed," he said.

"I thought you were the one following people."

"So did I. But I keep seeing the same car everywhere I go."

"You're sure it's the same car?"

"Pretty sure."

"Can you get a license number?"

"I haven't been able to. Hey, you got any cookies?"

"Cookies?"

"You know, sweet crunchy things?"

"Alan, I know what cookies are! Wait a minute, I may have some. Let me check." I opened a cabinet and found half of a package of Hydrox, and handed it to him.

"Bitchin'!" he said, shoving one in his mouth, then picking the milk carton back up and glugging half of it down.

"Back to the car," I said. "If you see it again, try to get the license number, even a partial."

"So you believe I'm not nuts?" He chugged the rest of the milk.

"You know what they say. Just because you're paranoid doesn't mean they aren't out to get you."

"Who says that?"

I sighed. "Woody Allen." I have no idea whether Woody Allen actually ever said that or not, but it was the first name that jumped into my head, and it sounded like the sort of thing he'd say. "The point is, you need to be careful."

"How do I do that?"

"Take streets you wouldn't ordinarily take. If someone is tailing you, don't let them figure out your regular routine, or else the next time they'll be waiting for you." *Maybe with a gun,* I thought, but decided to spare him. Then I changed the subject. "Since you're here, Alan, you mind if I ask a question or two?"

"Shoot."

"This is about the boys, Burton and Taylor."

"Whoever they are."

"Yes, assuming that you're right and that the twins I met are not your real sons. Before I can do anything, even go to the police with this story, I need to try and find out what might have happened to Ricky and Bobby. Outside of you and Nora, was there anyone else familiar with your sons?"

"I don't know," he muttered, scratching his beard and sitting down on a chair. "I was out of the picture before they started going to school, so I wouldn't know any of their school friends. Oh, wait, sure, there's Nora's mom, Natalie. She used to see the boys fairly often."

"Natalie Strange," I said, "and she's dead, too." Another dead end, pardon the pun.

"Natalie's maid, too," Kleinbach said. "She used to play with the boys while Nat and Nora talked."

Finally, a lead! "Do you remember her name?"

Kleinbach screwed his face up in thought, and said, "Naw, sorry. This was a long time ago."

"Okay, but please, if you happen to think of it or run across it, let me know."

"Yeah, all right. I'm going now."

"Remember what I said, Alan, be careful."

He grabbed the remaining Hydrox cookies and shoved them

in his pocket, handed the nearly-empty milk carton to me, gave me a peculiar salute, then without another word spun around and walked out of the apartment. I closed the door behind him and then went into the kitchen, but a moment later heard a knock on the door. Maybe it was the fact that I had just been misquoting Woody Allen about paranoia that made me so wary, but I approached the door cautiously. "Who is it?" I called loudly, standing to once side of the door, so that if someone did want to fire shots through the wood, they would miss me.

"It's Alan," Kleinbach's voice said. I opened the door and he said, "Katy."

"I beg your pardon?"

"That's the name of the Natalie's maid, Katy."

It sounded like he was saying "catty," and I repeated the word, hoping he would clarify it.

"Katy Gutiérrez," Kleinbach said, looking proud that he had remembered.

"Oh, do you mean *K-A-T-Y*, like Katy Jurado, the Mexican actress?"

"I don't know any Katy Jurado, but Katy Gutiérrez was Mexican."

"You don't know where she is now, do you?"

"Hey, I'm doing good to remember her name."

"All right, thank you." I started to close the door, but he held his hand out to stop it.

"One other thing," Kleinbach said. "You don't have kids, do you?"

"No, I've never been married. Why?"

"If I found out that someone had put my sons in a porno movie, I'd find him and rip his lungs out. I guess it's a good thing those two aren't really my sons. But if you find out who their father really is, you might find your killer." Letting his hand drop, he turned around and strode down the hallway.

After closing the door, I went to the window and watched him lope over to a parked motorcycle, get on, and then pull away without bothering to put on a helmet. No car materialized to follow him. Maybe he was simply paranoid. But paranoid or not, at least I had a bona fide lead.

Grabbing my laptop, I carried it to my small dining table, which I used more as an office desk than for dining, and started a data base search for Katy Gutiérrez, expected to find dozens of them. To my delight there was only one that seemed to apply: a Katerina S. Gutiérrez living in Culver City. Had I been seeking a Maria Gutiérrez, however, I'd be in serious trouble, since there must have been a hundred of them. Jotting down the address, I powered the computer down and decided to pay her a visit.

Even though Hollywood has always gotten the credit, a large number of the most notable movies and television shows in history have been shot in Culver City, which is about fifteen miles to the southwest, and was once home to the studios of MGM, Hal Roach, and David O. Selznick. Skull Island, Zenda, Tara, the Land of Oz, Mayberry, Stalag 13, the street where Gene Kelly sang in the rain, and a thousand other lands of make-believe were all at one time or other to be found within a few square miles within Culver City. All that is gone, though, most of it torn down for redevelopment, and the city's remaining classic architecture now dukes it out with ultra-modern structures on the same streets. The ghosts of the Golden Age still haunt the city, though only through such subdivision streets as Garland Drive, Astaire Avenue and Hepburn Circle.

Katerina S. Gutiérrez lived in one of the older residential neighborhoods of the city, in a modest looking Spanish home. After double-checking the address, I pulled up to the curb and got out. Going to her front door, I rang the bell.

"Who is it?" a woman's voice called from the other side.

"Are you Katy Gutiérrez?"

"Yes," the voice replied. "Who are you?"

"My name is Dave Beauchamp and I'd like to talk to you about Natalie Strange."

The door cracked ajar, prevented from opening all the way by a chain. "You're not one of those writers, are you?" She spoke with a faint accent.

"No, ma'am, I'm a private investigator."

"Can you prove that?"

She was smart. But unfortunately, I wasn't. I had given out all my business cards and had not bothered to replenish my wallet. "I'm sorry, Mrs. Gutiérrez, but I'm out of cards. If you have a Yellow Page phone book, you can look up my listing and dial the number, and you'll hear my voice on the answering machine."

"Let me see your driver's license," she said, and I took it out and slid it through the crack in the doorway. She examined it and then said, "All right, come on in, Mr. Beauchamp." She undid the chain and opened the door.

"Thank you," I said, stepping inside. "I appreciate your talking to me."

"I don't have anything else to do today," Katy Gutiérrez said, closing the door behind me. "I don't work anymore." She was petite, had very carefully coiffed dark hair, and wore a simple blouse and slacks. Her age could have been anywhere from fifty to seventy, it was impossible to tell. The inside of her house was magazine-photo neat and tidy, and there was a prominent picture of Jesus on one wall, under which were about a dozen school pictures showing the same two kids, a boy and a girl, growing up under the watchful eye of Christ. "Please, sit down."

She sat in an overstuffed chair while I seated myself on the couch, nearly sinking to the floor in the marshmallow cushion. "Are those your children?" I asked, pointing to the pictures on the wall.

"Yes, Carly and Rafael. They're grown now. She's a nurse and he's a firefighter. My husband passed away three years ago. Now, why are you investigating Mrs. Cousins?"

"You mean Natalie Strange?"

"I always called her Mrs. Cousins. What are you looking to find out about her? Book writers, they come around here sometimes and ask me questions about her, and they want me to tell the secrets, but I won't. I won't do anything to hurt her memory."

"Like I said, Mrs. Gutiérrez, I'm not a book writer. I was

a fan of both Natalie Strange and Steve Cousins, so I have no desire whatsoever to hurt their reputations. I'm actually investigating Natalie's grandsons, Taylor and Burton."

She eyed me warily. "Her grandsons were named Robert and Richard."

"I know, but their mother called them by their middle names."

Katy Gutiérrez's face darkened. "Their mother," she practically spat. "How such a miserable woman could have been raised by people as fine as Mr. and Mrs. Cousins, I do not know. I felt so sorry for those two boys, having a mother like that, and that father. They were two little golden angels."

"What did their father do to them?" I asked.

"He did not take them away from *her*. Alan was his name. The mother tried to claim that he was abusive, but he wasn't. He was just weak. But she said he abused them during their divorce, and he stood there and took it, and said nothing to defend himself. He never abused those boys, but he never stood up for them either. He ran away and drank. Mrs. Cousins took care of them more than he did, until the day...." Her voice trailed off, and I finished the sentence for her: "She died."

Katy Gutiérrez nodded. Clearly the death of Natalie Strange still affected her.

"Mrs. Gutiérrez, are you aware that Nora Frost is dead?"

"What?" she said, looking shocked. "No, I did not know."

"She was murdered."

"Santa Maria!" She folded her hands and bowed her head in a brief prayer. "I pray for her soul. Even with the love of the Blessed Virgin she is going to need all the help she can get. I wish I could feel more sorry about this."

"The boys, Taylor and...I mean, Richard and Robert...when was the last time you saw them?"

She appeared to age ten years before my eyes. "I don't want to talk about it," she uttered.

"Mrs. Gutiérrez, did something happen to them?"

"You *are* a book writer, aren't you? You've come here to blacken the memory of a fine woman just because she made a terrible mistake!"

"I promise you, I am not writing a book, a magazine article, a newspaper story, or anything else. Besides, these days, being a lesbian is not considered a mistake."

A strange, inscrutable look crossed her face and she began spouting something in Spanish, which I had no hope of catching. Finally she said, "You are here to talk about her...her bed life? How dare you pry into her private life?"

"I didn't mean—"

"Let me tell you something, young man. She and Mr. Cousins loved each other. They did! Yes, there were others. He had his men, and she...I did not agree with their actions, but it was not my place to judge. It was between them and their Maker, and it is up to Him to judge. So, they were...what is the word they use now? Jolly?"

"Gay," I said, making a mental note to put another entry in my notebook: *Rumors aside, if you want to discover the truth about anybody, ask the housekeeper.*

"Yes, so they were gay, but they were also the two finest people I knew. They loved each other." Her face suddenly broke into a smile. "One time...oh, I shouldn't be telling you this."

"I won't object, Mrs. Gutiérrez," I said. "I won't tell anyone else."

She smiled again, and shook her head. "*Jesu*, forgive me. On the morning of their fortieth anniversary I was going to clean the master bathroom in their house. I thought someone had left the shower running. I went in and pulled the curtain back and they were both there, in the shower. At that moment, they were *not* gay. They were more like two young people in love. They could not stop laughing at being discovered, and it was their *fortieth* anniversary! I wanted to crawl away, I was so embarrassed, but later they both kissed me on the cheek and made a joke that made me blush, and got me to laugh with them. They loved each other, young man. They always loved each other, no matter what. I loved both of them." She paused and then leveled a forefinger at me. "But not in *that* way!"

"I understand, Mrs. Gutiérrez. But what I am really trying to do here is find the boys."

"Find them?"

"They have disappeared."

"Gone? Where could they have gone?"

"We don't know, but the police are looking for them. They will be found."

She put her head in her hands and shook it back and forth. "*Dios ayúdame*! They are free of her. Finally, I can speak."

I leaned forward. "Speak about what, Mrs. Gutiérrez?"

"You are certain that Nora is dead?"

"Positive. Why?"

"Because now she can no longer threaten me."

"Why was she threatening you?"

"Because I knew what she had done."

"Mrs. Gutiérrez, tell me what Nora did."

The woman looked at me with an expression of bottomless sadness, fatigue, and maybe a trace of fear. "She killed her own mother," she said.

EIGHTEEN

It took a minute or so before I could say anything. Finally I got out: "Are you saying Nora Frost murdered Natalie Strange?"

"She might as well have plunged a dagger through her heart," Katy Gutiérrez replied. "*Dios*, after six years I can finally say things out loud, but I don't know if I should."

"Please, Mrs. Gutiérrez, anything you can offer might help me find the twins."

"Those poor boys," she shook her head again. "Nora was a demon in woman's skin! She kept trying to get the boys into pictures and television, but they had a problem."

"What problem?"

"Robert was very good. He was a natural, even at four years old. Bobby had such an outgoing personality. But Richard was the opposite. He was shy and quiet, and hated being photographed. She would force him to be on camera, but he hated it, and it showed. The two of them would be hired to play one part, because they were identical, but only Bobby's scenes would be usable. The directors would become so frustrated with the situation, they did not want to hire them."

"So, you couldn't tell them apart on camera, except for the way they acted?"

"They were identical in every way but personality. That was the only way to tell them apart."

So Alan was right after all…but where did that leave me? Or the Kleinbach twins? "What does the talent level of the boys have to do with Nora's killing Natalie?" I asked.

"Nora would take Ricky over to Mrs. Cousins' house and demand that she teach him how to act," Katy Gutiérrez said. "Mr. Cousins was already dead by this time, so I was there quite a bit, helping Mrs. Cousins out. Nora would try to drop Ricky off and take Bobby with her, but Mrs. Cousins would insist that both of the boys stayed. She hated the way Nora judged Ricky, saying he wasn't good enough in front of him and his brother. Mrs. Cousins always tried to treat them exactly the same. There were arguments with Nora, such terrible arguments."

She stopped, pulled out a handkerchief and wiped her eyes. I had known Nora just long enough to realize that she treated everybody like an employee, even her own mother.

"Did Nora fly into a rage and attack Natalie?" I asked.

She shook her head slowly. "One day Nora dropped the boys off and an argument started. Whenever Nora started yelling at Mrs. Cousins the boys would run away and try to hide until it was over, but this argument was the worst one. Nora was high on some drug, I think, and Mrs. Cousins started talking about taking Ricky and Bobby away from her. It was just awful... awful...it seemed to go on for an hour. I nearly called the police. I was afraid Nora was going to become violent and start hitting Mrs. Cousins, but instead she started calling her names, using words that I could not believe I was hearing. Then Nora stormed through the house demanding the boys come to her. She was going to take them and leave, you see. I ran out to be with Mrs. Cousins, who was crying and shaking. Then we heard a scream coming from her bedroom."

"What happened?"

Katy Gutiérrez shuddered. "We rushed in and I saw the boys lying on the floor, like they were sleeping. One of them was holding a pill in his hand. 'Oh, my God, my pills!' Mrs. Cousins shouted. She had been counting them earlier to see how many she had, and had left them laying out on her nightstand. They looked like candy, so the boys ate them."

"What were they?" I asked.

"Clonazepam."

"I'm not familiar with that."

"It's a drug for people who have anxiety problems. Mrs. Cousins had become increasingly agitated since the death of Mr. Cousins. She could not sleep half the time. She took these pills to relax her. The pills knocked the boys unconscious. I dialed 911 and an ambulance came for them, and took them to the hospital. Mrs. Cousins just sat there, weeping."

"Where was the twins' father at this point?"

"I don't know. Gone, I think."

"What about Randall Frost?"

"Who?"

"Nora's second husband."

"I don't know anything about him. I never saw the boys again after that day. Mrs. Cousins tried to call Nora to find out how they were, but she could not get her own daughter to pick up the phone. Finally, a week or so later, Nora showed up and accused her mother of trying to kill the boys. It was horrible. She claimed Mrs. Cousins had done it on purpose because she was jealous of them, which was loco. She told her mother that if she wanted to kill someone so badly, why didn't she kill herself? She said she was useless and old and senile…Mrs. Cousins was getting a little absentminded, but she was *not* senile…but Nora wouldn't stop. She called her those names again. Mrs. Cousins already felt so badly about making the boys sick, that she could not even look Nora in the face. Finally I ordered Nora out of the house. I picked up a candlestick and threatened to swing it at her head if she didn't leave, *Dios ayúdame*." She crossed herself quickly and then wiped her eyes again. "Within a month, Mrs. Cousins was dead," she said. "She never recovered from that argument with Nora, and when she got a new supply of pills…"

"So it was a suicide, not a murder," I said, my voice threatening to crack.

"If you drive someone to take their own life, that is murder!" she declared. "Mrs. Cousins would never have done something like that on her own. She would never have risked condemning her soul to eternal suffering if Nora had not driven her to it! At her funeral Nora came up to me. I tried to get away, but I could not. She said: 'That....' I cannot use the word she called her mother, '...died of an accidental overdose, and if you ever say it wasn't, your life won't be worth a refried bean.' That was how she said it. I never saw or spoke to her again. Now she's dead and I'm...."

Katy Gutiérrez totally broke down then and began weeping in her chair, while I sat by stupidly and tried to think of something to do or say. Before I could, though, I heard the sound of the front door opening. "Hi, Mom, it's me," a voice said, and a moment later one of the most muscular men I have ever seen walked into the room. He appeared to be about thirty and he had the kind of muscled arms that threatened to burst through the sleeves of his shirt, like a young Schwarzenegger. I recognized him from the pictures on the wall as Rafael Gutiérrez, though the school photos obviously gave no indication as to his physique, or perhaps it developed later. He looked at his sobbing mother and then turned his gaze toward me. "What's going on here?" he demanded. "Who are you?" He approached me in a semi-threatening manner, and I rose from the couch and held my hands in front of me.

"You must be Rafael," I said, lamely. *Good job, kid*, Bogie sneered.

"I know who I am, I asked you who you are," Rafael Gutiérrez said.

"Rafael, it is all right," Katy said through her sobs. "This man was asking me questions about Natalie."

"Did you get the answers your came for?" Rafael asked me.

"Um, I guess I did."

"Then, um, I guess you can leave this house and stop bothering my mother."

Even though his mother was mildly protesting, I was not about to argue with a guy who looked like he could juggle three professional wrestlers at one time. "A pleasure meeting you, Mrs. Gutiérrez," I said on the way out.

"Goodbye," she called.

"Mom, you can't just let people come in here like that," I heard right before I closed the door behind me. I couldn't really blame the guy for being a good son and wanting to protect his mother, and I doubt I would have gleaned any more information from her had he not cut the interview short. But what I had learned did not make me feel any better about this case, nor was I feeling any warmer and fuzzier about my one-time client, who had now transitioned from being a garden-variety B.O.W. to a possibly homicidal psychopath.

I headed back to the office, not having anything better to do. When I got there the light on my phone machine was blinking, which reminded me to unplug my cell phone from the charger and stick it back in my pocket. I punched the playback button, hoping for a nice, normal, boring divorce or skip trace gig; instead I the voice of Alan Kleinbach, saying: "Hey, I saw that car again, and I got the license number you were asking about." He proceeded to read it off on the machine, and I wrote it down. Then he said: "But y'know, there's something weird about all this. You're gonna love this, man, 'cause I'm pretty sure I've seen that car befo—" His voice then was cut off by my machine.

"Aw, sheez!" I said, jabbing the button again, knowing it would make no difference. Kleinbach's voice cut off in exactly the same spot. At least I had the license number, though there was little I could do to follow it up personally. I had never bothered to subscribe to the DMV database. Fortunately, I knew several people who had. Digging through my Rolodex, I finally found the number of a man from whom I had taken private investigation classes through USC extension, and punched in his number. When I finally got him on the line, I said: "Hi, Walt, it's Dave Beauchamp."

"Dave...oh, right. Hi, Dave," Walt Westermann said. "What can I do for you?"

Without going into detail, I read off the license number the Kleinbach had phoned in and asked him to run it through the DMV database.

"You really need to spring for one yourself, you know," Walt said.

"I know." I didn't mention that for the first time in a long time, I could actually afford to do so. But I needed the information now.

Unfortunately, Walt couldn't do it right now, but he promised to do the run at the first opportunity and get back to me. After a little more small talk, and profuse thanks, I hung up.

I sat and thought about this mess for a long time. Then I muttered, "It's the boys, it has to be the boys. They are the key to this whole thing, but how and why?"

Maybe they know something worth murdering for? Bogart's voice intoned inside my brain.

"Okay, but what?"

Don't ask me, I've been dead for a long time.

Great. Thanks.

Robert Mitchum took over: *Try using your own damned brain. Who knows, you might like the experience.*

"I've been trying!" I said in desperation. "I don't know where to go from here!"

Check out the house, Mitch replied.

"What house?"

Nora's house.

"Oh, yeah, right," I muttered. I was going to break into the house of a recently murdered woman, my client, cross and potentially corrupt a crime scene, and run the very good risk of landing myself into more trouble that it would be possible to get out of in one lifetime? Was I really going to do that?

Yes, Dave, you are, a new voice said. *You're going to do it for me.* It wasn't Bogie, Mitchum, or any of the other regulars.

It was Marcy DeBanzi.

Yes, I would do it for her. Of course, I would. And if I happened to be caught inside Nora Frost's house, snooping around a crime scene, I could always use Hollywood on Parade inside my head as the groundwork for an insanity defense.

I turned the lights off in my apartment and left, but I had not even gotten down the street before I began reconsidering the wisdom of this move. Was I truly going to break into a crime scene? *Sometimes a man's gotta do what he's gotta do*, Bogie said, but that was easy for him to say. He was dead.

As I headed in the direction of Nora's house in Hollywood I tried to come up with a logical explanation for my presence should I be seen or, worse, discovered by the police. Pretending to be a delivery boy wasn't going to work, nor was professed ignorance of the law. Were I a television detective, I would have a disguise kit and wardrobe at my disposal from which I could have made myself look like a perfect replica of Alan Kleinbach, should I be spotted.

Stopped for a light on Ventura Boulevard, my focus wandered over the curbside, where I saw that rarest of objects in today's world: a public pay telephone. That was it! As soon as the light changed I pulled through and parked at the curb in the red. I didn't expect to be here long enough for it to be a problem. I ran to the phone and picked up the receiver with a handkerchief, put in two quarters, and dialed my office number. When the machine picked up, I waited, and then in a high-pitched whisper I said: "Mr. Beauchamp, I have to see you. I've found something at Nora Frost's house. Meet me there, inside." Then I hung up. That would be my insurance policy if I was caught. Sure, if the cops really wanted to, they could run a trace on the tape and probably figure out that it came from a payphone within a couple miles of my office. If they really wanted to, they could run a voice print on the recording and prove it was my voice. But my hope was that they would have bigger things to worry about.

Traffic was with me, and once I got to Nora's place I was gratified to see no fleet of police vehicles out front. There was still a yellow crime scene tape across the front door, but I wasn't planning on using the front door. Parking a couple blocks away, I got out of the car and started to walk down the street like I belonged there. It wasn't quite magic hour—that time of the afternoon that filmmakers love, when the shadows are long and the natural lighting gold-tinged and evocative—but it was close.

As casually as I could force myself to appear, I went up the driveway beside the house to the garage in back. Once there I took a quick look around and then vaulted over the short brick fence that enclosed the backyard. Even though there were trees on each side which cut down the visibility to neighbors, I felt particularly naked standing there and more than particularly foolish. *You don't take chances, sonny, you don't get anything*, I heard. Thanks, Mitch. I hope you'll be a character witness for me from the great beyond if I get caught.

Going to the back door of the house, I pulled out my wallet and withdrew my homemade lock pick—a six-penny finishing nail, bent into an "L," with the head flattened just so. It's a trick that an old guy who was once a hotel dick showed me, and it's astonishing how well this works once you know exactly how to pound the head. It took a few seconds of wiggling the nail, but I managed to spring the lock, and unless there was a security chain on top, I was in.

There wasn't; I was.

I certainly knew better than to turn a light on inside, so I pulled out my keychain that had that little flashlight hooked on it. Up to this point in my career, this had been my most useful tool in my investigator kit, since I had never actually had cause before now to use the lock pick on a case. I was in the kitchen, and even though the smell of death permeated the place, it was not enough to overcome the reeking trash, which clearly had not been taken out since before Nora was killed. Taking care with each step, I slowly moved into the dining room, which was free of crime scene markers. From here I could see the bathroom door, which was sealed like King Tut's tomb with yellow tape and plastic sheets. There was no reason for me to go in there, thankfully.

The last time I had been here, when Nora was alive and the twins were drinking sodas in the kitchen; she had gone upstairs to her bedroom and retrieved the would-be threatening letter from the place in which she kept it locked up. If her bedroom was where she kept important papers, those papers might give me some sort of clue what was going on in this case.

You sure about that? Bogie's voice asked.

"Yes, I'm sure," I whispered. "Go away."

I crept over to the staircase and started up, trying desperately not to think about Martin Balsam in *Psycho*, who in similar circumstances met "Mother," wielding a butcher knife, at the top of the stairs. Once I had safely reached the landing, I approached the room I had earlier decided had to be the twins' and noticed a glow coming out of it. Peering in, I saw that a computer had been left on, its screen radiating a faint light. Either they left in a hurry and forgot to turn it off, or they intended to be back soon and didn't bother. Neither option was very comforting.

The room next to this one was a combination guest bedroom and storage room, with boxes stacked everywhere. Across the hall was a bathroom and next to it another large bedroom, this one with all the accoutrements of a female inhabitant: Nora's room. The last time I had been up here, snooping, I had not really bothered to examine the contents of the room, because I was looking to see if the twins were anywhere in the house. Now I was able to study the furnishings: a bed, unmade; a dresser and a chair; and an old-style vanity with a round mirror, and lots of makeup items on top. Did she keep her important papers in a safe? I wondered. The classic image of the wall safe hidden behind a painting was pretty much a Hollywood invention, but sometimes people kept small safes inside of a closet. Going to the large walk-in, I opened the door and examined the contents. There were plenty of dresses and outfits, and an unholy number of shoes, but nothing that looked like a metal safe. Turning back, I realized that the only other logical place in the room to keep something under lock and key was the vanity. Approaching it, I noticed an electrical cord coming out of one of the drawers, and upon carefully opening it with a handkerchief, saw it was connected to a hair drier. I opened the other drawers and found nothing much, until coming to the bottom one, which was locked. "Mm-hmm," I muttered absently, pulling out my lock pick and sticking it in the drawer lock, which was almost too small for it…almost. After a few seconds, the lock tripped and I was able to open the drawer. What I saw took my breath away.

There were at least a dozen banded stacks of hundred dollar bills in there, totaling, by my estimate, about fifty thousand dollars. All anyone would have to was reach in and grab one… or two…and nobody would ever know.

I knelt there, staring at all that money, waiting for a voice to tell me what to do, but none of my regulars seemed to want to volunteer. I was on my own for this one. I'm almost ashamed to admit that I was actually licking my lips looking at all those graven images of Ben Franklin. Maybe that was why I decided to leave each and every one of them where they were, no matter what my financial situation was.

Kid, you're all right, Bogie told me, as I remembered to exhale. But I continued to examine the stack of cash and soon realized that there was something underneath all the bills. Carefully picking the wads up with the handkerchief, I set them on the carpeted floor beside the drawer, and discovered there wasn't *quite* as much I had assumed. Maybe only twenty grand or so. Underneath was a large envelope labeled *San Gabriel*, which I carefully opened. It contained a series of invoices from a place called San Gabriel Valley Private Hospital in Sierra Madre. I could find no specifics as to the charges, though each monthly invoice was for an amount on one or the other side of four-thousand dollars. Could Nora have been paying off a facelift on the installment plan? "Oh, no," I uttered, as an even sicker idea struck me. Earlier pictures of the boys were identical, but now they aren't. Had Nora forced the kids to undergo plastic surgery so they wouldn't look alike?

We don't use the T word, I remembered her telling me. *It's demeaning to them as individuals.* Was she actually crazy enough to force them to undergo surgery so that they could look more like individuals? An even grimmer speculation was that she had forced only Ricky/Burton to have the surgery so the boys would be no longer identical, and Burton could not ruin

Taylor's career. Maybe that was why their own father did not recognize them.

While speculation may be great, it proves nothing, so I kept looking. Also in the secret drawer was an envelope with the return address for Pacific Investigations in Brentwood, an outfit with which I was familiar. They specialized in cases for celebrities and people who wanted not only the very best, but the quietest. Rumor had it that operatives from Pacific had been employed by the O.J. Simpson "dream team" of high-powered lawyers to track down witnesses to the murders and encourage the people to sell their stories to tabloid publications, all but ensuring that this would destroy their credibility as potential witnesses in the actual trial. In any event, Pacific Investigations (*PI...get it?*) was the firm one called for maximum results at a cost that was no object, which fit in with Nora's M.O. Elena Cates had said Nora hired a detective to find Marcy, so this was probably their report. But examination of the envelope argued against that, since it was addressed not to Nora, but to "Lt. Randall Frost."

Nora's husband.

Opening the envelope, I pulled out the papers inside with my knuckles and read the one on top, which was addressed to Lt. Randall C. Frost:

Dear Lt. Frost,

As per your instructions we placed a tail on Mrs. Nora Frost, regarding the matter that you initially communicated to us. After spending some fifty (50) man-hours on the assignment, I feel that I can report back to you with extreme confidence that nothing in your wife's actions as witnessed by us supports your concerns. In short, Lt. Frost, our best operatives have failed to uncover any evidence that your wife is engaged in any extra-marital relationships.

So the military hero suspected that Nora was playing squigillum with someone else. Trouble in paradise. The letter continued:

> *I feel, therefore in fairness to all parties involved, that we should agree between us to terminate the contract dated August 23, 2007. Should our accounts reveal that we have not utilized your entire retainer, a refund check will be issued to you.*
> *I hope this missive is satisfactory.*
>
> *Sincerely,*
>
> *Alexander McCarthar*
> *President, Pacific Investigations*

There was something that bothered me about this letter. It was the phrase *all parties involved*. I know I'm not the best or savviest PI in the greater L.A. area, but if I'm hired by a client, I work for the client, and don't spend a lot of time worrying about whether my investigation is going to step on the toes of investigatee. Maybe it was simply semantics, but using the words *all parties involved* implied that the object of the investigation—Nora—was included in this discussion to drop the matter. I put the letter back inside its envelope and set it down, and then reached for the next document in the drawer. This one was a letter from Pacific Investigations, but without an envelope. It proved to be the cover letter for a contract, addressed to Nora, spelling out the details of the work to be undertaken in the quest to find her missing sister.

Paperclipped to the bottom of the cover letter was the handwritten note: *Nora—The other matter of which we spoke, your husband's arrangement with us, it has been taken care of. AM.*

Alexander McCarthar. So Nora had been playing, or paying, the investigators to drop the case against her. Lieutenant Frost is happy that his worst fears are not confirmed, and Pacific

Investigations gets paid twice. Nice. I put the contract down with the cash and the other envelope. Next in the drawer was a manila folder containing photos. Most of them were of a happy looking young couple with two small blond children. The man appeared to be Lt. Frost, though it was a little hard to tell, since unlike his official military photo, he was smiling. But who was the woman? Several photos later, a strong possibility suggested itself: Frost was Nora's second husband, so it was highly possible that Nora was Frost's second wife, and the woman in the pictures was his first wife. But there were kids in the pictures, too. As I studied the photos more carefully, I developed chills. "Oh my god," I whispered. The two blond kids were boys, the same size, presumably the same age, but not identical.

The last photo showed only Lt. Frost, in uniform this time, and the two boys, looking about nine years old, but no Mom. Each of their faces wore a glum expression, but not so much so that I could not easily recognize the kids I knew as Burton and Taylor Frost.

This was the proof of Alan Kleinbach's suspicions; there *were* two sets of twins. Kleinbach was the father of one set, and Randall Frost was the father of the other set.

I flipped the picture over to see if there was any kind of notation on the back. Nothing was written there, but something was printed in tiny lettering. It proved to be the developer's notation of the date: *AUG 96.*

Whoa…that couldn't be right.

I turned the photo over again, and then back to the date. August, 1996 was what it said; fifteen years ago. Yet the boys looked about eight or nine. How was that possible?

Anything's possible in Hollywood, a strange high-pitched voice said in my head. Even though I recognized it, it took a few seconds for the meaning to register. "Oh, *sheez*," I uttered to the empty house. "Oh, no!"

But yes, that explained everything. What was that old Sherlock Holmes wheeze about how if you get rid of every impossible explanation, whatever is left, no matter how improbable, had to be the solution? What I was thinking now was improbable, to be sure, but it was not impossible. Proof of that was the voice that had clued me in, that of perennial child actor Willy Lipton, the guy who Mac at Edendale Video discovered had played a role in *The Mummy*, but whose regular gig was playing adolescents, even into his sixties, because of his physical condition. That took care of the impossibility. This photo proved the probability.

I picked the paperwork back up from the private hospital in Sierra Madre, and studied it more closely, now searching for words like *hormone* or *growth treatment*. That was only possible way those two kids could look twelve today and only slightly younger fifteen years ago...*they were really adults*. They were adults with some sort of affliction that kept them looking like kids, like Willy Lipton or Gary Coleman. This also explained why a porn producer would dare to use them in a film. It was because they were legal adults who *looked* like children; which while squirm-inducing, was not illegal. It also potentially answered the question of Burton and Taylor's abduction: they had not been abducted at all; they simply took off, because they were really old enough to drive. But if that were the case, it could mean....

"Ohhh," I moaned, no longer simply chilled, but frozen.

Go ahead, shamus, say it, Bogie taunted. *Say it out loud.*

"It means they could be driving a car and shooting at people," I replied. "It means it might have been the twins who took a shot at me, and who clubbed Marcy, and who...."

Finish it.

"...Killed Elena and Nora."

NINETEEN

Could it be that Burton and Taylor Frost were behind *every-thing*?

No, it didn't scan. I remembered Elena Cates saying she had picked the boys up at Nora's house at nine-thirty, and took them away for the day, so they would not have had a chance to kill Nora…at least not without Elena's knowledge.

You're not thinking improbably enough, old boy, said a very distinctive voice. It was Nigel Bruce, who played Dr. Watson in the classic series of films opposite Basil Rathbone as Holmes. While I really preferred the hard boiled genre to backlot Baker Street, at this point I was willing to accept help no matter from which part of my subconscious it came. Okay, fine, I'll think improbably: how could Burton and Taylor, one or the other or both of them, have murdered Nora without Elena knowing it?

"Oh, sheez," I uttered. There was only one way: they shot her before Elena arrived at nine-thirty to pick them up. Elena had told me that the last time she had heard Nora's voice was when Nora was screaming at her over the phone the night before, which meant she never saw her the next morning. What if the boys had simply *pretended* like they were saying goodbye to their mother in another room, and then came out and left with Elena, who would have been grateful not to be confronted by her employer?

Then the other shoe dropped inside my brain. *What if the two little freaks pulled the same trick on Marcy and me?* I thought back to their arrival at Marcy's house, ostensibly having been dropped off by Elena, yet at no time did I see or hear Elena. Instead the twins waved into the distance as though they were saying goodbye to her. What if they had already killed her and drove themselves to Marcy's house?

The sane part of my mind—the chunk that did not speak to me through the voices of old Hollywood actors—was playing devil's advocate, trying hard to tell me that this theory was just nuts. But that part was drowned out by a voice in my head that said: *Are you willing to risk Marcy's life on the theory that it's insane?*

It was my own voice I heard, and the answer was *no*.

Pulling out my cell phone, I dialed her number, but got the machine again. That was an ominous sign, since it was getting a little late for her to still be at work. She could be at the store, of course, or somewhere else perfectly mundane, but I a little cold ball of fear was forming in the pit of my stomach as I heard the beep after her phone machine greeting. "Marcy," I said softly, "it's Dave. This is going to sound nuts, but you have to believe me. It's the twins. They're not kids, they're adults. I think they're behind this. You have to protect yourself. Call me as soon as you get this message." I cut the call and put my cell back in my shirt pocket, so I'd hear it immediately if it rang.

After replacing the stacks of cash and locking the drawer again with my handy-dandy homemade pick (and locking things with it is a lot more difficult than unlocking things, for some reason), I made my way downstairs and prepared to leave the way I came. Creeping to the low wall, I scaled over and headed up the driveway, until I saw the police car slow down on the street. The lights were not flashing and there was no siren, meaning it was probably on patrol rather than responding to a call, but that didn't make the situation any better for me.

If they get out of the car and find you here, you're done, sonny, Robert Mitchum said inside my head.

Tell me something I don't know, I thought back, dashing behind a tree trunk.

You mean like how to be a detective?

Funny, Mitch; har-de-har-har. You're a laugh riot.

The car sat there on the street for what seemed like an eternity, and then one of the uniformed officers got out and walked to the front of the house. If he decided to come in back, I was as dead as Nora. But he didn't. After a minute, he got back into the cruiser, which took off. My pulse pounding through my temples sounded like a drum solo and my legs became watery. I sank to the ground behind the tree, forcing myself to breathe slowly and evenly, and not hyperventilate.

Sometimes I suspect I'm in the wrong business. But then there are other times when I'm convinced of it.

After resting a moment and finally putting the cuffs on my wind, I was able to return to my car without incident. Then I got out of Nora's neighborhood, and hoped I'd never have to come back.

The proper thing to do, of course, would be to call the police and tell them what I had discovered, and send them down to make certain Marcy was safe. The problem with that was that I had gleaned the information while in the act of breaking and entering, which would most likely not endear me to Detective Colfax, let alone Mendoza. The practical thing to do (as opposed to the proper thing) was to find some sort of corroborating evidence that the boys were not boys, which would absolve me of having to confess that I had ransacked Nora's desk illegally. As much as I wanted to race down to San Pedro, I knew I had to have some sort of legally-obtained justification before getting further involved, so I headed back home.

Once there, I immediately powered up my computer. The evidence to back up my theory was out there somewhere. All I had to do was find it. But that was why God made computers. Or was it the Devil? While waiting to connect, I noticed my phone message line was flashing. *Please be Marcy!* I thought as I punched the playback button.

It wasn't Marcy.

"*Hey, Dave, this is Walt Westermann,*" the voice of my former teacher said. "*I had a free moment so I ran that license plate through for you and got a hit. It's registered to someone named—"*

"Elena Cates," I said, speaking in unison with the recorded voice on the chip. That must have been what Kleinbach tried to tell me before my machine cut him off, that he recognized Elena's car, which he had followed earlier.

"If you're going to continue in this business," Walt's voice went on, *"don't forget what I said about getting the DMV database yourself."* Then the message cut off. Of course, this was not proof that it was the twins who were driving Elena's Taurus, but clearly *somebody* other than Elena was. I still had to dig some more.

The laptop was connected online now so I typed the name *Natalie Strange* in the search engine, figuring that was the easiest place to start. Dozens of entries popped up, but I settled on a newspaper obituary, which reported that she had died of an accidental overdose of medication in 2007, and even though her former maid had implied it was somewhat less than accidental, there was no proof for that. There was one strange thing about the obituary, however: it listed Nora Kleinbach as her only survivor. There was no mention of Richard Burton or Robert Taylor Kleinbach.

Next I typed in Lieutenant Randall Frost, and while the pickings were obviously much smaller, because of his status as a fallen soldier it was not hard to come across his obituary. It stated that he had been deployed in the summer of 2009 and was killed in combat with insurgents in October, 2010, at the age of thirty-nine and was survived by his wife of three years, Nora, and two sons, Burton and Taylor. That meant that Frost and Nora had been married in 2007, the same year that Natalie Strange had died. Was there a connection? It would be possible of course to search the databases and try to obtain death, birth and marriage certificates, but it would take weeks, if not months, to get the information back. I did not have that much time.

If only I knew the name of Frost's first wife.

"Think," I ordered myself, and the command must have

worked, because I thought to type in *Brothers Alpha* and saw their home page pop up. Most of the shots of the two boys I had seen in Nora's house, but there was a "Biographies" page, to which I linked. There I saw photos of the boys as genuine children. In one shot they appeared to be about two. In the others they looked maybe five or six, and even at that age it was easy to see they were not identical. Nora must have gotten these photos after she married Frost and used them on the site, because they were pretty generic candid shots. But shot of a couple of kids still proved nothing.

Then I saw it.

In one of the photos the boys were standing outside of a movie theatre. There was a poster in the background, which would have gone unnoticed to anyone other than someone obsessed (okay, I've said it) with movies. Examining it closely, I recognized it as the poster for an indie kids move called *Gordy*, which was about a talking pig. I quickly linked over to the Internet Movie Database and punched the title in. Like the similar, but far more successful film, *Babe*, *Gordy* had been released in 1995, but unlike *Babe* it had quickly disappeared from theatres. If you wanted to see it on the big screen, you had to be there on opening weekend. I knew now that the boys shown in the picture would have been six or so, even though they looked younger. That was not the point, however: had the boys really been twelve today, there is no way they could have been standing in front of a movie theatre in 1995. More pertinently, this proof was obtained online, not through an illegal break-in and search. I could now safely go to the police.

But there were still plenty of loose ends, including what had happened to Nora's real children. I started by Googling the names "Robert Taylor Kleinbach" and "Richard Burton Kleinbach," just to see if there were any news stories or obituaries for them, but it turned up nothing. Then on a whim I typed in the name *San Gabriel Valley Private Hospital*. That took me straight to their site, where I learned that it was not a clinic for face lifts or anything else, but rather a hospice for terminally ill.

That left one way to find out the truth. The website had a phone number, so I called.

"Hello, I'd like to speak with whoever is in charge of your accounts," I said to the woman who answered the phone.

"You mean the billing office?" she asked.

"Yes, thank you."

"I'm sorry, they're gone for the day."

"This is rather important, is there anyone in charge I can talk to?"

"Our head physician is here, but he can't—"

"Fine, I'd like to speak to him, please."

"Hold on."

While waiting I was subjected to about thirty seconds of really dreadful, elevator music, and then a man's voice came on. "This is Dr. Maxwell, how can I help you?"

"Dr. Maxwell, my name is William Pratt," I lied. "I'm an attorney representing the estate of Mrs. Nora Frost."

"Attorney? Are we being sued?"

"No, no, nothing like that. I'm calling regarding the children of Nora Frost."

"I don't know a Nora Frost."

"How about Nora Kleinbach?"

"Oh, god, the mother of Thing One and Thing Two," he said.

"I beg your pardon?"

"Sorry, Mr. Pratt, that's what we've taken to calling them here. But you said you represented an estate, didn't you? Is Mrs. Kleinbach dead?"

"I'm afraid so. The reason I'm calling about is to work out the details of continuing the funding of care for the boys through the estate," I lied.

"You need to talk to our financial people about that."

"Yes, I suppose I do, but as head physician, can you at least tell me roughly how long you think treatment is going to last."

There was a pause, and then Maxwell said: "Until someone pulls the plug, I imagine."

"I'm sorry?"

"Mr. Pratt, the Kleinbach twins have been in a permanent vegetative state for six years. They are being kept alive through feeding tubes. This is why, as awful as it may sound to a lay person, they have come to be known as Thing One and Thing Two, because it's a way of dealing with their situation. Nobody here ever knew them as living children. They were already comatose when their mother checked them in here. Apparently they ate a bottle of prescription medicine between them. We are not offering treatment, *per se*. We are keeping them alive."

"Oh…I see," I muttered. "I had not been made aware of the severity of their conditions."

"Quite frankly, Mr. Pratt, the death of their mother might turn out to be a blessing. These two are never going to recover. They are never going to have lives, only unconscious existences. Whoever it is that is now their legal guardian would probably be doing them a favor by removing the feeding tubes. Again, this may sound awful to you, but the people here spend each day with these poor helpless, wasted youngsters, and after a while, you can't help but think that there has to be a more merciful resolution."

"Well," I said, my voice cracking, "thank you for your time, Dr. Maxwell." I hung up and rubbed my temples. For years Nora had kept the boys alive in a private hospital, all the while pretending that Frost's natural kids were her own. Had she expected that they would someday recover? Or had the boys' tragedy, combined with the vengeance she enacted on her own mother, taken away her ability to think rationally?

I had everything I needed to pass the case on to Dane Colfax and let him find the missing boys, but I owed it to Marcy to fill her in first. I punched in her number again. If I couldn't get her by phone, I would go down there. Once more I got the machine, and started to leave another message, but this time she cut it off by picking up the line.

"Dave," she said, "I was about to call you. I got your earlier message, and if was anyone else but you, I'd say you were drunk or high."

"I wish that were the case, Marcy," I said.

"You really think the boys are doing all this?"

"Yes."

"You think they're the ones who hit me over the head?"

"Yes, and I'm afraid they might come back and try to finish you off."

"What should I do?"

"I'm coming down. Don't do anything until I get there. Don't answer the door and keep screening calls, okay?"

"Okay."

"If you see any sign of the boys, if they try to get in the house, call the police immediately. I'll be down there about seven-thirty, traffic willing." I hung up and took off.

As it turned out, traffic was not willing. Because of a wreck on the 110 South, it took me more than ninety minutes to get down to San Pedro. I did not get to Marcy's place until a little past eight. Racing to her door, I knocked, and was gratified to hear her voice demanding my identity before opening it. "Sorry I'm so late," I said as I raced in.

"I'm glad you're here," she said, embracing me. Sitting her down on the sofa, I gave her a detailed rundown of most of what I had discovered, including the parts of the puzzle I'd found inside Nora's house, where I didn't belong. I left out the porn connection, but even so, I could tell from her expression that she was having a hard time believing it. "You're telling me they're in their twenties?" she said, when I finished. "They look twelve, max. Do they have something like hypogandism?"

"What's that?"

"It's a condition that keeps you looking like you're barely out of childhood. It's more common in girls than boys, but it's not unknown in boys."

She worked in the medical industry, so I guess she would know.

"God," Marcy said. "Why would they keep up the pretense that they were really adolescents?"

"It had to be Nora's doing," I said. "She wanted them to be

young so they could be child stars, though from what I saw of them, they were not happy. Why they went along with it is anyone's guess, though they must have gotten something out of the deal. Maybe it was just their connection to Elena."

"What, they had a crush on her?" she asked.

I had to tell her everything. "Marcy, Elena worked as a porn actress, and the boys…I guess I should say the young men… they turned up in a porno, too."

That seemed to shock her. "Taylor and Burton did a *porn* movie?"

"I saw it. They weren't in a scene with Elena, but she had to be connection that got them there."

Marcy leaned back in the sofa. "Good god. I only met Elena once or twice, maybe, but she just didn't strike me as the street type."

"Just like the boys didn't strike either of us as adults."

"Sit with me, Dave," she said, and I didn't have to be asked twice. I plunked down beside her on the couch, close. "This is a lot to take in."

"I know," I said. "But now we have to figure out what to do. The boys are out there somewhere, driving Elena's car. We thought they were abducted, but they weren't. They hit you and then took off. I think they probably meant to kill you, too, but for whatever reason, they weren't carrying the gun the used on their mom and Elena, so they improvised, and then fled."

"This gets worse and worse," she moaned.

"No, it might be good, actually," I said, just having been struck with a thought. "If they think you're dead, then they'll disappear."

"That's good?"

"For you it is, Marcy."

I looked deep into her eyes and saw awareness flooding in. "But if they think I'm still alive, they'll come back and try to finish the job, is what you're implying."

"We can protect you, though. I can protect you."

"Oh, my god, Dave," she moaned, grabbing my arm with

both hands and holding on like it was a life preserver. "Have you called the police?"

"No, not yet. I wanted to make sure you were all right first."

"If I ever complain about having a boring life again, throw something at me, would you?"

I continued to look into her eyes, and could not help but notice that she was looking back, and then some. Slowly I leaned toward her, and she moved her head slightly toward me, then took her right hand off of my arm and put it on my shoulder, parting her lips slightly. I was just about to go in for the kiss when her phone rang, shattering the moment.

"Well, I know it's not you calling," she said, with a wry smile.

I heard her message play through, after which a male voice came on. "Ms. DeBanzi, this is Detective Colfax," it said. "I just want to let you know that we've located the twins."

In a flash Marcy was up and off the couch, practically knocking me to the floor in the process. She grabbed the phone and said: "Detective, this is Marcy DeBanzi. Yes. Where did you find them?"

I could just imagine what Colfax was telling her...probably a variation of what I had just told her, that the boys were old enough to drive and probably even have valid California licenses, and they were driving Elena Cates' car.

"Detective," Marcy said, "please forgive me, but I don't think I'm up to coming in tonight. This is quite a shock. Yes, okay. Thank you. Good bye." She hung up and turned back toward me. "You were right. The police found Taylor and Burton in Elena's car. It turns out they actually had drivers licenses under their real names. They're Eric and someone...I can't even remember. They're at the jail. The police wanted me to go down there, but I just don't think I have the strength right now."

"They deserve to spend the night in the slammer, and a lot more." I was trying to figure out a slightly less blatant way to say *Now, where were* we? when *my* phone rang! "Oh, sheez," I muttered, pulling the cell out of my pocket.

"No, Dave, don't answer it," Marcy said, rushing over to me.

"Let it go. It's probably Colfax, and I need you more than he does."

"You do?"

"I need you, Dave," she panted. "I need you now."

Cue the romantic music.

ZOOM into CLOSE-UP of the long, lingering kiss.

CUT TO: INT. NIGHT. MED shot of embracing couple, starting to take each other's clothes off with passionate clumsiness. Soon they are in a naked embrace and panting like a dog team after the Iditarod. The man picks the woman up in his arms as though she weighs no more than a tiny bird—a tiny, naked, beautiful bird whose lips are parting with desire—and sweeps her into the bedroom, and....

Okay, I'm not that strong, and my hand still hurt. But we made it to the bedroom anyway.

TWENTY

When I woke up the next morning, birds were singing outside a slightly open window. Marcy was next to me, still asleep, lightly snoring, her shoulder and back protruding seductively from the covers. I'm not sure how I had the stamina to be seduced again, but if push were to come to shove, I'd figure out a way.

With as little movement to the mattress as I could get away with I slid my legs out from under the blankets, stood up, and made my way, shakily, to the bathroom. Passing a clock on the way, I learned it was 6:47. The jewelry stores wouldn't open for another two hours and thirteen minutes.

Jewelry stores! Robert Mitchum roared at me. *Oh, brother*!

Maybe he was right.

What I really wanted right now (well, second on the list of things I really wanted right now), was a quick shower and something to eat. I was starving. I hoped Marcy wouldn't mind if I ransacked her kitchen when I was done cleaning up.

Keeping the flow down low, so as not to make too much noise, I quickly showered and reached for what looked like a guest towel folded up on the counter. Had she anticipated my staying over? No, it had probably been set out for one of the boys. Still naked as a jaybird, I went back out into the living room, where my clothes were strewn, and put on my shorts. Maybe I should do something nice, like make breakfast for her, too.

Quickly pulling on my shirt, shorts, and pants, I started for the kitchen, but then I heard a beeping coming from my cell phone lying on the floor. Picking it up, I saw the screen read: *One missed call*. Right; the one from last night. Pressing the retrieval button, I put the phone to my ear and heard the ubiquitous female introducing the call. That was followed by a male voice saying: "*Turn your damn phone on, Beauchamp! This is Detective Mendoza. Detective Colfax is calling your lady friend, and he wanted me to check in with you. Frankly, I rather blow a coyote, but orders are orders.*"

One thing about Mendoza; you always knew where you stood.

"*Those two kids, we found 'em. And guess what? They aren't named Burton and Taylor. They're really Eric and Ryan Frost. And guess what else? They aren't kids. They're twenty-four years old.*"

Since I knew this, I was about to cut off the call, but then Mendoza's voice told me something I didn't know; something that gave me the chills, which lasted even after I had listened to the call one more time and put on my socks and shoes.

For the next ten minutes I sat there on Marcy's couch, wondering what I should do. When a voice behind me purred, "How come you're dressed?" I jumped and nearly screamed. Marcy was standing behind the couch, almost wearing a bathrobe. "Damn, Dave, I hope you're not like this every morning."

"I, uh...Marcy...I...." I could see her eyes drop down to my cell phone.

"Did you take that call from last night?" she asked.

"Yeah."

"Who was it?"

"Detective Mendoza."

"I see. Did he tell you about the twins?"

"Yes, he did, including the part you failed to mention. The part about how they were both found yesterday in the back seat of a rust-colored Taurus, dead from gunshots."

"Damn," Marcy muttered, and for the first time I noticed that I could only see one of her hands. The other was being held behind her back. "I figured ditching the car in a mall parking

lot meant it would be weeks, months, before it was discovered."
Now she revealed her right hand, and the revolver it was holding.
Then she came around in front of the couch to face me.

"Please tell me this is a joke," I croaked.

"Sorry," she said, pointing the revolver in my direction.

"Are *you* the one who killed Nora?"

"No, the two little assholes did that, just like you figured.
They'd grown to loathe her, and who can blame them? They
were sick of the baby act."

Suddenly a white light went off in my head, like the old
cartoon light bulb cliché. "It was the twins who wrote that
threatening letter to Nora, wasn't it?" I said. "All this time I was
trying to figure out who was close enough to them to include
their first names, when it was them all along. They practically
signed the note for me, I just didn't see it. Did the twins kill
Elena, too?"

She nodded.

"So you killed them out of revenge for killing your sister."

"Hardly." She smiled and slowly backed up to a chair and
sat down, never taking the gun off me. Were I a movie P.I., I
would have charged her, overpowered her and taken the gun
away before she put the distance between us. Now if I even tried
to rise from the couch, I'd be dead. "I had come to hate Nora
even more than they did, so I gave them the gun and showed
them how to use it."

I had not expected this. "I don't get it, Marcy," I uttered. "You
could have simply gone about your business having nothing
more to do with her and the boys. Why plot to kill her?"

"Because she knew something about me that I really don't
want known. It's a little secret from my past that was uncovered
when she hired the private detective to find me. As long as Nora
was around, there was a chance that my secret would come out."

"I'm betting you're not going to tell me what it is."

She mouthed the word *no* without making a sound. Despite
my curiosity, I was actually relieved, because had she told me,
I was certain she would have felt obligated to kill me. This way,

maybe I still had a chance. Maybe. "Okay, if Nora had something on you, I understand why you would want her out of the way," I said. "I can also guess why you wanted the twins to do the dirty work. If something went wrong, they would get the blame. But I don't understand why the boys agreed to do it. Even if they hated Nora, they were adults. They could have told her to stuff it and taken off any time they wanted to."

"Sure, they could have, but if they did they'd lose any hope of being millionaires."

"Millionaires?"

"Nora's estate, most of which she inherited from her parents, is worth a little over four-million dollars."

"So that's what this is about? You wanted Nora dead because she was threatening you, but Burton and Taylor wanted to inherit her fortune."

"And just like Nora helped her own mother to an early grave, the boys did not want to wait for nature to take its course."

"Sheez. Hey, wait…how do you know what happened to Nora's mother?"

"Nora told me."

I was starting to get a headache. "I thought you weren't close enough for sisterly confessions."

"We weren't," Marcy said. "I guess you can say I forced the issue. I always knew there was something not quite right about the twins, and then one day Taylor let something slip. We had just had a small temblor and he casually commented that it was nothing like the Northridge quake, which he then went on to describe with convincing accuracy." She leaned forward. "But the Northridge quake took place in 1994, before they should have been born. When I mentioned this to Nora she tried to laugh it off, but I wasn't convinced. Then she broke down and told me that her real sons had died as a result of her mother's negligence."

"Wait a minute. She told you the boys had died?"

"Yes. She also said that she had to restrain herself from strangling her mother with her bare hands, but opted for driving her to take her own life. But that didn't bring back her babies, so she found her new husband, Randy Frost, on a website that connected the single parents of twins. She reeled him in and convinced him to marry her so his boys would have a mother. What she didn't tell him, at least at first, was that she was planning on having his sons continue her unfulfilled crusade for fame and fortune. But here's the sweet irony: Nora got conned back. She didn't learn the boys were so old until after the marriage took place. Frost knew his deployment was inevitable, and he wanted his sons taken care of. They were about seventeen then, still not quite old enough to be on their own, especially those two. When Nora found out about the hypogandism, well, I think whatever rationality she had left broke off and floated away. She forced the two to play their roles, I think out of spite, at first, but then she started to believe her own press again."

"And the boys just took it in hopes of inheriting?"

"I can't prove it, but I think she was drugging them to make them more acquiescent."

That also explained their zombified demeanors.

"And you never thought it strange that she was confessing all this?" I asked.

"Nora knew I wouldn't dare go to the police because if I did, she'd reveal what she knew about me, and while it would be very hard to prove that Nora had driven her mother to suicide, what I'm keeping hidden can be easily verified."

From where I was sitting, there wasn't much she was keeping hidden, given the way her robe was gaping. I was trying not to be affected by it.

"Okay, let's just get this over with," she said, raising the gun.

"What about Elena?" I blurted out. "Why did the boys have to kill her?"

"What's that phrase they use to explain why civilians have to die in wars?" she asked. "Collateral damage, that's it. Elena was collateral damage. She really thought those two idiots were adolescents, until she caught them driving her car. Then she threatened to call the police, and Burton, the moron, let it slip that she'd better not unless she wanted to end up like Nora. Elena called me, distraught, asking what she should do. I told her to do nothing, said I'd take care of it. And I did. I convinced the boys that they had to get rid of Elena."

I had a sudden, grim realization. Both Nora and Elena had two bullet holes in them. Each boy must have fired once. To them it was probably another video game. Then I had another flash of insight, which might maybe save my life. "You know you don't have to get rid of me if you killed the twins in self-defense."

"What are you talking about?" she asked.

"The twins were adopted, but you're related to Nora by blood, which makes you the legal next of kin, which mean you would inherit the estate, not them. They figured that out and planned to kill you too, but failed in the first attempt. You got to them before they could try again. You could tell that to the police."

She shook her head. "They never tried to kill me. That business of getting clubbed on the head, that was just an act to throw suspicion off of myself. After I talked with you on the phone, I told the twins to scram and then drove my head into the wall."

"Why?"

"Because *you* were the element in all this that I hadn't planned on," she said. "I figured I could dance past the police, God knows I've done it before, but you kept hanging around. I had to convince you that the killer was out to get me, too."

God knows she'd done it before? What did that mean?

Marcy continued: "There's no way those little bastards would have killed me. They needed me."

"I'm lost, Marcy."

She smiled and leaned forward. "That's what I like about you, that lost quality. Okay, try to pay attention. The twins had a big problem when it came to inheritance. Everybody thinks they're twelve, which means they'd either have to wait a decade or so to inherit the money, or fess up and tell everyone they're really in their twenties, which means their alibis for the murders get flushed. In fact, a revelation like that would probably propel them to the very top of the suspect list. Either way, they were screwed. But if *I* were to inherit Nora's estate, as legal next of kin, I could quietly siphon off some of the money and give it directly to them. That was the plan."

"Which you rewrote by shooting them."

"Four-million dollars is way too much money to share with anyone, particularly those little pricks." She leveled the revolver at my head.

"You know, Marcy, you have a problem to," I said.

"Yeah?"

"You're the last one standing. Everyone else is dead. If you kill me, you're the only suspect."

"Unless I convince the cops that the real killer came after me, and I was forced to kill him in self-defense."

Even though I was dressed and she wasn't, my guess is that I was feeling an awful lot colder than Marcy. "You mean me, don't you?" I croaked. "You're going to set *me* up as the killer."

She smiled, and dimples or no dimples, I didn't like it.

TWENTY-ONE

"What the police will learn," Marcy was saying through her smile, "is that you knew the boys were adults all along, and that they paid you to kill Nora and Elena. But then you wanted even more money, and they balked, so you killed them, too. Upon learning that control of Nora's estate passed to me, you came and threatened me as well, but it seems you underestimated my determination to stay alive."

I wanted to believe that this yarn would never stand up under police scrutiny, but the fact that Marcy had taken me for such a ride was a testament to her abilities as an actress, so it very well might. Add to that the fact that Mendoza, if no one else, would be delighted to hear that I was the murderer.

You gonna sit there and take this? the voice of James Cagney barked inside my head. *Give 'er a good one, right in the mush*! Unfortunately, I was all out of grapefruits, while she had a gun. Hold on...*was that the murder weapon*?

"I take it you're holding the gun that was used on Nora, Elena, and the boys," I said.

Marcy nodded.

"So if you use it to kill me, how are you going to make me look like the killer?"

"You have so little imagination," she said, rising and sashaying toward me, her robe completely open and revealing her spectacular body in the process. When she got close she held the revolver to my head and began making light circles with the barrel around my temple. Then she raised it and fired two shots behind me that nearly deafened me.

"Jesus!" I cried, diving off the sofa onto the floor. A couple seconds later, the revolver dropped down into my field of vision. I quickly grabbed it and then sat up. Marcy was standing over me, wearing a smile, and holding *another* gun, this one an automatic. "The gun you're holding is empty, so don't bother trying to use it. This one, however, has a full clip." She leveled the automatic at my forehead. "By the way, I wiped that one clean on my robe before I threw it, so the only prints the police will find on it are yours."

"You think of everything," I said, grimly.

"Yes, I do. Now get up."

I was thinking furiously, and coming up with little. Then, "Wait," I said. "Colfax knows someone took a shot at me."

"That wasn't my idea," she said. "It was those idiot kids. They came to enjoy firing the gun."

"But if you're trying to make me out to be the killer, how do you explain those shots?"

"Who witnessed the shooting?"

"Colfax took the bullet."

"But who witnessed the actual shooting?"

"No one, but—"

"Then as far as he knows, you staged the entire thing for purposes of misdirection. And since the bullets came from the gun you're holding, that's the proof."

This was going from bad to worse.

Leaning down to me, Marcy asked, "Anything else?"

Think! Ah! "You've forgotten something, Marcy," I said, feeling the perspiration forming on my upper lip. "You killed Nora because she knew your secret, but someone else does, too."

"Who."

"The detective she hired to find you. He must know."

"You know, Nora actually tried to use that against me as well. At first she said my secret would be safe with her as long as I was 'part of the team,' meaning at her beck and call. Then when I found out what she was hiding, she tried to use her investigator's knowledge as the chip that kept her on top of the situation. Nora hated even playing fields. But now that Nora's dead, all I have to do is find out who the investigator is and offer a deal. If he doesn't take it, then…." She raised the gun to the level of my head and made a popping sound with her mouth.

"The thing is, Marcy, I know who the man is," I said. "I saw his invoice in Nora's desk. If you kill me, that information dies with me."

She regarded me with amusement. Or maybe it was pity. "Except for the fact that you've just told me where to find it."

That tears it, William Powell's voice said in my head. *We're through, you and I. May flights of angels sing thee to thy rest.*

Marcy DeBanzi straightened up and motioned for me to get up off the floor with the gun. "Any more doomed attempts to save your ass you feel like trying before the inevitable occurs?" she asked.

"Didn't last night mean anything to you?" I groaned, slowly facing her. "We spent all night together, naked."

"Yes, and there's a black mole on your left side you should have checked out. Oh, wait, never mind. You'll be dead soon."

"Marcy…."

"You want me to say I enjoyed last night?" she asked. "Fine, I did, even though my primary reason for jumping you was to prevent you from taking that phone call, which I assumed would be the police. Had you taken it, we would have gone through all this last night. Instead, we had a little fun, and I take my fun where I can. You're a boy scout, Dave, a goofy, naïve puppy dog pretending to be a grown up. But oddly, you're not that bad in the sack."

"Thanks."

"Don't mention it. Now let's get this over with." She came closer and stuck the barrel of the automatic between my eyes, which I closed. "Oh, for crying out loud, get your damn eyes open and walk over to the fireplace," she ordered.

I peeked. "The fireplace?"

"You know, the place where you build a fire? Over there, and hurry."

I did as she commanded, but walked backwards, never turning my face away from her or the gun for more than a second. *Think! Either think of something or die!* "You know, Marcy, someone had to hear the shots you just fired," I said, back up and dropping the empty gun she had thrown to me down on the couch. "They've probably already called the cops."

"That's the idea. The cops will find you unconscious on the floor, two bullet holes in my wall from the murder weapon, covered in your prints, me half-naked and hysterical, having been raped—"

"Raped! Come on! The cops will see through your story."

"Not if I sell it well enough, and believe me, I will. I may have confessed that I didn't like acting, but I never said I wasn't good at it. Now stop." Keeping the automatic trained on me, she slowly reached over and took the iron fireplace poker in her other hand. "The police will be told you fired at me but missed, and then ran out of bullets, and I was able to get to the fireplace and grab the poker and hit you over the head with it."

"Wouldn't it be easier just to shoot me?"

"Not with this gun. If the cops were to trace the registration, it would lead them straight to the thing I'm trying to hide. That revolver over there is unregistered, and that's the only gun they'll find. Now kneel."

"What?"

"Get on your knees."

"You've already said you weren't going to shoot me, Marcy," I said, "so why should I?"

In response, she took a murderous swing at me with the poker, which I barely avoided by throwing myself onto the floor. Then she tapped me on the head with the end of it. For anyone who has never been threatened with an iron poker, even being tapped with it is extremely painful. But it also makes one a little angry. I tried to rise up, but she hit me again, harder this time, hard enough to make my vision go all red. "Damn," I muttered, sinking back to my knees. I knew if I tried moving again, she would start clubbing me in earnest, so the more I resisted, the more convincing my injuries would look to the police. Gazing up with eyes now tinted with pain, I saw her toss the Luger on the sofa. "I'll hide it later," she said, "after I'm done playing piñata."

If there was a way out of this, I couldn't see it. Or so I thought. Glancing past her to the front wall of her house, it came to me. It was a longshot, but I was out of shortshots. "Marcy, would you allow me one last question for old time's sake?" I begged.

"Christ. Make it fast."

"Do you watch a lot of movies? Television?"

She looked puzzled. "I knocked your brain loose, didn't I?"

"Humor me and answer the question."

"No, Dave, I do not watch a lot of movies or television. Besides, if you're thinking of asking me out on a date for dinner and a show, I think we're a bit past that in our relationship."

"I know, I know. It's just that you seem to be so proficient at planning crimes down to the last detail that I wondered if you'd gotten that knowledge from watching—" I stopped talking, and looked past her to the front window, which was mostly blocked by heavy blue drapes, except for a couple inches in the middle where the curtains didn't close. Looking past her, I widened my eyes. "Detective Colfax, thank god you're here!" I shouted, "Hurry!"

Instinctively Marcy spun around to look at the window, and as she did I leapt to my feet and, ignoring the severe pain in my head, launched myself at her, grabbing her from behind in a bear hug, and pushed forward with all my weight. She screamed as she tumbled face first to the hardwood floor, the fireplace poker falling beneath her. "Ow, *fuck*!" she shrieked. "Do you know how much that hurt, you asshole?"

"Yes, I think I do," I said, kneeling on her back, pinning the poker under her weight, while I grabbed her left wrist and twisted her arm with both hands, desperation and anger enhancing whatever natural strength I possessed. She screamed again, and I didn't care.

There had, of course, been no one at the window. The old look-over-the-shoulder-and-pretend-to-see-someone bit was the second oldest in the book (just after rubbing a pencil over a blank page to reveal writing indentations), but only someone who watched movies and television would know that.

"I think I've got a broken rib, you cocksucker!" she cried. I still didn't care. I gave her enough room to move her right arm out from under her, but only so I could also grab it and twist it behind her. The poker was still underneath her, and it had to hurt. Still, she put up a good fight, but I was bigger. When she ceased fighting momentarily, I was able to whip off my belt and use it to cinch her wrists together. Holding her arms in a make-shift lasso with one hand, I groped around for my cell phone. Finding it, I dialed 911 and reported a shooting. I didn't trust that a neighbor would have heard the shots. Marcy screamed and struggled underneath me, calling me names I wasn't sure had been invented yet, but I was able to ride her, bronc style, hoping she would soon surrender. When I had finished calling, I tossed the cell away, and lifted myself off of her and pulled on the belt, until I had pulled her torso up off the floor. It looked horrifically uncomfortable.

"I hate you!" she screamed.

"I think you're beautiful," I replied. "If I hadn't fallen in love with you, I'd go get that automatic and shoot you through the head."

Like hell you would! Bogie sneered inside my brain. *You're not the killer type.*

He was right, of course, but Marcy didn't need to know that.

Holding her with one hand, I was able to reach the revolver the other. I rubbed it all over my clothing, hoping that it was enough to eradicate, or at least blur, the prints. After about three exhausting, invective-filled minutes, a police car arrived at the house. The doorbell rang and as loudly as I could, I shouted: "Officers, come in, this is an emergency!" I could hear some pounding, accompanied by Marcy's shrieks for help, and a moment later, the door was forced open. I gratified to see

Fillmore and Baker enter the house, weapons drawn.

"What the hell is going on?" Fillmore demanded.

"He's crazy!" Marcy shouted. "He raped me, and he tried to kill me...."

"She's lying, officers," I said, calmly. "She killed two young men and is an accomplice in the killing of two women. There's an automatic somewhere over there that has her prints all over it, and just underneath her is a fireplace poker that she hit me with."

"It was self-fucking-defense!" Marcy screamed.

"When you find the automatic be sure to check the registration," I went on. "I think you'll find something interesting." I still didn't know what Marcy's secret was, but clearly I struck a nerve, since it sent her into a fury.

"Can't you morons see how he abused me?" she screamed. "He raped me, for god's sake!"

"We did have sex, officers, but it was purely consensual," I countered. "But that was before she threatened me with a gun and then wanted to bash me over the head with a poker."

"Get away from her, sir, nice and slow," Baker ordered, holding a gun on me, and I complied, easing her down to the floor, and then letting go of my belt, which was still restraining her wrists. Marcy used that opportunity to roll over and try to attack me with her feet.

"Whoa, whoa, whoa, hold it right there, lady!" Fillmore said, holding his gun inches from her head. Marcy got the hint and remained still, though she was panting like a dog and was virtually naked, her robe having fallen open. "Everybody, calm down!" Fillmore ordered. "You, ma'am, I don't want to see you do anything with your hands except cover yourself up. No sudden moves."

"Should I call for backup?" Baker, asked, pulling out her radio with her free hand.

"Yeah," Fillmore said. "I don't want this to get any more out of hand than it already is."

Baker made the call on the radio, and then turned to me

again. "What was your name again, sir?" she asked.

"Beauchamp. Dave Beauchamp."

"Aren't you supposed to be working for her?" She pointed at Marcy.

"I was working for her sister, whose death she facilitated."

"He's lying! He's a maniac!" Marcy cried. "Why are you taking his side? You're a woman, for god's sake!"

"Right now, ma'am, I'm a police officer." Baker said. "Don't worry. We'll get this straightened out. If he's guilty of anything, we'll find out."

Was I guilty of anything?

Stupidity? Robert Mitchum offered.

Give the kid a break, Bogie said. *Naïveté, maybe, but a dame turned on him. It happens to the best of us.*

While I was mentally thanking Bogart for his support, Fillmore had recovered the revolver across the room, and was bagging it.

The cry of another siren then pierced the air and before long two more officers were in the front room, one of them another policewoman. "See if you can get some clothes on her, but stay on guard," Fillmore instructed the recently-arrived female officer, who picked Marcy up and led her into the bedroom. Once they had left, he said, "You know, Beauchamp, we're going to have to take you into the station."

"Please," I said. "I'll enjoy the quiet."

"I'm going to have to handcuff you, too."

"Whatever. Will you be cuffing Marcy?"

"Yeah, but I'll let Baker do that."

"Ask her to make the cuffs loose, would you? I am afraid I had to get a little rough with her left arm to make her drop the gun. Oh, and if you could get Detective Colfax from Northeast Station to come down so I only have to give my story once, I'd appreciate it."

Once Marcy had emerged dressed from the bedroom with Officer Baker, she was cuffed and the two of us were taken into the San Pedro station, where Detective Dane Colfax arrived about an hour later, unfortunately, with Mendoza in tow. I was happy that Mendoza went to talk to Marcy, who was in a different interrogation room. Colfax stayed with me. I waived my attorney rights and gave him everything, absolutely everything I knew about the case. I know in the movies, private eyes always hold back some information from the police, either to protect a client or a love interest, or just to keep their professional mystique intact. But I had been played like a Steinway since the moment I met Nora Frost; that's why I had been hired, just so I could be played. The only reason I was still alive was because I either got lucky or smart, I'm not sure which. I'm not sure it matters. When I was finished Colfax said: "You know, as long as you were going to ignore my repeated instructions that you to drop this case anyway, the least you could have done is kept me informed along the way."

"Most of it didn't come together until last night, and then Marcy confessed the rest this morning."

"I hope you don't think Ms. DeBanzi's is in there confessing to Mendoza right now. She's ratting you out even more completely than you're ratting her out."

"Oh, I'm sure she is. But here's the thing, Colfax, I don't have a motive for any of this. Marcy does."

"I don't know, Beauchamp. It's still your version of the facts against hers. Maybe you had a motive that we just haven't discovered yet."

Something struck me then, something I had not yet considered regarding this case. On the one hand it was a tragic irony, but on the other, it was going to keep me out of prison. I leaned back and smiled, which seemed to take him by surprise. "Detective, I can settle this whole matter for you right now," I said.

"Yeah?"

"Yeah, because I know something Marcy doesn't, and when she finds out about it, she's not going to be happy."

"Spill it."

I reminded him about Nora's real children, Richard and Robert, lying comatose in that private hospital in the San

Gabriel Valley.

"Right," Colfax said. "It's a damn shame, but how are they going to help you?"

"By the simple fact that they're still alive," I said. "Nora told Marcy that they were dead, which was a lie, and Marcy believed it. She knows nothing about the private hospital."

"So?"

I leaned forward across the distressed table in the interrogation room. "Even though they are in vegetative states, Ricky and Bobby are Nora's legal next of kin until the courts decide otherwise. That means Marcy can't touch the estate. She orchestrated the deaths of four people for nothing. I think if you were to break this news to her, you would get an incriminating reaction."

"How do I know you're telling the truth about this?"

"Go call the San Gabriel Valley Private Hospital. They're in the book. Or use directory assistance, since any phone number I give you might be a phony that delivers you to a confederate of mine who's in on the plot."

"You've been watching too many movies, David."

"You're probably right, but still, go call and talk to someone named Dr. Maxwell, or anyone else there, for that matter. They will verify the boys' conditions. Then go tell to Marcy what you've learned. I'll wait here."

Colfax left the room for about twenty minutes, during which time I did my best to do nothing. Then he returned. "I don't suppose you know anybody named William Pratt, do you?"

"William Pratt?" I deadpanned. "Wasn't that Boris Karloff's real name?" Colfax uttered something that I couldn't make out, and I wasn't sure I wanted to. "Have you filled Marcy in on the situation?"

"Yes, and fortunately for you, Beauchamp, you guessed right. She went ballistic and incriminated herself enough to hold her until we can squeeze the rest of the story out of her."

"Am I also correct in assuming that you're not going to give any credence to the rape accusations?"

A strange smile crossed Colfax's face. "Part of Ms. DeBanzi's explosion was to leap up from the table, charge Hector Mendoza and kick him in the crotch so hard that he actually passed out. It took three male officers to restrain her."

Couldn't happen to a nicer guy, I thought, but only said, "Ouch."

"Hector's been taken to the ER. I mention this because it convinced me that Ms. DeBanzi is not the type to get raped without a fight. If she could fight off a squad of trained police officers, she would have killed you. Frankly, I'm a little surprised you survived the consensual sex with her."

Knowing what I now know, I couldn't really argue.

"She's now looking at an assault charge on top of everything else," Colfax finished.

And Detective Mendoza was looking at a solid week of standing in the shallow end of a swimming pool, learning to walk again. I only wish I could have been there to see the fight.

TWENTY-TWO

Officially the murders of Nora Frost, Elena Cates, and Eric and Ryan Frost were solved, with Marcella DeBanzi being charged directly for the latter two, and as an accomplice for the first two. There was much more information about the case to come out, and Detective Colfax was good enough to keep me in the loop. After fingerprinting Marcy, against which she fought so violently that she had to be restrained, the secret she had been guarding quickly came to light. Marcella DeBanzi was really Beverly Lynn Marshall, who in 2001 had been arrested for driving a car over her ex-husband in Las Vegas and killing him. She escaped that rap by eluding the police, disappearing, and changing her identity. When Nora's private bloodhound re-discovered her, Marcy/Beverly panicked at first, but Nora was able to lull her into a false sense of security, even telling her that she admired her style for offing her ex. She assured her that the investigator who found her was "part of the team" and his continued silence had been bought and paid for with money and sex, but that was only as long as Marcy stayed in line.

The most unexpected result of the case was that it shined a light on the operations of Pacific Investigations, which sent nervous ripples all through the Hollywood Hills. Alexander McCarthar found himself facing charges of obstruction of justice for not reporting to the authorities that his operatives had found Beverly Marshall. In addition, the DA was publicly threatening to launch an investigation into the firm itself. The word on the street was that all of Beverly Hills, Bel Air, and Mulholland

Drive were alive with the sound of celebrities shredding their contracts with PI.

Because of the sheer bizarreness of the circumstances, the case was working itself into yet another trial-of-the-century, due in no small part to how photogenic the woman I knew as Marcella DeBanzi was on television. Eventually the courts would find out how good an actress she was, too, which was only one of the reasons I was dreading being called in the eventual trial as the lead witness for the prosecution. Marcy had managed to lure the services of a high-powered celebrity feminist attorney, who specialized in taking headline-generating cases, so I assumed that she was already planning on how to try and rend me into little tiny Y-chromosome fragments. It was not impossible that Marcy would get off lightly, if not scot-free. This was after all Los Angeles, where more murderers freely walked the streets than streetwalkers. But even if they didn't hang her pretty neck, I wouldn't be there waiting for her.

Another mini-scandal connected to the case arose when it was revealed that Terrence Holving, the talent coordinator for Max Gelfan Productions, had been moonlighting as a casting director for the porn industry, sometimes using the people he found in contestant auditions in the skin flicks. Holving, it turned out, was the one who had gotten the Frost twins into *No Cuntry for Old Men*, and a couple other triple-X epics that I had the good fortune not to see. Having discovered that the boys were legal adults, Holving knew he would not be breaking the law by putting them in sex scenes. The twins were all for it, at least in spirit, since the medical condition that hindered their development also affected their sexual capabilities. But when Janelle Wynn—another of Holving's porn discoveries—kept bringing the twins for legit auditions because Nora was paying her to do so, it irritated Holving, who wanted to develop the boys exclusively as porn stars. Poor Elena Cates had nothing to do with the twins' involvement in porn; in fact, all available evidence confirmed that she really did believe the boys were adolescents. She truly was collateral damage.

Even though Holving had broken no actual laws by putting two young-looking twenty-four-year-olds in porno, the head of Max Gelfan Productions took a very dim view of the negative publicity the revelation generated, and fired him. It did not take a private investigator to figure out that Janelle was the one who ratted Holving out to both the production company and the press.

The hardest thing I had to encounter in the aftermath of the case was accompanying Alan Kleinbach to the San Gabriel Valley Private Hospital. He had managed to get himself as clean, neat and trimmed as possible, but as I watched him look at his emaciated, vegetative sons, who were hooked up to a variety of machines, I saw him die right in front of me. After a brief consultation with a doctor, Alan signed a paper to remove the feeding tubes, and then went out into the lobby of the hospital and broke down so completely that he had to be rushed back inside and sedated. I waited several hours for him, and once he had been released, took him back to his apartment, promising to stay in touch.

Robert and Richard Kleinbach died four agonizing days later, prompting a new burst of publicity for the trial. If there really is an afterlife, I hope those boys are getting the best of everything, because they sure got raw deals down here.

On the positive side, the publicity regarding my participation in the Frost case resulted in an increased workload for me, to the point where I was actually turning down cases and thinking of bringing in a partner. The thought had crossed my mind that Jack Daniels might be a good candidate. All he had to do was take some classes, and he could get his own license, or operate under mine. Maybe I'd call him about it sometime.

The other byproduct was that, for whatever reason, the Hollywood Golden Age Chorus had started to ebb away. They weren't gone entirely, but Bogie, Mitch, Bill Powell, W.C. and the gang were not chiming in anywhere's near as frequently. Could it be that my confidence in myself as an investigator had grown to the point where I didn't need the help?

You should be so lucky, Mitchum's voice said; but then, I had asked for that one.

On this particular day I was finishing up with a missing person case—the person in question turned out to have two families, and had decided to spend some quality time with the other one—when the phone rang. It was Mac from Edendale Video and Poster.

"Hey, Dave, according to the papers you're coming up in the world," he said. "Congratulations."

"Yeah, thanks, Mac. What's up?"

"Well, I've been following the accounts of this case you were on, the one with the twins, and I read that they were really in their twenties."

"That right."

"So those films they were in, the Triex things, those aren't illegal anymore."

"Right again."

"So because I destroyed my copy of *No Cuntry for Old Men* on your instruction, and gave the other to you, I figure you owe me $75.10 in replacement costs. If you still have yours, return it and I'll drop the amount down to $37.55."

Did I still have it? I'd have to check the fridge later. "Just put it on my tab, Mac," I said. "I'll settle up next time I'm in." I hung up, actually somewhat relieved that there were some aspects of my life that had not changed. Maybe I'd even stop by on the way home today and see what he and Bonn were up to.

I was contemplating closing up the office a little bit early so as to allow more time to swing by Edendale, when the tomato walked into my office. She was some tomato, too: red, round, and ripe. And underneath was a young woman: tall and dark-haired, with sultry Latin looks and great, shapely gams encased in dark green hose, which she wore under the huge, red tomato costume. I don't know how she squeezed through the door.

"Are you Dave Beauchamp?" she asked.

"Yes, ma'am," I said. I like getting the easy questions out of the way quickly.

"I need to talk to you."

She stepped closer and I could see that the tomato outfit was made of shiny fabric stretched over a wire frame. Up close it looked a little cheesy, but from even a short distance, like from my desk to the door, it was pretty effective. "Can you sit down in that thing, Miss...?"

"Luisa Sandoval, and no, I can't sit down. I barely made it up the stairs. I'm on my lunch break and have to get back soon, so I don't have time to take it off, either."

"Would you think me rude if I asked why you're dressed like a tomato?"

"I'm helping to promote the grand opening of a new Burger Heaven down the street."

"Oh, right, I remember seeing the signs."

"There are several of us working out on the street, waving to people and handing out coupons," she said. "One guy's dressed like a patty, another is a bun, another one an onion, you get the idea. But this tomato suit is really just a cover."

You mean you're really a pickle? Lou Costello's voice said in my head. I ignored it. "Cover for what?"

"I'm a reporter with the *L.A. Independent Journal*," she said. "I've been working undercover investigating the Burger Heaven chain, but I'm afraid they're on to me. I think I'm going to need professional help, or at least advice."

"I see. Why exactly are you investigating them?"

She came close enough that her round, red sides scrunched into the edge of my desk. "Mr. Beauchamp, you're not going to believe what they're putting in their so-called beef."

This wasn't the sort of thing I wanted to hear, given my devotion to Burger Heaven. But how could I refuse a hot tomato when she asks for help. "All right, Ms. Sandoval—"

"You can call me Luisa," she said. "Or Louie, which is what my friends call me." Then she smiled.

She had dimples. And a perfect smile.

I felt my pulse throbbing in my temples.

Louie, I think this is the beginning of a beautiful friendship,

Bogart said inside my head.
     I hoped he was right.

ABOUT THE AUTHOR

Michael Mallory is a short story writer, novelist, journalist, and occasional actor. He lives in the Greater Los Angeles area. You can visit him at:

www.michaelmallory.com